QUAKERTOWN

QUAKERTOWN

Lee Martin

DUTTON

DUTTON
Published by the Penguin Group
Penguin Putnam Inc., 375 Hudson Street, New York, New York 10014, U.S.A.
Penguin Books Ltd, 27 Wrights Lane, London W8 5TZ, England
Penguin Books Australia Ltd, Ringwood, Victoria, Australia
Penguin Books Canada Ltd, 10 Alcorn Avenue, Toronto, Ontario, Canada M4V 3B2
Penguin Books (N.Z.) Ltd, 182–190 Wairau Road, Auckland 10, New Zealand

Penguin Books Ltd, Registered Offices: Harmondsworth, Middlesex, England

Published by Dutton, a member of Penguin Putnam Inc.

First Printing, June, 2001
10 9 8 7 6 5 4 3 2 1

Portions of this book, in somewhat different form, appeared in *Texas Short Stories 2* and *Fish Stories: Collective IV.*

Ⓩ REGISTERED TRADEMARK—MARCA REGISTRADA

LIBRARY OF CONGRESS CATALOGING-IN-PUBLICATION DATA

Martin, Lee.
     Quakertown / Lee Martin.
         p.   cm.
     ISBN 0-525-94583-0 (alk. paper)
     1. Denton (Tex.)—Fiction. 2. Afro-American neighborhoods—Fiction.
3. Gardeners—Fiction. 4. Relocation (Housing)—Fiction. 5. Segregation—Fiction. I. Title.
     PS3563.A724927 J87 2001
     813'.54—dc21
                                                                                00-050340

Printed in the United States of America
Set in Sabon
Designed by Leonard Telesca

PUBLISHER'S NOTE
This book is a work of fiction. Names, characters, places, and incidents are either the product of the author's imagination or are used fictitiously, and any resemblance to actual persons, living or dead, business establishments, events, or locales is entirely coincidental.

This book is printed on acid-free paper. ∞

For the story of Henry Taylor (1854–1937)
and
For Laurie Chittenden, with thanks

ACKNOWLEDGMENTS

I am grateful to the National Endowment for the Arts, the University of North Texas, and the Texas Commission on the Arts for their support during the writing of this novel. Again, I thank Phyllis, Sonia, Susie, and Jordan for all their help, and I give my love to my wife, Deb, whose presence makes the journey easier.

A lilac, all a lilac . . . not even a silent resemblance, not more care than just enough haughty.

—GERTRUDE STEIN, *Rooms*

Prologue
1921

He wouldn't boast. No, sir. Not a speck. Not Mr. Little Washington Jones. But under the right conditions—perhaps on a May night in 1921, when the mimosa trees were pink, and the magnolia flowers had bloomed, and the catalpa trees were thick with blossoms, and he and his wife, Eugie, had just strolled through their front gate after a trip to RCO's Ice Cream Parlor—he might admit that yes, indeed, he truly did have the finest, most well kept lawn in the entire neighborhood of Quakertown, in all of Denton, maybe, and, though he hated to have to say it, but there it was, slap in front of his eyes, perhaps the loveliest in all of Texas.

Consider, he might say, the American Sweetheart tea roses, and the verbena, and the periwinkle, not to mention—well, if he must—the rare white lilac bush.

And if he paused, then, at the low picket gate, and lifted his hand to one of the white blossoms, just for the sheer joy of letting the velvety petals skim his work-worn palm, who would fault him? Surely no one who knew how he had found the white lilac growing wild along Pecan Creek, showy and magnificent among the scrub of mesquite and bramble, how he had uprooted it, wrapped its ball in damp burlap, and hauled it in his wagon the two miles to Quakertown, hauled it first down Oak Street, past the grand homes and their green, green lawns where young men in white linen trousers played croquet, and ladies in ankle-length skirts batted feather shuttlecocks back and forth across badminton nets. Little sat up straight on the bench seat of his buckboard, gave the reins a shake, and listened to the jingle of the mule's harness, the cloppety-clop of its shoes over the cobble street. He heard the *pock-pock* of the croquet games fall silent, a rocker squeak as someone leaned forward. "I swan," he heard a woman say, that single voice, a voice of amazement and admiration he would carry with him for years. And he knew that what his father had told him was true: a black man with a talent could always make white folks take notice. "Find something they prize," his father had said, "and do it better than they can. You'll always have a place with them. You'll make yourself an easier life."

And so it was true for Little. He had a talent with flowers and trees and shrubs, and people in North Texas treasured anything green or brilliant with color, determined as they were to make something grow from some of the worst soil in the world, a gummy mess of clay they called gumbo.

Each morning that summer, Little ate his breakfast on his front porch so he could watch his neighbors walk up the hill to the women's college where they worked as maids and cooks and janitors. As they passed, he called out to them. "Mornin' Osceola, mornin' Miss Simms, mornin' Mr. Smoke." He sat on a cane-bottom chair, a red bandanna tucked into his shirt collar, and sipped his tea, his own blend of comfrey and sassafras, and waited for someone passing to compliment his lawn, to stop, perhaps, and admire the white lilac or the Chinese pistachio.

From time to time, Eugie called him a high-hat nigger. "I declare," she told him once. "Look at you. Sitting up there like the sun done set in your pocket."

That night when he stood in the dusk near the white lilac, she accused him again of putting on the swank. "You're as proud as Lucifer," she said, and to their daughter, Camellia, who sat near the front window, tatting lace for her wedding dress, it seemed

like the good-natured teasing she had heard pass between them
for years.

But then Eugie said, "Little, you're a yardman. That's the true
by and by of it. You carry white folks' dirt home under your fin-
gernails, but does that make you white? No, sir. Nothing ever
going to make you white."

Much later, Little would tell her that had been the start of all
that happened afterward. Although he doubted that she intended
any harm, the fact was her words stung him. Her own father,
Captain Jiggs, had been a white man, and like Camellia, Eugie's
skin was light-toned. "Yella," the women at Miss Abigail Lou's
said when they were having their own coarse hair oiled, and
someone mentioned her name. Her skin was "yella," not brown
like Little's, and her hair was straight, its black sheen tinged with
auburn. Little thought her beautiful, but when she said what she
did about him not being white, he heard disappointment in her
voice, and it took every bit of heart he had to laugh and say,
"Well, maybe *my* lawn's not the prize. Maybe that's a stretch.
After all, there is one other contender. Mr. Andrew Bell who lives
on Oak Street. Mr. Andrew Bell, of the Farmer's National Bank.
Do you know Mr. Bell?"

"Little," said Eugie. "Quit acting the fool."

She did indeed know Mr. Bell and his fine lawn because it was
Little who managed it all for him, Little who had the magic
thumb. He could make a brickbat grow daisies, Mr. Bell told him
once. "Honestly, Little, you're a wizard." And Little, though he
didn't want to be prideful—at least not overly so—could not, for
the life of him, disagree.

One day, not long after Eugie's comment at their front gate, he
was pruning a live oak in Mr. Bell's backyard. Mr. Bell came to
the door and called him down from his ladder. "I need you, Little." He reached up and patted him on the back. Little marveled
over that intimate gesture. "This city needs you. Will you help
us?"

"Yes, sir," Little said, drawing back his shoulders, standing as straight as he could. When had he ever said no to anything Mr. Bell had asked?

Mr. Bell stuck his fat thumbs into the pockets of his vest, and the shiny material stretched across his ample stomach. His gold watch chain sparkled in the sunlight. "Good. That's the spirit. That's just the sort of civic pride we hope your neighbors will have."

"Oh, they're good folks," said Little.

"Of course they are," said Mr. Bell. "That's why I'm sure they'll know opportunity when it knocks." He held the door open for Little. "Come inside, Little. I've got something I think you ought to see."

When Little got back to Quakertown that evening, he saw the janitors and maids and cooks coming down the long hill from the college. They were laughing among themselves, throwing up their hands, relieved to be rid of work for the day, thankful to be away from the college where they had learned to move about with their eyes cast down to the floor, to mumble, "Yes, miss," when need be, or "No, miss," or "Sorry, miss."

Now they were back in Quakertown, the neighborhood of homes and businesses their ancestors had managed to build in the years following Reconstruction, subscribing to Booker T. Washington's philosophy of self-help rather than returning to the plantations. On Frame Street, there was Nib's Grocery, and above it, the rooms where Dr. L. C. Parrish practiced medicine. Next door, Poot Mackey operated the Buffalo Bayou Cafe, and across the street, RCO's Ice Cream Parlor advertised Dairy Maid Custard. And there was Bat Suggs's Shoe Repair, and Miss Abigail Lou's, and Billy Moten's Apothecary, and Griff Lane's Hardware Store.

In the evenings, someone out for a stroll might hear the clack of dominoes slapped down on a kitchen table, the call of "Box-cars. Now how you like that?" Or the voices of the AME Church

Choir going to work on "Couldn't Hear Nobody Pray." Or, if it was Saturday night, a blues singer at the Buffalo Bayou Cafe—Mabel Moon, maybe, or Big Mama Annie, Hocey Simms or Choo Choo LaDeau. Third Sundays, the Heroines of Jericho put out a feed. They laid plywood sheets over sawhorses the length of Frame Street, and everyone came toting kitchen chairs, sat down, elbow to elbow, and packed away catfish gumbo, garlic grits, Cajun cabbage, sweet potato pudding, red beans and rice, pork chops, barbecued chicken, baked ham, hot rolls with peach peel jelly, apple pie, sugar pie, black walnut pound cake. "Lord," someone would say. "Heaven have to go some to beat this."

At his home, Little stepped up on his porch and saw Eugie and Camellia sitting across from each other in the living room, their knees touching, the folds of Camellia's wedding dress draped over their laps. Eugie was showing Camellia how to sew beads to the bodice. They were sitting in a patch of sunlight, and the silver beads were glittering, and Little felt a chill pass over him. For an instant, he imagined that he was a stranger, peeking in at this woman, Eugie, and this girl, Camellia.

He opened the screen door and stepped into his house. His shadow fell over Eugie and Camellia, and when they lifted their faces, it was easy for him to imagine that they were looking at him with heat in their eyes as if he had just interrupted something consecrated and hallowed. He knew the words from Mr. Lincoln's address at Gettysburg, an oration Washington Jones, Sr. had recited time and time again.

Little knew what the words meant. They meant there were things in the world no one ought to disturb, places only a savior or a tomfool would ever venture to walk.

"Moms, Baby-Girl," he said.

He came closer to them, intending to tell the story of what Mr. Bell had asked of him. But just then a silver bead dropped from Eugie's hand and rolled across the floor until it bumped against the toe of Little's boot. He knew that she had saved back a dollar here and a dollar there from the money she earned doing alterations at Neiman's Department Store downtown on the square where the white folks went to shop, and she had bought the lace she would need for the bodice. Camellia had pitched in what she could spare from her teacher's salary, and they had gone to Miss Diane's fabric shop and had special-ordered five yards of white satin. Nights, they had worked side by side, first cutting the pattern and then stitching the pieces together at Eugie's Singer, the rocking of its treadle as constant as blood through veins.

Little got down on his knees and plucked the silver bead from the floor. He carried it to Eugie and laid it on her palm as carefully as he had once put their sleeping Baby-Girl in her arms. Something about the delicate motion shamed him, caused him to consider how sweet life was in Quakertown, not only for him and his family but for all the other families who had made lives there, and he couldn't bring himself to say what he had agreed to do.

One

1

He never could have known it was coming—Mr. Bell's request—back in December when he delivered Christmas trees to the homes along Oak Street. He was Little Jones, the yardman, the one who came to care for the lawns and gardens all spring and summer, to rake leaves in autumn, to deliver the pine trees at Christmas and collect them after the holidays had gone.

Mr. Bell's son, Kizer, could remember waiting on the porch when he was young, anxious for the sound of Little Jones's wagon, heaped high with pine trees, creaking and groaning as it came down the street. Kizer watched the other neighborhood children gathering on the sidewalk in front of their houses, jumping up and down, their bodies, whole and full of good health, hardly able to contain the excitement that was sweeping along Oak Street. Now that the Christmas trees had come, Santa Claus wouldn't be far behind.

Kizer's crippled left leg, shorter by a full inch than his right, kept him from hopping about like the other children, but he felt a smug satisfaction because he knew what they didn't; he was the most excited of them all because when Little Jones came he not only brought the Christmas trees but also his daughter, Camellia, who was the most wonderful part of Kizer's life. She was kind and sweet, this little Negro girl whose skin was light-toned and creamy. Sometimes she held her bare arm next to his to gauge the difference in color, and sometimes they touched each other with shy fingers. He could recall their lovely caresses even now after so many years had passed. He remembered how he and Camellia had found places to hide, hoping to forestall the inevitable moment when Little, finished with his work, would call for her. They hid in closets, under beds, behind draperies.

"Let's pretend we can't see," she said once, "and the only way we can know each other is by feeling with our fingers."

They touched each other's faces, arms, legs. Kizer let his fingers linger on her lips. He touched the delicate bones of her wrists. He found the swell of her calf muscle and let his hand slide up to her knee. All the while, she was touching his slender neck, the hollow where his throat joined with his collarbone. Then she touched his lame leg, and he trembled, for it was the first time that anyone had touched him there with tenderness; the doctors had always poked and prodded with their rough fingers and their hard instruments. Camellia stroked the length of his leg with her small hand, and Kizer thought the sensation wonderful.

Even now, he could close his eyes and let his own hands move through the air around him and reshape her, this girl he hadn't seen in years but who had once been closer to him than anyone in all the time that had followed, years that had sent him to boarding school in the East and then later to New Orleans to take his degree at Tulane. He had graduated in the spring—Class of '20—and had come home to work in his father's bank, the Farmer's National. Now it was nearly Christmas, and when Little Jones brought in the pine tree, the house suddenly fragrant with its sharp, clean scent, Kizer remembered the days when he and Camellia were children and how she had been the only one he had trusted with his secrets.

He told her that his mother sometimes drank too much of her nerve tonic and then lay down and slept a very long time. When she finally woke and he tried to talk to her, she looked at him with a blank gaze as if his body had somehow vanished and his voice had become only a whisper of air.

"I don't think my mama likes me," he told Camellia, "because of my leg. I think she wishes she had another boy."

"She's got to like you," Camellia said. "She's your mama, and mamas have got to like their babies no matter what."

Kizer had thought of that conversation often over the last six months, had used it to reassure himself that it was true: mothers and their children were bound by love no matter how much they might disappoint each other.

After all, there were times when things were pleasant with his mother. They might be sitting some evening in the drawing room, and Mr. Bell might play something on the piano—Liszt's *Consolation* No. 3, perhaps—and Kizer and his mother might clasp hands and let the music speak their love. Or they might drive out into the country some lovely autumn day just for the joy of moving through the warm air, lazing on a Sunday, driving past the cotton fields, white with open bolls. Once, a fluff of cotton, caught up in a breeze, floated to them, and Mr. Bell plucked it from the air. They thought it the most marvelous thing; already they were imagining how they would tell the story again and again. It would become part of their family history, a part that would have nothing to do with sadness, and for that reason it would always be marvelous. They took turns holding the cotton in their hands, rubbing it over their faces, remarking on how soft it was, how much it pleased them.

And there were Saturday nights when they went downtown to the Dreamland Theater to a picture show, to laugh at Charlie Chaplin or Harold Lloyd, to thrill to Tom Mix or William S. Hart, or to fall in love with Clara Bow or Coleen Moore. After the show, they strolled about the square, window-shopping. They stopped at Neiman's Department Store to remark on the shortened hem of the new hobble skirts or the latest walking boots for ladies that reached halfway to the knee. They lingered at Ever's

Hardware so Mr. Bell, an avid gun collector, could admire a Rider pocket revolver, or at W. J. Griggs's automobile lot where Mr. Bell promised to buy Kizer a new Hudson speedster when he graduated from Tulane. For those moments, they were like the other families strolling about the square, ordinary people out on a Saturday night. If their neighbors knew anything of the ugliness that could rise up in the Bell home—and how could they not, Kizer thought—they pretended that they didn't. They said, "Good evening," "How did you like the picture show?" "What weather we're having," and then went on, leaving the Bells full of gratitude for the wonderful feeling that they were ordinary and undistinguished by their misery.

These moments didn't come often—so many nights were spent at home in silence, or with Mrs. Bell sobbing, or worse yet making some scene because she was drunk—but when they did come, Kizer felt the hope that lay dormant beneath his family's sadness, and he prayed for more moments like them when that hope could rise and bloom and fill them with love.

There were also times when his mother could speak of her drinking and all that had led to it with dignity and compassion, and Kizer could feel humbled; his body had failed him through no fault of his own, but his mother knew she was to blame, would readily admit as much, for the weakness of spirit she was trying so desperately to overcome. People lived through horrid episodes all the time, she told him, and somehow they managed. She only wished she could be as stouthearted and brave.

"Come sit with me," she said one evening, and Kizer did, thinking, It's almost Christmas, 1920. We've almost made it through another year.

He joined her on the settee by the fireplace, and she told him the story she had told time and time again, the story of the last evening of her girlhood. The only light was from the fire and the Christmas candles burning in the windows, and he could imagine her, all those years before, sitting in the dark at Wright's Opera

House on the night the Allen Musical Company performed *The King of Kokomo*. She would have been nineteen, Tallulah Reins, the slender girl with the bright smile, the girl everyone called Tibby. "I was absolutely charmed," she said to Kizer though twenty-five years had passed and so much had changed for her.

He pictured her, as he always did when he heard this story, stepping out of the opera house into the spring night and looking up at the sky filled with stars. She had sat in the dark those two hours, living the lives of the characters onstage. "I don't know how to describe what I felt," she said. "Only that I was in love—in love with the whole world." He preferred to think of her as that girl, overwhelmed by how easily she could escape herself, go out into the universe, thread her way through the lives of others, instead of this woman now before him who kept searching the dark passages and blind alleys of her own life.

On occasion, she locked herself away in her bedroom and didn't come out for days. At other times, Kizer heard her pacing the floors at night, roaming through the house, unable to find a place where she might take some measure of comfort. He imagined at these times that she was thinking of her own mother on the night of *The King of Kokomo*. He had never known his grandmother, Loreli, but he had long been aware of her story. She had fallen in love with a married man from Dallas and had tumbled into despair when he had gone back to his wife. He had broken things off with Loreli on the very night when Tibby stood outside the opera house looking up at the stars, sensing how everything was of a piece—she and the actors on the stage, the characters who only lived through their bodies and voices, and the other theatergoers drifting past her, all of them stunned by how the sky opened above them and dazzled them with stars.

She didn't know—and this was the part that always broke Kizer whenever he thought of the small moment of grace allowed his mother—that Loreli had already stepped off the second-story sleeping porch, impaling herself on the spiked fence below. Tibby would come home and find her there and would never be able to get back to the girl who only minutes before had been so enchanted with the world

"That night everything seemed so wonderful," she said. "At least for a while. And then. Well, just wait until you've lived through something horrible. Then you'll see what life can do to you."

Her comment wounded him. Did she think it had been easy living as a cripple—the butt of jokes, the object of stares? He didn't know how to say as much to her without disregarding her own pain, but suddenly he didn't have to because she squeezed his hand and said, "Oh, listen to me rattle on and on. The past is the past. Shoo. Let it go." And he knew, then, that she was sorry.

On Christmas Eve, he came home from the bank at noon and saw her sitting on the porch in a wicker chair with a fanned back. She was sitting very straight, her hands folded in her lap. It was one of those warm Texas days in early winter that always gave her hope. Kizer came up the walk leaning on the crook of his cane where the mahogany was worn smooth from the pressure of his hand. The sight of his mother wearing a white dress she had obviously chosen for how bright it would look, how full of promise, overwhelmed him.

"Mother," he said, and she reached out her hand and waited for him to come to her.

"Tomorrow's Christmas," she said. "Feel how warm the sun is. Do you think your father will like his present?"

They had bought him the Rider pocket revolver for his gun collection.

"I'm sure he'll like it just fine," Kizer said, glad to be talking of ordinary things, to be caught up in the excitement of the holidays. "I think he'd adore anything you'd give him."

Tibby smiled sweetly at him. "Thank you for that. Sometimes I forget that I'm still a person someone can love. It's all going to be wonderful, isn't it?"

"Yes, Mother. It's going to be grand."

Mr. Bell did indeed adore the Rider pocket revolver. "Oh, Tibby. It's just the thing," he said the next morning when they were all gathered around the tree. "You remembered how much I admired it that night in the window at Ever's Hardware."

His gift was one for both Tibby and Kizer, a trip to Hot Springs.

"The mountains?" Tibby said, her face bright with anticipation.

"That's right," said Mr. Bell. "We leave tomorrow. The three of us. A holiday getaway. Won't that be fine?"

The next day, they rode the train across the North Texas plains, into Arkansas, where they began their climb into the mountains. Tibby thrilled to how fresh the air was. "I can smell the pine trees," she said, and clapped her hands together.

Kizer was content to watch her shoulders draw back with her breath and her face relax until she finally settled her head on Mr. Bell's shoulder. She rested her hands in her lap and soon she was asleep.

"I don't mind telling you it's been a rough go." Mr. Bell whispered so as not to wake Tibby. "Your mother's nerves," he said. A sad look came into his eyes, and his chin broke into gooseflesh as if he could barely keep himself from breaking down. "Let's just say we both can use a rest."

Kizer watched his mother sleep, rocked by the gentle sway of the train. He imagined the locomotive powering the string of cars higher and higher up the mountain, and he could almost believe in the healing power of will.

"I'm going to the club car." His leg ached, and he wanted to move about. "Care to join me?"

"You go on," Mr. Bell said. "I wouldn't want her to wake up and find me gone."

Kizer had always admired his father's devotion to his mother no matter the upsets and turmoil. "The ones like your mother," he had said once, "they're the ones we have to keep loving. Poor souls. They have such a hard time loving themselves."

Now, as Kizer entered the club car, he wished that he could someday know the sort of love his father did, a love without condition.

The club car was empty except for an elderly gentleman sitting in a leather wing chair. He lowered the newspaper he had been reading and smiled at Kizer. "I'm going to Hot Springs for the baths." There were thin spots in the white whiskers of his out-of-fashion mutton chops and moustache, and Kizer could see the pink skin beneath them. When the man squinted, the sun glinted off the small round lenses of his spectacles. " 'For I will restore health unto thee,' " he recited, " 'and I will heal thee of thy wounds.' That's painted on the wall of the lobby at the Fordyce Bath House. Jeremiah, chapter thirty, verse seventeen. As I've gotten older, I've begun to believe in God. Do you believe in God, young man?"

Some nights, Kizer lay awake, listening to the wind screaming across the plains, and he imagined the only sound heaven could make was that roar. If God had ever tried to tell him anything, Kizer decided—had ever tried to comfort him, or explain why he had been born lame—it had been with a clamor and a din beyond his understanding.

"It seems to me," he told the man, "we're pretty much on our own."

The man folded the newspaper and tapped the spine against his leg. "Miracles happen at Hot Springs," he said. "For the Indians, it was a place of peace where tribes could lay aside their feuds and let the Great Spirit fill them. The springs can make even the most hopeless of us feel holy. I swear, son. It's true."

Kizer wished more than anything that his mother could be well, that she might find the girl she had been that night she had stepped from the opera house and felt herself connected to the stars above her. "I'd like to believe that," he said to the man. "But really, it's just water."

"It starts out as plain old rainwater," the man said. "It seeps through the chert and novaculite on the face of the mountain and travels down through the crust of the earth for years—God knows how many years. The deeper it goes the hotter it gets. Then it hits the cracks and faults of the sandstone and these cracks bring the water back up in thermal springs on the slope of the mountain. Imagine that! The rain that falls today will be healing people who haven't even been born. If you ask me, that's the miracle—this evolution from rain to elixir." The man waved his newspaper at Kizer's leg. "You must believe there's a chance. Why else would you be going to the springs?"

Kizer realized, then, that the man thought him the pilgrim, the supplicant desperate to be healed. It pained him now to make his way to the door, knowing the man was watching him with pity. At the door, Kizer turned back and said, "You don't even know me."

"We're all ruined," the man said. "All of us in one way or another. There's no shame in that."

In Hot Springs, Kizer and his parents took two rooms at the Arlington Hotel. Each morning, Tibby went to the Fordyce where a trainer, as she told Kizer later, put her through her paces. There were pulling machines and striking dummies, turning poles and strides. Afterward, she soaked in a delicious bath of thermal water. Then maybe a hot bake in the thermo room and a massage to take out all the kinks. Afternoons, she and Mr. Bell went hiking up the face of the mountain. They came back to the hotel with their cheeks red and glowing, the clean scent of pine on their skin. "Tomorrow you must join us," Tibby said to Kizer each evening at dinner, but he never did. Not even for bowling in the basement of the Fordyce. "The pins just scatter," his mother said. "They're in their neat little triangle, and then you knock them down."

And through all this, for two weeks, she didn't have a drop of gin. Kizer was happy for her. Maybe the gentleman on the train had been right; maybe Hot Springs was a place of miracles.

Their last night there, they dined in the Fountain Room at the Arlington. Tibby kept petting Kizer's hand. "I've had the best of times," she said. "It's a new year and everything's off to a fine start."

Later, they went out into the lobby where a dance band was playing. "Oh, listen." Tibby grabbed onto Kizer's arm. "Will you dance with your mother?"

The thought of himself clomping across the floor with his ragged steps appalled him. "My leg," he said.

"Pish," said Tibby. "You'll be fine."

She held out her hand for him to take, and he understood that this was her way of saying she was sorry for all she had done to hurt him. Still, he couldn't bring himself to dance with her, to have the eyes of the other dancers following him. Perhaps, he thought, there was something shriveled inside him, his heart withered like a dried pea, but he couldn't accept the invitation. "Father, will you do the honors?" His mother let her hand rise to her throat, and Kizer saw how he had wounded her. "I believe I'll step outside for some air."

While his mother and father danced, Kizer strolled down Central Avenue, along Bath House Row, where the wind rattled the green, waxy leaves of the magnolias. Along the lawns of the bathhouses, holly shrubs had been neatly trimmed into low hedges. The electric streetlamps were on. Kizer stopped in front of the Fordyce and rested a hand against one of the fluted green poles. On the plaza between the Fordyce and the Maurice, steam lifted from a jetting fountain of water. A woman wearing a fox stole around her shoulders took off her glove, stuck her hand into the spray, and jerked it back with a cry of surprise. "Jigs, that's hot," she said to her friend, a young man in a high-backed wooden wheelchair, a tartan blanket spread over his legs. "Sure, it's hot," he said. "That's the ticket."

Kizer averted his eyes as the couple passed by him. Through the front windows of the Fordyce, he could see people in rocking chairs in the lobby. On the third story, a row of seven arched doorways led to balconies. One of the doors was ajar, and Kizer could hear piano music and a woman's voice singing "In the Gloaming." It was a haunting voice, full of sweetness and sorrow—a clear, strong voice rising in the dusk, and suddenly he was trembling, sorry for the way he had refused his mother. He would make it all up to her if only he could. If he could just go back and dance with her, not caring how clumsy, how pathetic he was. He imagined her dancing with his father, the movement of her body familiar to her and sure. Tomorrow, they would go back to Denton to face the coldest months. The dark would come early, and they would hunker down and wait for morning, eager for the coming of light. Perhaps, Kizer thought, his mother might heal the sadness and want inside her. But he could do nothing about his leg. When he had slipped from her body, his own had been marked for life.

2

That winter, it was Camellia's habit to get to school before dawn so she could build a fire in the coal stove and take the chill out of the room before her pupils arrived. She sat alone in the dim light, listening to the roar of the fire, and her heart sank, imagining as she did that this would always be her life—an old-maid school-teacher like so many she had known at Bishop College.

When the children came, she helped them off with coats and hats, scolding those who had rushed out of their houses bare-headed or who hadn't bothered with scarves or gloves.

"Do you want to get sick?" she said to them.

And they said, "No, ma'am, Miss Camellia."

"Then stop being melon-heads. Goodness, I swear sometimes you don't have the sense God gave a goose."

Three children had died in Sanger just before Christmas. How would it be, Camellia fretted, if she were to lose a single one of her own? Tuberculosis, typhoid, the Spanish influenza. Just that week, a man from the Public Health Administration had lectured the students on cleanliness. Camellia made sure they had clean handkerchiefs, their own drinking cups. She taught them how to cover mouth and nose when they sneezed. She wouldn't let them sample food from one another's dinner pails, and when they whined and complained, she threw up her hands and said, "I don't want to hear your grumbling. I mean to keep you well, so you might as well get used to doing what I say. What did I tell you? An ounce of prevention is worth what?"

"A pound of cure, Miss Camellia."

"That's right. Now there's something you can take to the bank."

Each evening, on her way home, she stopped at Billy Moten's Apothecary to buy a newspaper. Later, after she had helped her mother with supper and marked her pupils' lessons, she went to her room and sat on her bed, reading the front-page articles about Miss Clara Harmon who was on trial in Oklahoma for killing her lover, a Mr. Stephen Mays.

Camellia was ashamed of herself for taking an interest in what her father called "trashy white folks," but she couldn't resist the drama of it all, particularly there in winter when everything was so gloomy. If the story of Clara Harmon could spice things up for a while, who was she to ignore it?

She could barely imagine the scandalous things she read. She, herself, had never even been with a man, not because she wasn't pretty, but because she had yet to find someone who appealed to her. She knew it was a common notion in Quakertown that she was choosy, and maybe she was. At least, she told herself, she wouldn't end up like Clara Harmon—so trampy she got mixed up with a married man and now faced charges of splitting his skull with an ax.

One evening, Camellia read an article about a white man from Dallas. A mob of masked men rousted him out of his home in the middle of the night, took him to the bottom land along the Trinity River, stripped him to the waist, and lashed him with a horsewhip because he was living with a Negro woman.

Suddenly, Camellia's hands were trembling. Only once, so she imagined, had she ever come anywhere close to loving a boy, and she had been so young she hadn't even known what love was. His name was Kizer Bell, the son of Mr. Andrew Bell. "Kizer has taken a shine to your girl," Camellia heard Mrs. Bell tell Little one day. "It's no wonder. She's so sweet to him."

Camellia sat with Kizer on afternoons while her father worked in the Bells' flower beds and gardens. She especially remembered the time when Kizer had just come home from the hospital, and his leg was wrapped in a plaster cast.

"They busted my bones," he told her.

"Why'd they bust up your bones?"

"I was born wrong. This leg's shorter than that one. Now they're trying to make it longer."

"You're some kind of brave to let 'em bust up your bones."

"Sometimes I'm scared," he said. "What if it doesn't work? I don't want to be a crippled boy."

Camellia made up stories about the two of them. They hunted for buried treasure, rode wild horses across the plains, stowed away on cargo ships, and sailed to the Far East. And when trouble came, as it always did in Camellia's stories, she spun the tales out through breathtaking twists and turns until it seemed that all would be lost. "And then," she always said, "Kizer the Brave came to the rescue." She gave him daring and strength and told how he saved them both from peril. "Oh, Kizer," she said at each story's end. She laid her head sweetly onto his shoulder. "My hero."

"You're my friend," he said to her once. "You're my best friend."

She hadn't thought of Kizer Bell in years, but now the article about the white man in Dallas had brought him back to her. Night after night, she dreamed of him. Sometimes he was the little boy with his leg in a cast; sometimes he was grown. She was always the age she was now, either holding the child on her lap, rocking him to sleep, or walking with the man, clutching his arm. In either scenario, she was there to comfort him as she had all those years ago. She woke from these dreams feeling as if she had lost something dear, something she had spent the rest of her life trying to replace. She knew that her loss had something to do with a feeling she had cherished when she and Kizer had been children, the feeling that someone needed her. If she could only touch him the right way, rub her hand over his lame leg, she might heal him. She had wished that, then, though she hadn't known how to say it. Now, she ached for the sweetness she had known with Kizer before her mother had finally put a stop to it. "I don't want you going over there, Camellia," Eugie had said. "World can't stand too much cozy between black and white. Believe me. I know."

Camellia could remember the last time she had seen Kizer. She had been in her father's wagon, looking up at Kizer's bedroom window where he sat on the window seat. It was drizzling, and she could barely see him through the rain-streaked glass. But she could tell that he had his hand pressed against the window as if he were reaching out to her, as if he somehow feared that this was the last time he would see her and wanted to let her know that wherever they went he would be with her and she with him. Her father shook the mule's reins, and the wagon lurched forward. Camellia twisted around on the bench seat and lifted her arm. She felt her fingers stretching out toward Kizer, but the distance was too great and the wagon was gathering speed, and soon there was only the rain and the fading light—dusk falling, and the grand homes of Oak Street vanishing behind her.

3

In January, when Tibby didn't feel like leaving the house, she couldn't help but think of her mother and the note she had left before stepping off the sleeping porch: "I'm bringing the curtain down on this dreary show." With her mother's death, Tibby found herself surrounded by drama. Wherever she went, she saw people draw close and mumble as she passed. *Such a scandal. Loreli Reins and a married man from Dallas. You know what they say? Apple never falls far from the tree.* Tibby heard them. She felt their eyes on her. She knew what everyone thought, particularly the boys who wanted her. Her mother had been a woman of dubious character, and surely she would be, too. She threw herself headlong into their expectations. She became the saucy Tibby, the dangerous Tibby. She found herself at one party or another, drinking liquor, falling into the arms of this boy or that, who expected her to be wicked like her mother. Only Andrew had seen in her some sweetness that had been hers before her mother had taken her dramatic leap, and for that reason alone, she married him. There was a time after when she didn't drink. She saw to her house and her husband, kept her affairs in order, proud to be a young wife. She and Andrew had all their lives before them. Then Kizer came, and when she understood that his leg was deformed, she blamed herself; surely she had done something wrong when she had been pregnant. She sank into a deep despair, and soon she was drinking again.

Now, on gray days, she lay in bed as long as she could, dreaming herself back to Hot Springs—to the warm water of the baths that had soothed her. Not a drop of gin. Those two weeks, not a drop.

In Texas, the flat plains stretched out so far and the sky opened all around her, and she feared if she took so much as a single step, she would disappear into all that space. Sometimes at night she heard the wind and she curled herself into a ball and sobbed because her place in the world seemed puny and without merit. What had she ever done that was good and would last? She hadn't been able to save her mother; in fact, that last night, just before she left for the opera house, they had argued. "People are talking," she had told her mother. "They say you're a whore." Oh, how she wished she could take back the word. Sometimes, when she drank, she got to the point where she left the here and now and found her mother in the spirit world, and she said to her, "I'm sorry," and her mother forgave her. She had tried to say the same to Kizer that night in Hot Springs when she had asked him to dance, but he had turned away from her.

She longed for a drink, for the warm glow of gin in her throat and chest, the fog in her head until she was finally free from misery and guilt—at least until morning when she woke.

"My sweet Tibby," Andrew always said to her when she cried in their bed at night. He wrapped his arms around her and rocked her against him. "Sh, sh," he said. "I'm here."

But he wasn't. Not really. He was at the bank all day, and evenings he was off to this meeting or that—the Board of Regents at the women's college, the City Commission—or else staying too long at the Knights of Columbus Lodge. He loved this city—*his* city, he often thought, not that he wanted to boast, but he did take great pride in everything that his influence had been able to accomplish: the paved streets, the arc lighting, the new bronze clock on his bank that chimed each quarter hour. He loved the long, tree-lined length of Oak Street and the gentle rise to the downtown square where the courthouse clock tower stretched up to the sky. He loved the comings and goings of trade, shoppers chatting as they squeezed by one another on the walkways. There were Victrolas to buy at Palmer's Music Store, and the latest calf-length skirts for the ladies at Neiman's, and groceries at G. W. Gibson's, and headache powders at Allison's Pharmacy, a new pair of shoes at Beyett's Booterie, a fresh cut of meat from Ben Sullivan, a tailored suit at W. S. Wheatley's, a portrait made at Cole and White's. A gent could get his hair cut and his face shaved at R. M. Mitchell's shop and then stop by Ever's Hardware to see what new gadgets might be on display or duck into W. R. Allen's to check on the market prices for cotton, or buy a hot lunch at the Lone Star Restaurant and maybe an ice cream later at Lipscomb's Soda Shoppe. Now that the war was done, and people's spirits were high, Mr. Bell loved to be out and about in his city. He had even coined a slogan for his bank to go along with the growing downtown traffic: "Go Slow. Keep to the Right." He thought it sound advice for life's whole journey, as well as for the passing moment in the street.

Kizer, these nights, sometimes slipped away to the picture show or the travelogues at the college; sometimes he stayed home and holed up in his room, reading travel books, dreaming of foreign lands and how he might one day visit them.

One night, Tibby knocked on his door. When he heard the meager tap, his back stiffened because he knew why she had come. He sat awhile longer, hoping the knock wouldn't come again, but it did, and this time his mother called to him. "Kizer," she said, and her voice was so small, so pleading and yet full of dread, that he couldn't resist it. It sounded the way he imagined his own voice had all those years ago when, after the surgery on his leg, he had called for her. "Kizer," she said again. "Please."

He went to the door but didn't open it. "I can't." He laid his face against the wood. "You know that."

"But my hands. Oh, Kizer. You should see how they shake."

He heard a jagged scratching on the other side of the door, and he knew she was holding her hand to it, letting her fingers skitter and scrape. It was that sound that finally undid him. He couldn't bear to hear it. He opened the door so the noise would stop, and there was his mother, her face streaked with tears. She put her trembling hands on his chest. "Kizer, please." She clutched at his shirt front, and he knew the only way to stop her would be to let loose of his cane. "Kizer, won't you help me?"

He felt weak with what he knew she was asking, hated himself already because he knew he would give in. This was the thing about loving someone who was weak and wounded—the hard thing about loving his mother. He had never been able to fully steel himself against her, though he knew that was what she needed if she was ever going to be well. How much could he let her suffer toward that end? It was simple, when only thinking about what had to be done, to say, "All right now, we'll face the worst. We'll face it over and over, as many times as we have to, until we get to the other side." But when they were in the middle of her anguish—her shakes, her screams, her sobs—that was a different matter. Then it was so difficult to say what was right. Kizer found himself willing to do anything to make her stop.

He knew a bootlegger in Quakertown named Mr. Smoke, and often he went to him to buy bathtub gin for his mother. It was better, he thought, then having her drive down there herself as she had done once and the yardman, Little Jones, had found her, fallen down drunk in the street, and had brought her home in his wagon.

But now they were trying to save her, he and his father. Kizer knew that. They were trying to see her through the grim winter days. "One at a time," his father had said, but when the dark came and the house seemed so gloomy and the nights so long, his father was gone and it was Kizer who had to try to resist his mother's threats and despair, and he longed for someone with more courage and forbearance to tell him the right thing to do.

When Mr. Bell came home from the Knights of Columbus, he saw the rooms of his house blazing with light. It was late, nearly midnight, and he was still trying to get a firm grasp on the talk that had exploded at the Board of Regents' meeting and continued at the Knights of Columbus, swirling and pulsing and taking on a life it would be nearly impossible to stop. A young lady at the college, the daughter of Mr. Neiman of Neiman's Department Store, had been accosted one evening on the college grounds. A boy from Quakertown, she claimed, had followed her, had spoken vile, lurid things to her ("Gonna get you, baby," he had said. "Gonna get me some of your honey pot.") before she had run for the safety of her dormitory.

Mr. Bell remembered how the men had pounded on tables and said the coloreds weren't to be trusted. They weren't a hundred percent American, and if someone wasn't a hundred percent American, who knew what they might do. Look at the IWW—*anarchists*—and the socialists—*reds*. The white men said they had to nip this Quakertown in the bud, said the coloreds were getting too big for their britches. Just like the Germans when they sank the *Lusitania* and started the war. Like the goddamn communists—*radicals*. That's what those coloreds down in Quakertown were, especially those ones who fought in the war. *Lookit here, lookit here, right here in this NAACP magazine:* "Make way for democracy! We saved it in France and by the Great Jehovah, we'll save it in the U.S.A., or know the reason why." That way of thinking, the white men decided, by-God had to be stopped.

Mr. Bell had cringed, hearing such hateful talk. When it came to the coloreds, he couldn't say with any certainty, the way so many others could, that they were suspect. In fact, over the years he had developed a genuine warmth for Little Jones, thought of him sometimes—though he admitted this only to himself—as a friend. The night he had brought Tibby home from Quakertown in his wagon, he had said, "Mr. Bell, I wouldn't want to see Miz Bell hurt herself." He had said it with concern and affection, without passing judgment, and Mr. Bell was still grateful to him for that kindness. But now he went weak with the thought of Tibby in young Miss Neiman's place, Tibby drunk and wandering through Quakertown. Who knew what might happen to her if there were a next time, or to any of the girls at the college. Maybe the men at the Knights of Columbus were right. Maybe Quakertown was a dangerous place.

Now, when he saw the lights on in his house, he felt the same panic that had risen in him the night he had seen Tibby in Little Jones's wagon, her head lolled over against his arm, her hat cock-eyed—a fear that one day she would sink so low she would be gone forever. Mr. Bell let his Hudson idle in the driveway, afraid to look on his own house, brilliant with light, for fear of what he might see.

The doors to the upstairs balcony opened, and Tibby's shadowy form rushed out. She lifted her arms to the sky, and light from the hallway behind her glinted off the bottle in her hand. "The stars," she cried in a drunken voice, the voice Mr. Bell had been hoping to never again hear. "All the pretty, pretty stars."

When he had finally gone into the house and quieted her, had put her to bed and held her until she slept, he found Kizer outside on the front porch, sitting in a rocking chair, his head tipped down into his hands.

Mr. Bell dropped the empty gin bottle in his lap, and Kizer, too slow, failed to catch it before it fell to the floor and shattered.

"I'm sorry," Kizer said. "Father . . ."

Mr. Bell held up his hand. "You've always been weak, and so have I when it comes to your mother. But after that trip to Hot Springs, I thought we had a chance. Now look what it's come to."

"Sometimes," Kizer said, "I feel like going away. Somewhere far from here. Europe maybe. I swear, sometimes I can't bear being here in this house."

The night was cold, the wind moving the bare branches of the trees in an eerie dance and sway that seemed to Mr. Bell both a beckoning and a reaching out. He didn't know what to say to Kizer. He only knew the cold night, the swinging of the branches, and the feeling that something was stirring, some ugliness kindling, ready to spark and fire.

4

The first time Camellia saw Ike Mattoon, he was downtown in Neiman's Department Store, a pair of wool trousers folded neatly over his arm. She had come through the back door from the alleyway, as Mr. Neiman had insisted she do on Saturdays when she brought her mother a hot lunch. Today it was chicken and noodles, toted in an old syrup pail. Normally, Eugie would have stopped her sewing machine and stretched her back, and she and Camellia would have eaten the lunch in the cramped room where Eugie did her alterations. But today, she put her finger to her lips, signaling for Camellia to keep quiet.

Camellia could see Ike Mattoon through the gap in the green curtain that separated the alteration room from the rest of the store. He was wearing a handsome suit of clothes, and the collar of his white shirt was bright against the dark skin of his neck, the darkest skin she had ever seen on a colored man, as dark and as shiny as the mahogany counter behind which Mr. Neiman stood, a yellow tape measure around his neck, a pencil behind his ear, his arm lifted so he could point his finger to the changing room behind Ike and the sign on the door that said WHITES ONLY.

"You see that sign?" Mr. Neiman said.

There were several ladies in the store, white ladies, who were gathered at the garment rack that held the new winter coats. Even from her distance, Camellia could smell the perfumes and powders they carried on them—the scents of gardenia and lilac. They drifted to her on the cold air the women had brought in from outside.

When Mr. Neiman spoke to Ike, the women's chatter and the whisk of hangers over the clothes rod stopped, and all Camellia could hear was the creak of the floorboard as Ike shifted his weight, took one step toward the counter. She felt the floor vibrate beneath her feet, and she swore that Ike's step had sent a tingle up her leg.

His voice, when he spoke, was loud and clear. "I need to try on these trousers for size."

Mr. Neiman let his arm drop to his side. "Those trousers?" he said. "Boy, you can pay for those trousers, then you can take them on back to Quakertown and try them on all you've a mind to."

"Pay for them first?" Ike laughed, and it was clear that he was laughing at Mr. Neiman, at the absurdity of his suggestion. "I declare you're pulling my leg. Yes, sir. That's what you're doing, having some fun with old Ike. Oh, gracious. That's a good one. Yes, sir. Buy a pair of trousers without trying them on? Now, sir, what if they don't fit?"

"My point exactly," said Mr. Neiman. He was a short man with a skinny neck and red-tipped ears that made it seem that he had been sorely embarrassed once and had never recovered. "You think I could sell them then? After it got around that you had them on?"

Ike was at the counter now. He laid the trousers out on the black mahogany. He stretched out the legs. "I'm a war veteran," he said. His voice was as soft as Camellia imagined his hand would feel if it rubbed along her skin, slow and gentle, the way it now smoothed and petted the wool. "I served this country in France."

"I don't give a lick what you did in France," said Mr. Neiman. "You're not going in that room. All you coloreds up there in

Quakertown are getting too uppity. Being places you shouldn't be. Saying things you've got no right to say."

"All right, then." Ike reached into his coat pocket and drew out a straight razor. The blade, once he had opened it, gleamed in the sunlight streaming through the front window. "Yes, sir. If that's the way you want it, sir."

Mr. Neiman stepped back from the counter. The pencil fell to the floor with a clatter. "Careful, boy," he said.

Ike found the seams of each leg and sliced through the cloth with his razor. When he was finished, he held the trousers up above the counter, and the legs, split into ribbons, dangled and danced in a stir of air. Camellia watched the brilliant light as it flashed and waned in the spaces where only moments before the cloth had been whole. She had seen a man hanged once on the courthouse lawn in Fort Worth, a colored man who had raped a white woman, and his legs had jerked and twitched as he had spun at the end of the rope.

"Boy, you're going to pay for those," Mr. Neiman said.

Ike let the trousers drop to the counter. "Oh, yes, sir. I'll pay." He took a wallet from his breast pocket. "Just for the satisfaction." He tossed some bills at Mr. Neiman. They struck him on the chest and fluttered down to the floor. "Go on now," Ike said. "I want to see you get down on your hands and knees, want to see you crawl around for that money."

Mr. Neiman shook the end of his tape measure at Ike. "I'll call the constable on you."

Ike gathered up the trousers. "My name's Isaac Mattoon. You tell the constable to come on down to Quakertown if he wants to find me. I reside at Miss Sibby Long's boardinghouse." He turned and bowed to the white women at the coat rack. "Ladies," he said, "I'm sorry for the spectacle." Then, shoulders back and head level, he walked out of the store.

Camellia's hands were trembling as she set the syrup pail on her mother's work table.

"That boy's trouble," Eugie said, but already Camellia was hurrying to the alley, out into the cold wind. Never had she seen a colored man so bold. Not even her father who was, as her mother always said, a bantam rooster. Even he knew to duck his head when he spoke to a white man, to never look him in the eyes, to knock quietly on the back door when he had finished his yard work, and to wait until someone carried out his pay.

Camellia caught up with Ike at the corner in front of the Farmer's National Bank. She could hear the works whirring in the clock above the bank's doors, could hear the gears moving as the hand scraped off another minute. Ike was waiting to cross the street. She was afraid that if she didn't reach out and touch him, she would lose her chance, would let him walk away from her.

She put her hand on his arm. He spun around. The legs of the cut trousers brushed across her hand.

"I saw you," she said. "There in the store. I saw what you did."

Ike took in a breath, and his brilliant white shirt stretched across his chest. "So you saw me. Yes, indeed. And how is it I don't remember seeing you? I expect I'd a noticed if you'd been anywhere near my sights."

"I was in the back," she said. "With my mama. She does sewing for Mr. Neiman."

Ike held up the cut trousers. "Reckon she could sew these?"

"What a thing to do," Camellia said. And then, because it still amazed her to think of it, she laughed. "Cut up those britches and then pay good money."

A look came over Ike's face like the scowl he had presented to Mr. Neiman. "Is that what you stopped me for? So you could laugh at me? Tell me what a mooncalf I was to buy a pair of britches and then ruin them?"

That wasn't what she had meant at all. He had misunderstood.

She had wanted to tell him that what he had done had left her breathless. How courageous he had been. She had never seen anything like it in her life. She could still hear the ripping sound the razor had made through the cloth, and the silence—so tantalizing—that had followed.

Now all she could do was stammer. "I didn't mean . . . I wasn't . . . I thought . . ."

"There." Ike threw the trousers on the ground. "Let the damned things rot," he said, and then he marched across the street, leaving Camellia to gather them up, to hold them against her, to think what a mess she had made of things. How stupid she had been. How utterly stupid.

That afternoon, at her mother's sewing machine, she laid out one leg of the trousers, overlapped the raw edges of the torn cloth, and stitched a seam. She repeated the process with the other leg, hoping that there was enough material left to make a proper fit.

As she worked, she told Little, who was around the house more now that winter had come and the lawns had gone brown, what she had seen with her very own eyes in Neiman's Department Store.

"He stood up as big as you please," she told him. " 'I served in France,' " he said. " 'My name's Isaac Mattoon.' "

Little was sitting on a stool by the sewing machine. "Dark-skinned, you say?"

Camellia nodded. "As black as this wool."

"I'll go out and talk to a few folks." Little stood up and slapped his hands together. "See what I can find out."

By evening, when Eugie came home, he had the lowdown on Mr. Isaac Mattoon.

Little told Eugie and Camellia everything he knew as they ate their supper. The light above the table cast a shimmer on the slick oilcloth. Ike Mattoon had come from Tennessee, and yes, he had served in the war. A barber by trade who intended to open a shop on Frame Street. He had paid three months in advance at Sibby Long's boardinghouse. Little winked at Camellia. "Mr. Money Bags. No wonder he turned you all sideways."

"Papa," said Camellia. "You're making up stories now."

"Story me this," said Little. "Who's the one spent all afternoon sewing up that man's pants?"

Eugie balanced her butter knife on the rim of her plate. "Is that what you done, Baby-Girl?"

"She most certainly did," said Little. "Chattered away like a squirrel. 'Oh, he done this. Oh, he done that.' 'My name's Mr. Isaac Mattoon,' he said.' "

"Well, you better snatch him up fast," Eugie told Camellia. "Sounds like he won't be around too long for the taking."

"Other ladies got their eyes set on him?" said Little.

"Oh, I wouldn't doubt that's the truth." Eugie nodded her head. "Fine-looking man. But he's uppity."

Little pulled his shoulders back. "Nothing wrong with being proud."

"You should've heard Mr. Neiman ranting and raving after Mr. Isaac Mattoon left the store." Eugie shook her finger at Little. " 'Since the war,' he said, 'coloreds think they own the world. One of them was after my daughter one night. 'Gonna get you, baby,' he said. *Baby*. Just like that. Just like he was a white man.' "

"Up there at the college," Little said. "I heard the story. Truth is that young Miss Neiman was sneaking around with her beau— Mr. Arthur Goody's boy, I believe he is, and he got a might too fresh, if you know what I mean, and she storied, said it was a boy from Quakertown who gave her the trouble."

"Well, I know Mr. Neiman worked me extra hard," said Eugie. "Made me tear out a whole passel of hems. Swore they weren't straight. Little, even you know better than to talk to a white man the way this Mattoon boy did, and you're about the proudest colored man I know."

Little bowed his head. His voice, when he finally spoke, was flat and dull, and Camellia knew that he was ashamed of all the times he had said, 'Yes, boss,' and 'No, boss,' to the snooty white folks who hired him to tend to their gardens and lawns. "I reckon a man fight for his country," he said, "he got a right to stand up for himself."

"Stand up," said Eugie. "Nothing wrong with that. But no need to cause trouble for the rest of us."

"No trouble at all," said Little. "Unless you go looking for it."

After supper, Camellia carried the trousers to Miss Sibby Long's boardinghouse and knocked on Mr. Isaac Mattoon's door. She could hear music inside, Dixieland jazz, and when Ike opened the door, the clarinets and the horns blared out into the hall.

"You," he said. His white shirt was unbuttoned, and she could see the swell of his chest muscles rising up above the neckline of his undershirt.

"Camellia," she said. "I'm Camellia Jones."

"I remember you. You're the one who laughed at me."

"I didn't mean to." She handed him the trousers. "I meant to say that you were wonderful."

Ike unfolded the trousers and held them to his waist. "Sewed them up." He grinned. "Well, what do you know about that?"

"Didn't take much," said Camellia. "I'm sorry you thought I was making fun."

She turned to go, but Ike grabbed her hand. "Here now. Don't run off. Don't you want to know if they fit?"

"I'll wait out here," she said, "while you try them on."

"You won't run away?"

"No," said Camellia. "I won't run."

He closed the door, and Camellia heard him lift the needle from the phonograph record. Everything was so quiet then. She heard footsteps coming up the stairs, and the voices of Mavis Brown and her friend Hocie Simms. Camellia pressed her back to the wall. How would it be if someone saw her, a schoolteacher, loitering outside a strange man's room? It wouldn't do at all. She did the first thing she could think to do: she opened Ike's door and stepped inside.

He was standing by the bed, his shirttails hanging down over his bare legs. Camellia put her hands over her eyes.

"See no evil," he said with a laugh. "You get anxious?"

Mavis Brown and Hocie Simms were passing in the hall.

"And that Miss Abigail Lou," Mavis said.

"Fifty," said Hocie. "If she a day."

Ike spoke in a whisper. "Busybodies," he said. "Don't worry. I won't give you away. Now let me get these britches on." Camellia heard a rustle as Ike stepped into the trousers, and she imagined the wool sliding over his legs. "Wait a minute now," he said. "This doesn't look good."

She was still afraid to open her eyes. "What doesn't?" she said.

"You sewed the seams crooked."

"No, I didn't. I'm sure I didn't."

"Maybe you just think you didn't. Maybe you're cross-eyed."

"Who's cross-eyed?"

"You're cross-eyed."

She felt the air move about her, saw a shadow settle in front of her face. She took her hands away from her eyes, and there was Ike.

"Says who?" she said.

"Says me," he told her.

And then he leaned over and kissed her. It was a sweet kiss, unhurried and shy, that seemed to say, "If you want more, that's fine. If not, that's all right, too." Camellia rose up on her tiptoes, surprised that she had even known to do that.

"What you must think of me," she said. "I shouldn't be here. I don't even know you."

Ike bowed to her. "I'm Mr. Isaac Mattoon," he said. "Miss Camellia, I'm proud to make your acquaintance."

So that was the first time he kissed her, and soon it was clear to everyone in Quakertown who saw them at the Palace Theater, RCO's Ice Cream Parlor, the Saturday night dances at the schoolhouse, that it had finally happened: Camellia Jones had fallen in love.

And, oh, how she did fall, backward and forward and every which way around until her head was spinning and she came home from school in the afternoons amazed by everything around her—the smell of coal smoke from the chimneys, the rasp of her father's file as he sharpened shears and hoes, the very weight of the books she cradled in her arms—everything so ordinary before, made grand because he had kissed her. Ike Mattoon had kissed her. And suddenly she more than moved through the world. She heard it, touched it, tasted it, smelled it, and she let it touch her.

"Mama," she told Eugie one night. "It's all so wonderful."

"What is, Baby-Girl?"

Camellia put her arms out to her sides and spun around in the kitchen. "Everything," she said.

With Ike, she always believed that something thrilling was just around the corner. "That Ike Mattoon could make a top dizzy," Little said once.

That was Ike. He could dance all night, smiling and laughing, his face shiny with sweat. "You watch out now," he'd tell Camellia. "I'm just starting to percolate."

At the Heroines of Jericho suppers, he'd roll up his sleeves and eat and eat and eat. "*Ooohee,*" he'd say. "That's so good, it'd make you slap your mama."

He had a way of making Camellia laugh. He could leave her ready to burst with the sheer joy of living.

And he could be sweet. One day, he gave her a box the size of a block of ice. It was wrapped in glittery silver paper and tied with a red bow. Inside was another box, a bit smaller, with the same paper and the same bow. She opened three more boxes before she got down to the last one, a matchbox. She imagined Ike wrapping it with his big fingers, working to tie the dainty ribbon. There was nothing inside. She turned the box upside down and shook it, but nothing came out.

"That's the minutes of every day," Ike said, "when I'm not thinking about you."

It was the way he treasured her that she loved most of all, the calm strength of him she felt every time he touched her elbow to usher her through a doorway or to help her from a curb. Never had she imagined herself so cared for, so cherished and protected, so truly and wholly loved.

After all the days of buckling her students' galoshes, tending to their bloody noses, swabbing Mercurochrome on their cut knees, saying, "Hush now, honey, hush. Miss Camellia's here," Ike's firm but gentle touch was heaven, and she gave herself to it with all the gladness in her heart.

One night, he walked her home from the Palace Theater, and at the front gate, he paused. The moonlight caught the satin band around his hat. "Camellia," he said, "I've been thinking we've known each other awhile now."

And she said, "Yes."

"I've got my shop, and I make a good living."

And she said yes again.

"This is the one place I want to stay, and you're the only girl I mean to love . . ."

And before he could finish, she said, "Yes." "Yes," she said. Then she kissed him, and she ran into the house where she called out, "Mama, Papa. I'm going to marry Ike Mattoon."

Who could blame her, then, for starting to believe that whatever she wanted for her wedding trousseau, she only need ask and Ike would make it hers: the blue willow china, the lace tablecloth, the patent-leather shoes with the dainty straps that clasped above her ankles. Oh, she knew it was shameless, but she couldn't help herself. After all the times she had seen to her students' whims, she fell in love with whatever caught her eye.

Like the dress her mother had shown her at Neiman's Department Store, a white-on-white brocade with a mesh bodice and gauzy sleeves and mother-of-pearl buttons up the back. The most elegant dress she had ever seen. The perfect dress to slip into after the wedding when she and Ike would go to the depot and board the train to Dallas for their honeymoon.

"It's stunning," she told Ike, and she liked the sound of the word so much, the way it felt in her mouth, that she said it again. "Stunning," she said. "Oh, Ike."

"Now, sugar, don't fret," he said. "You want that dress, it's yours."

She never worried about how much something cost. Ike's barbershop was doing well, and he had saved his army pay. So money never concerned him.

One Saturday, they went to Neiman's Department Store, and Camellia found the dress on the rack. She held it up in front of her and told Ike to feel the brocade.

"What do you think?" she asked him.

"Stunning," he said. "Is it your size?"

She nodded. "A perfect fit."

"Like it was made special for you."

"Then we can buy it?"

"Whatever you want. You just name it. I'll buy you the world."

A salesclerk, her heels clacking over the wooden floor, was saying to a customer, a young woman with blonde hair and bright red lipstick, "It's over here. White-on-white. You'll look like an angel."

"Bro-cade," the blonde woman said, drawing out the syllables, making the word last.

Camellia clutched the dress to her and looked at Ike, her eyes wide with alarm.

"Here now," the sales clerk said. Her name, Camellia knew,

was Miss Priscilla Eddey. "Gal, if you're through playing dress-up, Miss Neiman here would like to try on that dress."

"I adore bro-cade," Miss Neiman said, and her red lips puckered into a pout, the way they must have, Camellia thought, the night she had told her lie about the boy from Quakertown.

Eugie had told Camellia how sometimes Miss Priscilla Eddey would sneak back into Eugie's workroom and sit down to rest her feet. "You and me," she would say to Eugie with a wink, "we're both working gals."

Camellia imagined that if she reminded Miss Eddey who she was, everything would be all right. "Miss Eddey," she said, "it's me, Camellia Jones. My mama does alterations here. You know her. Eugie Jones? The two of you chat from time to time."

Miss Eddey drew back her shoulders and lifted her chin. "We do *not* chat," she said. "Don't try to be familiar with me, gal." She turned to Miss Neiman. "Really, the idea."

Camellia held the dress against her, held it even when Miss Eddey grabbed onto the hanger. But Miss Eddey was stronger, and, when she pulled, Camellia felt the dress slipping away from her hand. She felt Ike move beside her as he took a step toward Miss Eddey. Camellia remembered the colored man she had seen hanged on the courthouse lawn in Fort Worth. If she were to say, "Ike, no," she knew he would stop. And she wanted to say it. She felt some line about to be crossed, and she wanted to keep them on the other side of danger, but that dress, that beautiful, beautiful dress. So when she spoke—when she said, "Ike"—it was in a wounded voice that she knew would spur him on to her defense.

He grabbed the dress and gave a yank, and Miss Eddey, the hanger coming out of her hand, stumbled backward, fell into the rack of dresses, which came down upon her with a crash.

"What's the commotion here?" Mr. Neiman charged up the aisle. Miss Neiman tried to find Miss Eddey in the tangle of dresses. "Oh, I see." Mr. Neiman stopped and pointed his finger at Ike. "It's you. It's Mr. Isaac Mattoon. Making trouble again."

Ike was still holding the dress. "That's good," he said to Mr. Neiman. "You remember my name."

"Oh, I haven't forgot you," said Mr. Neiman. "You're trouble with a capital T."

"No, sir. I'm not the trouble," Ike said. "It's you. You and the ones like you. You're the trouble every colored man ever had in his life. Now I'm going to take this dress. It don't even pay a smidgen of everything you owe."

"You can't do that. You can't walk out of this store with that dress."

"Sir, that's exactly what I mean to do."

Ike turned to Camellia, and she said to him, "No, Ike," and this time her voice was hushed. She touched him on the arm. "It's not worth the misery it'll cause." She took the dress and handed it to Mr. Neiman. That beautiful dress, the brocade slipping over her hand one last time.

"You're letting it go?" Ike said.

"For you," said Camellia. Then she took his hand and walked with him down the long aisle and out of the store.

It was a different love she felt for Ike that evening as they strolled down Frame Street to the dance at the schoolhouse, a love more settled and perhaps not as thrilling, though she couldn't have said that with any certainty as she was still enchanted with the idea of herself saving him from doing something foolish, something she felt sure they both would have ended up regretting.

He was sullen. He walked with his hands stuck into the pockets of his trousers, the ones Camellia had mended for him. His shoulders were hunched up around his face.

"That dress," he said once.

"Hush," she told him.

They kept walking until they were at the end of Frame Street and they could see the lights of the schoolhouse off to the right. A dog barked. The wind sent dead leaves scuttling along the street.

"A man's got to keep his pride," Ike said, and Camellia wished he hadn't said it because she was thinking then of the dance. She could hear a raspy saxophone, a few piano notes, a horn blowing scales as the band tuned their instruments. She thought of the women, the few bold ones like Hocie Simms in flapper dresses, beads hanging down to their knees, and the others who at least had the courage to curl their eyelashes and rouge their cheeks. The men would be wearing freshly pressed suits. Some of them would have their hair oiled. They would slip out of their suit coats and roll their shirtsleeves to the elbows so they could dance. There would be bottles of Coca-Cola, still wet from the ice in the metal coolers, and paper cartons of ice cream, and slabs of caramel cake. And she was a part of it all now that she was a woman about to be married. "Pride," Ike said again. "When a man wants to stand up for you, Camellia, you got to let him."

"What do you think would have happened," she said, "if we'd tried to walk out of there with that dress?"

"White folks been getting away with too much all this time."

"It was my fault," she said. "I got greedy. Maybe your fault, too. You put stars in my eyes, made me think I could grab the moon."

"You got a right to have what you want."

"I want to go to the dance," she told him.

"Yes, ma'am." He took off his hat and bowed, sweeping his arm in front of him. "The dance. Whatever you say. You're the one running the show."

"Don't say it that way, Ike. Don't be mean."

"You know I got meanness in me. That's why you come to my room that night."

"Maybe so." She was ashamed. He had known it all along, known that what had first drawn her to him had been this untouched part of her that had hungered for nerve and grit, for some force to lift her and send her marching through the world with spirit and might, no longer the modest, the solemn school-teacher. The day Ike had cut through the seams of the trousers in Neiman's Department Store he had set something loose in her, but still she knew there were limits. There was reasonable living. You could want too much in the world, and end up losing it all. "Yes," she said, agreeing with Ike again. "I fell in love with you because you made it so easy. You made me believe all I had to do was imagine something, and it would come true."

Just then, a motorcar stopped along the curb, and Camellia saw the men inside: four of them, each wearing a white hood over his face. She grabbed Ike's arm, pulled at him, but he wouldn't move.

The men came out of the car. Two of them carried ax handles.

Ike shook away from Camellia, took a few steps forward, and dropped the first man with a sharp jab to his forehead.

Then one of the men with an ax handle swung it against Ike's knee, and he fell to the ground. The man pinned him there, the butt of the ax handle pressed into his throat, and another man dropped to his knees and vised Ike's head between his hands.

"Mr. Isaac Mattoon," the third man said as he bent over Ike, "we understand you think you're something special with a straight razor. Well, boy, now we come to do the cutting."

Camellia heard the razor click open and saw the blade in the man's hand. "No," she said. She ran at the man, but the first one, the one Ike had punched, was on his feet now, and he grabbed her.

Then the razor sliced through Ike's cheek, and she heard him cry out. "You think about that next time you take a notion to cut something," the man with the razor said, and the four of them got back into the motorcar and drove away.

Camellia crouched down by Ike, and saw the blood spilling from the wound, running onto the white collar of his shirt. "Don't you look at me," he said. There were tears in his eyes. "Don't you damn look at me."

He spit the words at her, and she turned her head, did what he told her, but only for a moment, long enough to feel his shame.

5

Dr. L. C. Parrish came out into his waiting room and told Camellia it had taken twenty-two stitches to close the wound on Ike's face. "Just remember, scars fade with time." Dr. Parrish sat down beside Camellia and patted her hand. "Older you get, less you notice them."

"We're going to be married," she said.

"I know you are," said Dr. Parrish. "Don't worry. Nothing's going to change about that."

But in that moment when she had crouched down beside Ike, and he had told her not to look at him, she had felt something leave them, the joy they had managed. She had convinced herself, after the episode in Neiman's Department Store, that she had sacrificed the dress she wanted so much for the sake of all the days she imagined she had to come with Ike. What she hadn't known—what only became clear to her when he said, "Don't you damn look at me"—was that already they were becoming different people. She had brought him to Neiman's Department Store, had helped to provoke anger, and once she had, the rest of their lives had gone on ahead of them.

Now, as she waited for him to come out of Dr. Parrish's examining room, she knew every time she looked at the scar on his face she would feel wicked and guilty. She would have to make herself forget, make Ike forget, too, by loving him more, by caring for him more.

"No, nothing's changed," she said to Dr. Parrish. Then Ike came out of the examining room, and she rose to meet him.

At Sibby Long's, she tried to help him with his shirt. "Let's get this off you." She reached up to loosen his necktie so she could unbutton his collar, but he grabbed her wrist and eased her hand away.

"I'll see to it," he said, not in a harsh voice but a dull one, so unlike the first time she had heard him speak in Neiman's Department Store.

She let her arm fall to her side. He fumbled with the knot in his necktie.

"I want to help you, Ike."

"Sugar, I know you do."

"Then let me."

She loosened his necktie and moved her fingers up to the collar button at his throat. She thought, though she couldn't be sure, that she could feel the heat from the wound on his cheek. She imagined how it would feel if she were to touch it, damp and hot, the ridged weal puckered with Dr. Parrish's stitches. She felt Ike move his head back, lean away from her. His neck stiffened, and she understood this was the posture he had learned as the men had held him, as he had waited for the razor's cut.

In the weeks that followed, whenever she touched him, she felt this resistance, and though he never turned cruel to her—never closed her off completely—he was a different person from the one she had fallen in love with. He was distant now, unapproachable, as if he had slipped over into some other world and left her behind to mourn his leaving.

It wasn't long before he started talking about Africa. It was the only place, he said, where coloreds could live free. "I thought things would change after the war," he told her one evening in his room. "I heard about Quakertown from the porters on the trains that came through Chattanooga. Little piece of colored paradise, they said. Looks now like this Marcus Garvey is right. That's what I'm saving my money for. To help Marcus Garvey take us home."

They had stopped going to RCO's Ice Cream Parlor, or the Palace Theater, or the dances at the schoolhouse. They spent most evenings in Ike's room, one blues record after another playing on the phonograph.

"Africa?" she said. She was standing at the window, looking down at the street where couples were passing on their way to the dance.

"It's where we came from."

"Why, I've never seen Africa in my life."

"Don't have to see it to know it's home."

"How do you know that?"

"I know the way I feel here."

She could hear a woman's laugh fading away as another couple passed. "I always thought Quakertown was heaven."

"Until I made trouble. Is that what you mean to say?"

She turned away and saw him sitting on the bed, hidden in shadow, and she told him what had never been spoken between them. She knew, coming from her now after what the men had done to him, it was the most hurtful thing she could say: "I'm part white."

"White," he said, and she could hear the pain in his voice. "I knew you were lighter than most, but I didn't know . . ."

"My mama's daddy. She told me once that my own daddy sometimes thinks he doesn't measure up for her on account of her being half white. I'm a quarter. Maybe Africa wouldn't have me."

"A quarter, a half. Don't matter how white you think you are. You're colored. Face it, Camellia. You're a nigger just like me."

One Saturday night, when Ike still refused to go to the dance, Camellia walked up the long hill to the college, climbed the fire escape outside the administration building, and sneaked into the balcony of the auditorium where so many times she had sat, undisturbed, as the slides from a travelogue changed on the screen below her.

She liked to listen to the hushed voice of the narrator, full of wonder and awe, as he commented on each slide. "Venice," he might say. "City of Canals."

Tonight, it was Paris, *la ville lumière*—The City of Light. She sat far back, in the dark, where, if anyone below might happen to turn and look into the balcony, they would never see her. She followed the stream of light veeing out from the projector and spreading over the tops of people's heads. She could hear the narrator's voice above the projector's whirr, a murmured "aha" from an audience member as the slide changed.

"The Rue de Rivoli at night," the narrator said. "The gaslights receding to Vincennes."

How enchanting she found the lights along the Champs Elysées compared with her notion of Africa—its jungles and deserts. She loved the slides of Paris: the flower sellers in the blue twilight, the garden restaurants with bulbs strung from the trees and ladies stretching out white-gloved hands for gentlemen's kisses. With each slide, she let herself slip farther and farther from Quakertown and Ike, who had begun to keep company with the Masonic Joppa Lodge, with men like Tilman Monk and Nib Colter and Mr. Smokey Joe Moore, otherwise known as Mr. Smoke. She imagined herself wearing white gloves, the kind she would button at her wrists, and a wide-brimmed hat with a spray of feathers, perhaps her shoulders bare, and the velvet band of her choker at her throat.

Then she saw a man rise up in the crowd below her and start making his way to the center aisle. She could hear him muttering, "Excuse me, pardon me, so sorry," and she could tell he was having a clumsy time of it because of his hobbled gait and the cane he carried. She could hear the cane knocking against the legs of the wooden folding chairs.

At first, she thought he must be an old man, but when he was finally out into the aisle and the projector's light fell over him, she could see that he was young. He raised his hand to shield his eyes from the projector's glare, and she saw the pale skin of that hand, unwrinkled, and the long fingers, and the knobbed wrist as his shirtsleeve drew back along his arm. She thought of the young boys at school, the seventh and eighth graders, at the age when they were growing, trying to fit their new bodies—how they could break her heart with a sudden graceful turn or one faltering step. The young man in the aisle wasn't moving now. The slides were flashing on and off across his face—rivers and gardens and monuments—and on the screen behind him his shadow loomed up, and people started to grumble.

"Sit down," someone called out.

"For pity's sake," said someone else.

And then the young man spoke, and his voice, so thin and halting, seemed to Camellia the most timid and lonesome voice she had ever heard, and somehow she knew it belonged to Kizer Bell. "My cane," he said. "The tip of my cane. It's caught in a heating grate."

She wanted, at once, to come down from the balcony and help him free his cane and lead him out of the harsh light, but she was caught, too, hidden away in a place where she wasn't supposed to be. She hurried to the fire escape door, unable to watch another moment while Kizer waited for someone to help him.

A few evenings later, Eugie took Camellia's measurements so she could cut the pattern for the wedding gown. She wrapped her tape measure around Camellia's waist. "Baby-Girl," she said, "you're such a slip of a thing."

Little sat at the table, honing the edge of his jackknife with a whetstone. "That's what I said today. Yes, sir, just today, I said, 'Why Camellia's about to dry up and blow away.' " He held the stone in his palm and ran the knife's blade back and forth until the air filled with the scent of hot steel, and Camellia could barely stand to watch, thinking as she was of the night the men had cut Ike's face.

"Papa, you didn't," she said. "Who'd you say that to?"

"Mr. Andrew Bell's son. I was over to their place to prune back the roses."

"Mr. Bell's son?" Eugie said.

"That Kizer," said Little. "That crippled boy. Sad thing about that boy. A good-looking man otherwise, and good-mannered. 'How's your daughter, sir?' he said to me. Imagine that, calling me *sir*. 'Your daughter, Camellia?' "

She thought, then, of those days when she had sat with Kizer, telling stories about the two of them. At the end of that summer, the doctors had taken the cast from his leg and still he had been hobbled. Then school had started, and Camellia had stopped coming to the Bells' house with her father. She and Kizer had grown up apart from each other. From time to time, Little carried home news. Another operation on Kizer's leg hadn't worked, and shortly after he had gone east to a private boarding school. The years had gone by in such a rush, then, and little by little, she had stopped thinking about him as much as she had after they had first been separated. In fact, she hadn't seen him again until that evening at the travelogue. "He asked about me?" she said to Little. She stood the way Eugie told her so she could measure for the length of the skirt. Little stopped honing his jackknife. "Me?" she said again. "Kizer Bell?"

"*Sir*, he called me. 'How's your daughter, sir? Camellia?' "

Camellia recalled how she had felt all those years ago, alone with him in his room, her head laid over on his shoulder—as close to anyone her age as she had ever been. And now he remembered her. Kizer Bell. He remembered her name.

On Monday, after school, she walked to the square and stood outside Neiman's Department Store, looking in through the glass.

The white-on-white brocade dress was still hanging on the rack—
Miss Neiman hadn't taken it after all—and Camellia watched
first this woman and then that one pluck the dress off the rack
and hold it in front of her, the way Camellia herself had done that
day she had thought it would be hers.

The air was so cold she could feel her ears burn. The wind flat-
tened her dress against her legs. She stuck her hands deep into the
pockets of her coat, knowing she should leave, knowing how silly
it was to stand in the cold, keeping watch over a dress she would
never own. She was too ashamed now to ask Ike to buy it for her.

When she turned, she bumped into Kizer Bell, and his cane fell
from his hand and went skittering along the sidewalk. "Oh, my,"
she said. "My goodness. I'm sorry. Oh, my."

"My cane," he said, and she retrieved it for him.

"I didn't see you," she said.

He was wearing a coat with a fur collar, and a cap, the kind
with a snap on the brim, and a pair of thin gloves the color of
butter. He took the cane and anchored himself with it.

"I've been watching you from the bank," he said. "There must
be something extraordinary in this store to keep you standing out
here so long." He hunched up his shoulders and shivered. "Glory,
it's cold."

"It's a dress," she told him.

They stood together at the window, and she pointed out the
white-on-white brocade.

"It is grand," he said. "Your heart must be set on it."

There was something in the way he said it, something about
the enchanting sigh of his voice, so much like the narrator's at the
travelogue, that warmed her, made her feel as if he alone knew
what it was to want something so beautiful.

"I'm Camellia," she said because she couldn't bear any longer
not to say it. "Camellia Jones."

She was afraid to look at him, but she couldn't help but find
his reflection in the glass—the same sweet face she had admired

all those years ago. He had needed her company, then, and she had obliged, one of the first times she had given herself to someone else's need. And now here they were, next to each other. Although she worried that someone might see them there, standing so close, she didn't dare move, charmed as she was by the sight of them.

"I remember you," he said, his voice nearly a whisper now. They were standing so close that, if she dared, she could lay her head on his shoulder, feel the soft fur of his collar on her cheek.

"I saw you Saturday night," she said. She was afraid to admit this because she feared it might shame him. "At the travelogue. I wanted to help you when your cane got stuck, but I was up in the balcony—I climb the fire escape and sneak in, you see—and I couldn't give myself away."

"The balcony," he said. "No one can see you up there."

"That's right," she told him.

"Glory." He closed his eyes. "Don't you just love sitting there in the dark, looking at how lovely the world can be?"

For a moment, she imagined the two of them there in the balcony, and the thought filled her with guilt. Mercy, she was engaged to be married, and here she was, admiring another man.

"I'd like to go abroad," Kizer was saying. "I'd like to see all those grand places. Like Paris. Wouldn't you?"

She imagined life with a man like him, tender and moonstruck, a man who saw travel as romance, not survival the way Ike did, insisting now that one day she would live with him in Africa. And she told Kizer, yes. "Oh, yes," she said. "I would."

That evening, Ike offered to take her to the new Mary Pickford picture at the Palace Theater. "Been moping around here too long," he said. "Got to show my sugar pie the town before she goes sour." He grabbed her around the waist and twisted up his mouth like he had just sucked on a lemon. She couldn't help but laugh. "Ike." She gave him a playful swat on his shoulder. "You're putting on."

"Putting on the swank," he said. "Step up now, sugar. We're going to the show."

She was glad for his spirit. How alive he again seemed. She had been dreaming over and over the moment with Kizer outside Neiman's Department Store, and now Ike had made that all go away.

At the Palace, he insisted they sit far back in the last row of seats even though Camellia pointed out how difficult it would be to read the captions from that distance.

"It's just a made-up story," he said. "There's not a word of it true. Besides, Milly Menthol's organ-playing tells you when it's happy or it's sad."

It was pleasant, sitting there with him. Camellia felt guilty for having imagined what she had about Kizer—that the two of them might . . . *How silly,* she thought. She leaned over and kissed Ike on the cheek, not thinking that her lips would fall upon his scar.

"Stop it." He jerked his head away from her. His voice was a fierce whisper in the dark. She knew, then, that he had wanted to sit as far away from the screen as he could so the light wouldn't flicker over his face and show the scar that curved from his cheekbone to the corner of his mouth.

"You," she said. It was all she could think to say. "You," she said again.

"That's right," Ike said. "Me."

And she knew that what he meant was, *his* skin, *his* scar, *his, his, his.*

The night of the next travelogue, Camellia climbed the fire escape and sneaked into the balcony of the auditorium where Kizer was already sitting, his cane angled across his lap.

"You're right," he said in a whisper. "No one can watch you up here. It's out of the way. Come on. Sit down. You've already missed the sunset over the China Sea."

She hesitated. What would happen if someone found them there? But if she were to turn and leave, what would Kizer think? She sat beside him and watched the slides change: junks with their elaborate sails, pagodas with their stacks of curving roofs, Panda bears, cherry trees filled with pink blossoms, waterfalls in rock gardens.

"Marvelous," he whispered. "Splendid."

"Yes," she said. "Yes."

At one point, his arm brushed against hers, just the slightest touch, and she felt such a delicious thrill. She stretched out her pinky finger, moved it into the dark space between them, and held it there. She closed her eyes, waited. She told herself that if he somehow found it there, it would be a sign.

And he did. She felt the tip of his finger touch hers, such a light, quick touch, she could almost believe it hadn't happened. But she knew it had. She knew she had wanted it to, and now she was terrified.

"I have to go," she said.

"Camellia," said Kizer, "wait."

"No," she told him. "I have to go."

It wasn't long before she started finding trinkets on her desk at school—a velvet ribbon, a locket, a cameo brooch—and she never once suspected that they might be from Ike because she wanted them to be from Kizer. She knew that he had found some way to sneak inside the schoolhouse—Kizer, the Brave—and leave his presents for her to discover.

She took them home and hid them in a drawer in her chifforobe. At night, while Eugie and Little slept, she brought out the velvet ribbon and stroked the smooth length of it. She used scissors to snip her face from a photograph. Then she put it in one half of the locket. The other half, she left empty until one day she found a photograph of Kizer in an envelope on her desk.

Her life with Ike went on. He wasn't as sullen now that he had started a "business concern" with Mr. Smoke.

"What business?" Camellia asked.

"What's the difference?" Ike told her. "As long as it brings in the cash."

There were times when it was almost the way it had been before the men had cut his face. He strutted down the street, Camellia's arm entwined with his. He opened the door to RCO's Ice Cream Parlor and swept his arm before him. "Ladies first," he said.

But some nights, he only sat in the dark of his room and stared at the wall, his eyes narrowed, and she felt the rage simmering inside him. "Baby," she said to him. "My baby." And he let her say it. One night, he lay on the bed with her and let her hold him. "Shh," she said when she felt his shoulders tremble. "It's all right. Shh, baby. Everything's all right."

She knew how much he ached, how badly he needed her to love away the anger that had filled him. There could be a bloom on the maimed or the wounded—she had seen it on Kizer—a radiance like the golden nimbuses around the heads of the saintly in the Gothic paintings she had studied in college. She had never been able to resist it. She saw it now on Ike, and she felt it draw her to him.

He started to undress her, and she let him. It wasn't so awful, was it, she thought. She was a woman of a certain age, and she and Ike would soon be married. She let him slip her dress from her shoulders, run his hand along her stomach. His fingers were trembling. How much he seemed to need this now, this lovemaking, and she couldn't deny him.

But he turned out to be a hurried, forceful lover, and, when he was done, she was surprised to find herself crying.

Ike lay over her, kissing her neck. "You're crying," he said with concern. "Sugar, did I hurt you?"

She wrapped her arms around his back and pulled him to her. "I'm just happy, Ike. That's all."

But the truth was—and it startled her to know this—she was

crying because she was thinking about Kizer and how, when they were children, they hid themselves away and touched each other with shy caresses. She was crying because she feared no one, not even Ike, would touch her that way again.

Then it was spring, and one evening, when Camellia was walking home from Nib's Grocery, a motorcar with bright-spoked wheels and whitewall tires and shiny running boards pulled to the curb, and the driver, Kizer, said, "Quick. Get in."

She had found herself, at various times of the day, no matter how hard she had tried not to, imagining just such a moment as this, the moment when Kizer would come for her. So she got into the motorcar, convinced she had willed him to appear, and now that he had, she had no choice but to go wherever he decided to take her.

"I haven't been able to stop thinking about you," he said.

She was holding a bag with five peaches in it, and she folded the top of the bag and curled the paper lip into her palms. "Me?" she said, as if she were innocent and hadn't been dreaming of him. "I'm engaged to be married."

"Yes. Glory. I know I'm taking a chance."

He drove her out of the city, deep into the dark country. It was spring now, and she could smell honeysuckle and hear the peepers' shrill calls. She and Kizer didn't speak again until he pulled down a rutted oil lease road and shut off the motor.

"It's the best place I know to look at the stars," he said.

She saw them through the curve of the windshield glass, the glittering stars, and she felt her breath catch at the sudden brilliance of them. She sat there with Kizer, and they took turns naming the constellations: Orion, Taurus, and the six stars of the Pleiades. She opened the bag of peaches, and they shared one, passing it back and forth, letting the juice run down their chins.

"What a mess," she said.

He took her hand and kissed it. "Glory," he told her. "You do taste good."

One night, when they had again driven out to their secret spot, Kizer told her to close her eyes. "Keep them closed now," he said. "Don't peek."

She heard him open the door, listened to his cane moving through the buffalo grass. The trunk lid opened and then shut. Then he was back in the car, and he told her to open her eyes. When she did, she saw, in the moonlight, the glow of the dress from Neiman's Department Store, the white-on-white brocade.

"It's for you," he said. "I bought it for you."

She felt a surprising anger rise up in her. "You're trying to buy me, Kizer Bell."

"Glory, no." There was a wounded look in his eyes, the way there had been the night his cane had stuck in the heating grate at the travelogue, and he had been trapped in the bright glare from the slide projector. "I know what it's like," he told her, "to want something you can't have. I've spent my life wishing I wasn't crippled, wishing I could walk without this cane. I've watched you on the playground at school. I've seen the way the girls and boys clutch your hands, the folds of your coat. I've heard how you talk to them. 'Honey,' you say. 'Oh, honey.' How could anyone keep from falling in love with you. Even me—especially me—as miserable as I am."

"You're not miserable," she said. "You're beautiful." She touched his face. "Gorgeous." She loved the sound of the word. "You're gorgeous, Kizer Bell."

Then she was crying. "Camellia," he said. "What's wrong?"

"This dress," she said. "This beautiful dress. I'll have to hide it. If anyone ever saw . . . if Ike saw. . . ."

Kizer's voice sounded so far away. "Will you wear it now?" he said. "For me?"

"Here?" she said.

He nodded. "I'll close my eyes. You can go outside and change. I won't look. I promise."

She couldn't resist. She stepped out into the dark, slipped out of her shift, and into the white dress. She couldn't manage the buttons up the back so she asked him to come out and help her.

He found her in the dark, and they clung to each other.

"Camellia," he began.

"Hush," she told him. "Just hold me."

He wrapped his arms around her, and without his cane for balance, he teetered to the side, and his weight pulled at her. It was all she could do to hold him up, to keep him from falling, to keep both of them from tumbling to the ground.

"Marry me," he said. "I want you to marry me."

She wanted to say yes. "Yes," she wanted to shout. But then she thought of Ike and how badly he had wanted to buy her the dress she now wore, the brocade that touched her, touched Kizer.

How could she have ever suspected that she would fall in love with him, with his sloped shoulders, and his lame leg, and his old wooden cane? And so quickly she had fallen, but really, she thought, maybe not so quickly at all. The truth was she had fallen in love with him when they were children, before she had even known the word for what she felt, and now it seemed that they were only acting on what had been inevitable from the beginning—that they be together. But what would the world think of her if she were to marry him? Camellia Jones, the schoolteacher, fiancée of Ike Mattoon. Eugie had told her about the people who had called Granny Jiggs a nigger whore to a white man.

"Do you think it's that easy?" Camellia said. "Do you think it could ever be easy for us?"

He let his arms fall away from her. He brought his cane down and took a few halting steps backward. "No, it would never be easy," he said, "but it would be *us*."

The dress slipped from her shoulders, and she held it to her chest. It was at that moment—the instant when she felt the gauzy sleeves start to slide down her arms—that she thought of all the ways people could find to step into lives they could barely dare imagine: the colored man she had seen hanged on the courthouse lawn in Fort Worth, Ike who had slit the legs of those trousers with his razor. The thing, she thought, must be to go too far, go to the point where ordinary life was no longer possible. She let go of the dress. It slithered over her breasts, her stomach, her thighs until it lay in folds on the ground. She stepped free from it, moved closer to Kizer.

She had never seduced anyone in her life, but she knew that was what she was doing now—tempting him, tempting herself. Years before, she had imagined that if she could only touch his lame leg tenderly, softly, she might heal him. She felt the same way now as she stood before him, nearly naked. She knew her skin was the color of creamy butter in the moonlight. She took another step, and he didn't turn away.

6

One afternoon at the end of May, Kizer drove to Quakertown and walked into Camellia's school. It was late, and the students had gone. He found her at her desk, marking papers with a red pencil. He stood in the doorway, content to watch her awhile— to take in the graceful sway of her back as she leaned over to write, to hear her mutter to herself, "My, my, my."

Somewhere down the hall, a bucket scraped over the floor, and the janitor's mop slapped and swabbed. Kizer gave a shy whistle, the two-note call of a bobwhite, to catch Camellia's attention. She ran to him and pulled him inside the room. "What's wrong with you?" She shut the door. "You want someone to see us in here?"

He didn't care. He had decided he was through with all the hiding and the sneaking around, driving out to the oil lease road and lying naked with Camellia under the stars, making love— such sweet, sweet love, as shy and as full of desire as the moments when they had hidden themselves away as children and closed their eyes and touched each other. Now he wanted to let the world know that Camellia was his girl. They would have a life together, no matter what they had to endure. How could they not? They were too crazy for each other now for it to be otherwise.

The first night they had made love, Kizer had said, "Camellia, we should stop," not because he wanted to, but because he was pretending that it wasn't too late to come to their senses. She took him in her hand, there in the night, the two of them lying on the blanket beneath the stars, and brought him into her. They lay there, joined, not moving, and that was the sweetest time he had ever known.

"We can stop if you want," he said. "We can get dressed and drive back to town and never see each other again."

She threw her arms around his neck and clung to him. "I couldn't bear it," she said. "Not for a minute."

Now he had come to her school to tell her that she was the one good thing in his life, the girl he wanted to be with always. But before he could speak, she turned away from him. She crossed her arms over her chest and bowed her head, and he felt what he did whenever his mother drank—something dropping away inside him as if he were falling and he waited to see how far.

"Camellia," he said.

She spun around to face him. And then, in a quiet voice, she told him that she was pregnant. She put her hands over her ears as if she couldn't bear to hear her own words. "Since that night at the travelogue when our fingers touched, it's like we've been in a fast train and I keep trying to find the emergency brake, but there isn't any, and we just keep speeding ahead." She took her hands away from her ears. "Now look what's happened."

The clock on the wall ticked off the seconds. "A baby," Kizer finally said. "Your baby."

"And yours," she told him.

"Not Ike's?"

She couldn't bring herself to admit that this might be true. "I can't believe you'd think that." She stamped her foot. "Do you really believe I'd be giving myself up to both of you?"

"Our baby," he said. He opened his arms and started to go to her.

She held up her hand to stop him. "It's wrong," she said. "So wrong. Now everyone will know."

Kizer reached out his hand to her, but she wouldn't take it.

"I'm the one to blame," he said. "I should have stopped us that first time."

"It was my fault." She moved away to the window and stood looking out on the playground. "I'm the one who started it all. I kept telling myself I'd stop. 'You walk away, Camellia,' I said. 'You marry Ike.'" She placed her hand on the window and let it slide down the glass with a squeal. "I knew I couldn't go on seeing you forever, not if I was going to be with Ike, but you were the sweetest thing I knew."

Kizer was beside her now, his arm around her shoulders. "So now marry me."

"I can't," she said. She thought of the night she had told Ike she was a quarter white—"You're a nigger just like me," he'd said—and now, as Kizer stood looking at her, she realized Ike had been right all along. Even her mother had known it long ago when she had kept Camellia from Kizer. It was true. World couldn't stand too much cozy between black and white. "I can't," Camellia said again. "I promised myself to Ike."

"So you're choosing?"

She nodded. "It's the right thing to do."

"Does it feel right?" He put his hand on her chest. "Here in your heart?"

She took his hand and lifted it away from her. "It's right." She folded his fingers into a fist and then kissed each knuckle. "It's all I can do."

"And the baby?" he said.

"You should go now," she told him.

"But, Camellia . . ."

"No." She closed her eyes. "Don't say another word."

She stood there, refusing to open her eyes, as if this were all a dream and sooner or later she would wake. Finally he had no choice but to leave. All the way home, he imagined her opening her eyes and finding him gone—no one in the room but her and the baby growing inside her, the baby that was his.

7

That night Camellia and Eugie were sitting on their back steps, looking up into the sky, waiting for the first star, and before she could stop herself, Camellia told her mother about the baby.

"Ike Mattoon?" Eugie said with disgust. "You been laying down with that man? I knew he was trouble the first time I laid eyes on him."

"No, not Ike." Camellia said the first thing that was in her heart, a thing she hadn't planned. It pained her to make this confession, to unravel the slightest thread of a lie, but she felt so helpless, desperate for someone to tell her what to do to make her life right again. "It was a white boy," she said. "It was Kizer Bell."

"That crippled boy?" Eugie put her hand gently to Camellia's cheek and turned her face so they would have to look at each other. "I tried to keep you clear of him when you were young'uns."

"I tried to stay away from him, Mama. I did."

"He come after you?"

"Yes, Mama." There wasn't much of a lie to what Camellia was saying. Kizer had found her downtown in front of Neiman's Department Store, he had waited for her in the balcony of the college the night of the travelogue, he had sneaked into her schoolroom and left his gifts, and finally he had told her to get into his motorcar that evening when she had been walking home from Nib Colter's grocery store. "That's what he did, Mama. He came after me."

"And he forced himself on you. I know how these white boys can be. Tell me, Baby-Girl. Is that the way it all shook out?"

There it was—an opportunity to save herself—and maybe, she thought, this is what she had wanted all along, a chance to once again be respectable. It was becoming clear to Camellia that somewhere deep inside her she wanted to do what was right, and what was right, she had convinced herself, was to make a good and proper marriage to Ike, to be above reproach. So she let Eugie believe that what she was suggesting was true.

"Oh, Mama." Camellia laid her head on her mother's shoulder and sobbed. How easy it was to let the lie go out into the world. "Mama, help me."

"Hush, girl," said Eugie. "You listen now."

She told Camellia about the rented house on Oak Street where Captain Jiggs had brought Eugie and her mother to live because the Cherokees were raiding the ranches near Bolivar, and he had decided to move his cattle operation farther west.

"I won't have to worry about you here," he told them. "I've asked Tom Gleason to keep an eye out for you. Whatever you need, he'll see to it."

Tom Gleason lived across the street in a house he had built from pink marble brought over on ships from Italy. The house had a courtyard in the front that featured a fountain and marble benches and trellises lush with climbing vines. The yardman was Little Jones, and often, when he worked, Eugie watched him from her upstairs window. She listened to him as he talked to the flowers and plants. "Mr. Marigold, you're looking proud today. Miss Hibiscus, aren't you one for putting on a show?"

But what caught Eugie's eye more than anything was the way Little strolled through the courtyard, his shoulders thrown back, his head held high. From time to time, he stopped, put his hands on his hips, and slowly turned his head, looking at all around him like a man who owned it. She began to make up in her mind a dream of the two of them and a house like the Gleasons' with a courtyard where they could sit at twilight, listening to the gentle lapping of the fountain, breathing in the sweet scent of the trumpet vines.

"What are you, girlie?" Tom Gleason's son, Bert, said the first time he saw her. "A belle or a nigra gal?"

"I'm Eugenia Jiggs," she told him. "My mama is Lesta Jiggs, and my daddy's Captain Horace Jiggs of Bolivar. He's a friend of your daddy's, and you're supposed to look out for us."

Bert Gleason was a skinny boy who wore a derby hat and kept a matchstick jouncing around in his mouth. "Oh, I'll be looking all right." He took a matchstick from his pocket, scratched his thumbnail over the tip, and tossed the flame at her. "Girlie, you can count on that."

That evening Eugie watched the white girls strolling past on the sidewalk. Their long blonde hair was done up in Gibson Girl knots; their parasols were open against the sun. She held up the ivory-backed hand mirror her father had given her and studied her face. Despite Captain Jiggs's fair complexion, she was caramel-skinned like her mother, but with the delicate features of the girls passing below her. Her lips formed the same dainty bow as theirs, and her nose came to the same button tip. She was slim of waist and her hair was black and sleek. She knew she was pretty, and she knew that boys like Bert Gleason, no matter how horrid they might act, were enchanted with her looks.

So nights, when she saw him hiding in the shadows of the oak trees, she sat at her bedroom window, sometimes wearing only her chemise, and she brushed her hair, delighted to know how simple it was to make him ache for her, this stupid boy who had called her a nigra gal and thrown a match at her. Now all she had to do was turn off her light and leave him out there in the dark, dreaming of her dusky skin and how it would feel if he were to touch it.

Then one night, when she went out to the alley to empty the supper leavings into the trash pail, he was there, Bert Gleason, and he grabbed her and pulled her into the old carriage house where the landlord had once stabled horses. There, Bert Gleason spit his matchstick out onto the old straw and then, very gently, with a tenderness that surprised Eugie, he kissed her.

"Don't you tell anyone," he said. "Not a soul."

She remembered what her mother had said once about Captain Jiggs. "That man's been good to me, and good to you. Color don't make no difference. Don't mind what folks say. Love is what matters. Find it where you can, Eugenia. Only a fool would turn away from it."

"I won't," Eugie said to Bert Gleason. "I promise."

Each night, they met in the carriage house, and in the few minutes she could risk being away from her mother, she let Bert Gleason kiss her and sometimes press his face into her hair.

Soon the promise she had made him became too much for her, and she told one of the pretty blonde girls who strolled past her house with their parasols that she and Bert Gleason were in love.

The next time she went to the carriage house, he wasn't there. She waited as long as she could, but all she heard was the scrabbling and cooing of pigeons coming to roost in the rafters, and the creaky swing of a shutter loose on its hinges.

Later that evening, Tom Gleason and Bert came to call.

"It's that girl of yours," Tom Gleason said to Eugie's mother. He owned the Alliance Flour Mill, and because he knew the long hours of grinding and sifting it took to rid the flour of bran, he didn't believe in wasting time. He got straight to the point. "She's spreading lies about my Bert. Claims the two of them are sweet on each other. Says they're going to run off and get married. Sounds like she's taken a shine to the boy, and why shouldn't she, he's a catch, but it goes without saying, it won't do to have such a rumor get around."

They were in the dining room, and Eugie was helping her mother dust the bone china teacups Captain Jiggs had given her as a wedding gift. "So white," her mother always said whenever she handled them, "and so easy to break. You have to take extra special care."

Lesta set one of the teacups on the dining table, put her hands on her hips, and said to Eugie, "Is that true? What Mr. Tom says? Have you been telling stories?"

Eugie lifted her eyes just enough to see Bert Gleason standing by his father with his shoulders slouched. He was holding his derby hat in front of him, both hands clutching the brim. He seemed so frightened, not brazen the way he had been the first time he had spoken to her, and something in Eugie—something she wanted to call love—begged her to protect him. But she couldn't bring herself to take the role of a liar and a starry-eyed fool, so she said, "He kissed me. Every night in the carriage house. Just ask him if he didn't."

Tom Gleason chuckled. "Oh sure, maybe Bert did that, but ask yourself, Lesta, why would Eugenia—no offense, I trust—be addled enough to think it meant anything? You know yourself, that women of the—how should I say this—the exotic races have always been tempting to men who are more commonly colored. John Smith and Pocahontas, for example."

"I don't need a history lesson," Lesta said. "Did you ever think that your Bert might love my Eugenia?"

"Is that the case, Bert? Do you love this girl?"

"Ask her what she done at her bedroom window those nights." Bert waved his derby in the air. "Sitting there half-naked so I could see."

"Naked," said Lesta.

"In my chemise," Eugie said.

"Well, there you have it," said Tom Gleason. "I suggest you control your daughter."

The next evening, Bert Gleason was again waiting for Eugie in the carriage house. But this time, she refused to let him kiss her.

"If you want to woo me," she said, "we'll have to be respectable."

"But I love you, Eugie."

"Tell everyone else that."

"I can't. Not now. Cripes, Eugie. What would people think?"

She slapped his face, and the matchstick flew out of his mouth. "You're a horrid boy," she said.

The next morning, Little Jones came across the street, took off his straw hat, and bowed to Eugie who had come out to water the yellow rosebush that grew by the front steps. She was holding the water can over the top of the bush, and Little took it from her and crouched down to water only the soil around the roots.

"Damp leaves is asking for fungus," he said. "A rosebush takes a load of loving. Some knows that and some just never learn."

She remembered how she had seen him pruning the climbing vines around the Gleasons' courtyard, how careful he had been. "And you're one who knows," she said.

"Yes, miss. I've got the touch." He set the water can on the ground and stood up to face her. "There's a minstrel show this evening at the schoolhouse in Quakertown. Would you go with me?"

"I suppose I might."

He smiled. "All right, then." He set his straw hat back on his head. "Indeed. This evening it is. I'll call for you at seven."

When he came for her in his wagon, she saw Bert Gleason watching from his courtyard. Little helped her up onto the wagon seat, and she noticed, then, that the mule was wearing an old derby hat, holes cut so the mule's ears could poke through the crown.

Bert Gleason stormed across the street, his own derby pushed back on his head. "You better take that hat off that mule," he said to Little.

The reins lay across Little's palms, his hands cupped as if he were holding water. "Oh, I can't do that, sir. No sir. That mule needs that hat. Otherwise folks are liable to see him for what he is—just a stupid old jackass."

Little gave the reins a shake, and the mule started down Oak Street.

"That boy," said Little. "Don't mind him. He was just being a white boy."

They were passing under the spreading oak trees, through the cool shade, the gray dusk.

"My daddy's white," Eugie said.

"Yes, miss," said Little. "I know."

"I don't know what that makes me."

"I figure it makes you Eugenia. That's your name, isn't it?"

"Yes," she said. "Eugie."

The wagon rocked over the cobblestones, and she could feel Little's arm against her own.

"Eugie," he said. "That's a pretty name. That's a name I could get used to saying."

In Quakertown, she sat in an auditorium with people whose skin was as dark as her mother's, and for the first time in her life Eugie felt that she was finally in the place where she belonged. That was the night, she told Camellia, that she fell in love with her father.

"What happened to that boy?" Camellia asked Eugie. "That Bert Gleason?"

"He burned our house."

"Burned your house? And you've never told me that story?"

Eugie told Camellia about Granny Jiggs waking her that night. The smoke, Eugie said, was already stinging her nostrils. The fire had started in the kitchen, and as she and her mother made their way down the stairs, she could see the flames spreading up the walls. Together, in their nightdresses, they ran out onto the front lawn, where already neighbors had started to gather. Fire bells were ringing in the distance.

"My teacups," Lesta cried out, and before Eugie or Tom Gleason could stop her, she ran up onto the porch and through the front door they had left open when they had come out onto the lawn.

"Mama," Eugie cried. She could see her mother's shadow running toward the flames that had moved now into the dining room.

"Fool woman," someone said.

"She'll die in there," said another.

That's when Bert Gleason came out from the shadows of the oak trees, and ran up to the porch. He stopped at the doorway, and for a moment, it seemed that he would enter. But then his father caught up to him, took him by the shoulders, and led him back toward the street.

Bert Gleason stood on the lawn, his shoulders shaking, his face twisted with agony, and he screamed out at Eugie, "You made me do this. You, you, you."

Then Lesta was back, coming from the porch, her nightdress held up above her waist, the teacups, swaddled in its folds, her nakedness no concern to her until she had kneeled on the lawn and eased the teacups, all eight of them, down onto the grass. Then she smoothed the gown around her legs, and she sat there, guarding the teacups. "So pretty," she kept saying, and Eugie wasn't embarrassed because she knew her mother had saved what had mattered most to her in that house, her daughter and the teacups, both of which her husband had given her.

"Why would Bert Gleason do a thing like that?" Camellia said. "Why would he burn your house and then confess it?"

"Maybe he loved me, loved me so much he did a crazy thing. Or maybe he was just mean-hearted. Maybe it was that." Eugie pointed up at the sky. "First star," she said. "Quick, make a wish."

Camellia closed her eyes, and when she did, she saw Kizer the way she had seen him that first night at the travelogue when he had shielded his eyes against the projector's glare. A life with him would always be that kind of life, always feeling caught, always wondering who was watching.

"We do this and we do that," Eugie said, "and pretty soon we've made a life. Maybe not the one we thought we'd make, but, still, there it is, the only one we've got. It's up to us to find a way to love it."

8

By this time, Mr. Bell had a plan. He had heard the story of Isaac Mattoon and the scene at Neiman's Department Store and the way the Klan had gone after him and cut up his face. Mr. Bell thought that there were two sorts of men: those like him and Little Jones who wanted to live decent lives and those who were filled with rage and hell-bent on violence. He knew of the race riots in Memphis and Omaha and even closer to home in Waco where he had traveled on bank business and seen the burned-out buildings downtown. Such ugliness, such waste. The riots had devastated lives, white and black, and had very nearly ruined cities. The same thing could happen in Denton, and that was what Mr. Bell intended to stop.

So one night at the City Commission meeting, when the men began talking about finding a way to persuade people to move away from Quakertown—maybe even go as far as to send the Klan down there, maybe burn a few homes—he tried to reason with them. "You can't just burn people out," he said. "There are laws."

"We're talking about coloreds," Mr. Arthur Goody said. He was a stout man with a flowing red moustache.

The men sat around a long mahogany table in the courthouse. Their voices echoed off the high ceiling with its pressed-tin tiles.

"We're talking about people," said Mr. Bell. "People with families like you and me."

"You've got some nerve saying my family is anything like yours." Mr. Goody leaned across the table and pointed his finger at Mr. Bell. "Maybe you want to save Quakertown so you'll always have somewhere to buy your wife's gin."

Mr. Bell bowed his head, silenced by the humiliation that filled him now that someone had made a direct reference to Tibby's drinking. He had always tried to put on a brave face, to present himself as a man of principle and substance, and people had allowed it, people who had to come to his bank to ask for a loan. But now Mr. Goody had ruined the pretense; he had made it clear that people were wise to what went on in Mr. Bell's family.

"We could do this legally," Mr. Bell said, now using his banker's voice, determined to regain some measure of dignity. "We could move Quakertown. All it would take would be a bond issue."

He explained that a public vote could acquire Quakertown for the purpose of civic improvement. The city could buy the properties, move the houses they could, tear down the buildings they couldn't. Denton could build the one thing it lacked—a park, a magnificent park like the one in Dallas. Wouldn't that make a showpiece, Mr. Bell said, for the parents of all those girls at the women's college when they came to town?

"Move Quakertown where?" Mr. Goody wanted to know.

"A few miles east," Mr. Bell told them. "I own some land there, enough to divide into lots. I'll sell it to the city, and the city can make its money back by selling lots to the coloreds."

All of them except Little Jones, he thought, whom he intended to save.

Bert Gleason rolled the ash of his cigar in a cut-glass ashtray. "I won't be part of anything ugly," he said. "You all know I made a mistake once in my life, and I'm not about to be thought of as a hooligan again."

Mr. Bell knew that Bert was referring to the time he had burned the house Captain Jiggs had rented on Oak Street. The story was well-known. Bert, using his father's influence, had escaped punishment by volunteering for the army and going to Cuba to fight the Spaniards. There, he had told Mr. Bell when he finally returned, he had seen the concentration camps where thousands of Cuban civilians had died of disease and malnutrition. Now he owned the Alliance Flour Mill, having inherited it from his father, and spent his days satisfied to be making a product that fed millions of people.

"I won't see anyone treated like an animal," he said to the men. "We'll do this in a decent way, or we won't do it at all."

He would never forget the night he burned Captain Jiggs's house by sloshing fuel oil over the back porch and then throwing down a match. He had watched the house burn until nothing was left but the front steps and the stone fireplace to show that it had ever been a house. Eugie and her mother had stood there watching, too, their eyes wide in the glow of the flames. They had looked about them and taken a few steps first in one direction and then in another, unaware that nothing was expected of them but to accept the kindness of their neighbors. Someone brought blankets to wrap around them, and then Bert's father led them across the street into the pink marble house where they slept that night and the next until Captain Jiggs could arrive. By that time, Bert was on a train to San Antonio. "Maybe Cuba will do you some good," his father had told him. "You'll see people die, and, if you're lucky, you'll come home and live a decent life."

"This land out east," Bert said to Mr. Bell. "Will it be a good place for these folks to live?"

"You know how the creek floods Quakertown each spring?" Mr. Bell said. "That won't happen on this land out east. Bert, you know that there are better places waiting for us all the time. The misery comes when we can't bring ourselves to imagine them."

*   *   *

One afternoon, a few weeks later, Mr. Bell called Little in from his yard work. He offered him a glass of lemonade. Then he showed him the design for the park he had commissioned a landscape artist to draw. He spread the drawing out on the desk in his study and showed Little the flower beds, walking paths, gazebos, foot bridges, picnic pavilions, band shell, swimming pool.

"Someone has to be the caretaker of this park," Mr. Bell said, "and the City Commission, on my recommendation, of course, has decided that you're the man we want."

"Why, Mr. Bell," said Little. "I don't know what to say."

"Say you'll accept, Little. Say you're our man."

"Mr. Bell, you know you can count on Little Jones."

"Outstanding. Now look here, Little." Mr. Bell tapped his finger on the drawing. "Just get a good look at this."

Mr. Bell was pointing to a sketch of Little's house. The landscape architect had drawn the cedar shingle roof, the beds of marigolds and alyssum and candytuft, the tea roses, the pinkie hawthorn shrubs along the foundation, and in the yard, the Chinese pistachio, the flowering pear, and the white lilac at the picket gate.

"Mr. Bell, sir, that's my house."

"Caretaker's got to have a place to live, doesn't he?" Mr. Bell was ashamed of how easily he could entice Little, and for a moment he almost lost his nerve. "And that house of yours is a showpiece," he said.

"But, sir, that's Quakertown."

Mr. Bell laid his hand on Little's shoulder and squeezed it. "We need that space, Little. Will you help us convince your neighbors to move?"

"Move where, sir?"

"Don't worry. The city will buy those houses. Lots will be made ready a few miles east for anyone who wants to buy. It's better land than what you folks have now. Higher ground. You know how the creek floods Quakertown each spring."

"That's a fact. Still, Quaker's always been home."

Mr. Bell took a deep breath and then blew it out. "Little, if you don't do this, it might be hard for you to get yard work. You know what I'm saying? After the word gets around. I wish this wasn't the way. You know I've always been fond of you and your family. But the truth is the city will move Quakertown with or without you. And if you don't cooperate, you'll lose your home. What's more, this whole city might be ruined. You know the way things are getting hot around here right now. All these little squabbles. Little, you know me. Listen to what I'm telling you. This is what's best."

9

Little's father had been a traveling man. Wash Jones liked to boast that he had seen most there was to see of the country, had given it to his son in lithographs he had drawn in thousands of cities, always a quick sketch made for Little and sent back to Texas where he waited with his mother.

Bird's Eye Maps, Wash Jones called the drawings—detailed renderings of communities as they might be seen from the air. He had developed this aptitude for cartography when he had been the assistant to an officer who drew maps for the advancing Union forces. When the war ended, the officer gave his inks and leads and pens and paper to Wash Jones, claiming he never intended to draw another map as long as he lived.

So Wash started going into cities and producing, by subscription, perspective maps. He used engineering maps as sources and then replicated every street, railroad track, tree, barn—every object, in fact, that someone might see from a perspective above the city.

It was in one of those cities—Denton, Texas—that he loved a girl and married her despite the fact that he would be gone more than he would be home. "That," he told his bride, Ruth, "was the big picture."

Little knew his father most intimately through the scents of paper and ink, the domes of capitol buildings, the spires and steeples of churches and city halls, the spans of bridges, the switch and turn tables of rail yards. He learned the cities' names—Cedar Falls, Vinton, Waterloo. He imagined his father soaring above them or walking on a broad ray of sunlight, breaking through the clouds, the way Jesus did in the calendar picture his mother kept on the wall though the year, 1886, had come and gone.

Then, the spring when Little was ten, Wash Jones took him to Lincoln, Nebraska. On the train, they sat on hard wooden benches in a car for Negroes. They ate the butter-and-jelly sandwiches Little's mother had wrapped in paper. At small stations along the way, when the train stopped, they went out into fields or down alleys, and Wash Jones told Little to pee. "There's no shame in it," Wash said, but Little knew that was a lie.

At the Lincoln station, a young man was standing on a baggage cart, shouting and shaking his fists. He was a white man with wavy black hair, and when he raised his arms, Little could see the glossy lining of his cutaway coat. The lapels were shiny, too, as was the cravat tied in a bowknot at his throat. He was a short man, but his voice was majestic. "As deep as a well," Wash Jones said, and Little thought of the pipe organ at the white folks' Presbyterian Church in Denton, the church his mother cleaned, and how sometimes when the two of them would be there, someone would be playing that organ, and he would feel the tones rumble around in his chest, and he would think how wonderful it would be to fill the air with such might.

He experienced a similar envy when he heard the white man speak—something about the railroads and how they were making it hard on the farmers—but really, Little wasn't listening to the words, only the godly ring of the man's voice.

Although Little adored the push of that voice, its force made him feel very small and aware of how far he was from home. He didn't know whether to blame the voice, or his father who had brought him there to hear it, or the white people who wanted to keep him as far away from them as they could. He didn't want to blame anyone, truth be told, but he couldn't help feeling he should hold someone responsible for the fact that he was suddenly unhappy to be who he was.

It was evening there at the station, and arc lamps were burning brightly along the platform. "That's Bryan," Little heard someone in the crowd mutter. "That's the Boy Orator, rabble-rousing for the Populists again."

Another white man, this one carrying a walking stick, approached Little and his father. The man was wearing a stovepipe hat, and his face was nearly covered with a white moustache and mutton chop sideburns. Only the red knobs of his nose, his cheekbones, and his chin were bare.

Little snuggled in close to his father, and hid his face, as best he could, behind the folds of his coat.

The white man hooked the walking stick over his forearm by its handle, and Little saw it was the head of an eagle fashioned from bronze and worn smooth by the pressure of the man's palm. The man reached into his coat pocket and took out a tin. Without a word, he opened it and held it out to Little. Little saw the candies inside, smelled the horehound drops. His father nudged him, and he took one of the candies, then, and slipped it into his mouth.

"You must be Wash Jones," the man said. He took a candy for himself and then returned the tin to his pocket. "I'm Cook. I'm here to take you to my hotel."

Wash Jones gathered up his valise, and the three of them started walking toward the doors to the station. Then the man with the booming voice—this Bryan—stopped them. "I saw you, Cook," he said. "A candy for the boy. A sweet lump that dissolves in an instant. Here, son. Here's something that will stay with you, something to nurture you a lifetime." He pressed a small card into Little's hand and hurried away into the station.

Cook took the card from Little and read it aloud. "'He that troubleth his own house shall inherit the wind: and the fool shall be servant to the wise of heart.'" Cook tore the card into scraps and tossed it up into the air. "That Bryan is a Bible beater. Thinks he knows how everyone should live."

Riding in the hansom to the hotel, Little could still feel the card in his hand, its stiff stock, the raised letters of its engraving. He could remember the sound it made when Cook tore it, and how when he threw the pieces into the air, they flew and dove like moths toward light.

At the hotel, a Negro carried Wash Jones's valise to his room. The Negro was dark-skinned, much darker than Little or his father, and the gold chevrons at the wrists of his scarlet waist-jacket were brilliant vees of honey. The fringed epaulets at his shoulders shimmied when he pushed open the door to the room and then swept his white-gloved hand through the entry. "Here you are, sir," he said to Wash Jones. "Your room, sir. I'm sure you'll be comfortable, sir. You and the young master."

Inside, the man switched on the electric lights, the first Little had ever seen, and turned back the bed's quilted coverlet. He helped Wash Jones off with his coat and then did the same for Little. He hung the coats in a tall armoire with ornate scrollwork on the wooden doors. Little peeked through the slot where the panels of thick draperies met and saw the lights of the city spreading out below him. The people on the walkways, when they passed through the glow from the street lamps, were small— puny britches, which was what Little's mother always called him—and it gave him a special satisfaction to stand there in that hotel room and look down on all those people, to be so high above them.

Then the man in the scarlet waist-jacket said, "Yes, sir. Snug as a bug in a rug." Little suddenly spied his own reflection in the window, and he stepped away, ashamed, because what the man had said was what Little's mother said every night when she pulled the cover over him, and hearing it made him think of her, at home without him. He imagined her in her white cotton night-gown kneeling at the side of her bed to pray as she did every night, praying now for him, that he would be safe and come home to her. And just then he had been thinking how grand the hotel room was compared to the house where he lived with his mother, and now his father was calling to him. "Little," he was saying. "March yourself over here, boy. I've got something for you to give the man."

Little took the coin from his father. It was a copper penny with the head of an Indian chief engraved on it. "Go on," his father said. "Step smart."

So Little laid the penny on the soft palm of the man's glove, and when he did, the man said, "Thank you, young master," in what Little's mother would have called a snitty way, and Little's father said, in an ugly voice Little had never heard him use, "Don't use that vinegar tone with my son."

"Sir?" Little watched the man close his white-gloved hand over the penny as if he could hide what had just taken place. "I meant no harm, sir."

"We won't tolerate any smart-alecky talk from a jackanapes like you." Wash Jones raised a finger and flicked the fringe on one of the man's epaulets, recalling how in the army, he had stood in mess lines to fetch the mapmaker's meals, had shaved him, and helped him dress. He had blackened his boots and kept his leads sharp. "Say you're sorry now, and we'll forget it."

Little could see the man's jaw muscles tighten, and his nostrils flare open as he took in a breath, and Little understood that the man would sooner swallow that penny whole than say he was sorry.

But he gave a deep bow to Little, and then he said, "Please for-give me, young master. It's just my ignorant upbringing showing through."

Wash Jones sat down on a chair with a tufted back. "Just one thing more. Before you go, I'd like you to loosen my boots, please."

The man got down on his knees and undid the buttons from their hooks. "There you are, sir."

"And while you're here, I believe they could use some of this dust wiped off."

"Yes, sir. I'll just step out and fetch a cloth."

"No," said Wash Jones. "I want you to use those nice white gloves of yours."

The man held his hands up in front of his face and studied the gloves. "That's like to dirty them up, sir."

He started to rise from his knees, but Wash Jones caught hold of his waist-jacket and pulled him back down to the floor. He balled the cloth up into his fist and drew the man close to his face. "Don't you know who brought me here? Councilman August Cook, the same Mr. Cook who owns this hotel. I wouldn't want to have to tell him that you insulted my son and made me very unhappy. Would you want me to have to do that?"

"No, sir." The man tilted back his head and stuck out his chin as if someone had suddenly put a knife to his throat. "I wouldn't want that for the world."

"Then I suggest you start wiping."

The man swiped his gloved hands over Wash Jones's boots, and Little knew the white cloth was darkening with the dust and grit of railroad cinders.

Wash Jones glanced up at Little, and gave him a smile. "This is livin', ain't it, Little? High on the hog, hey, little man?"

Little felt an ache come into his throat. He knew why his father was happy to spend so much time away from him and his mother. So he could stay in fancy hotel rooms, look down on the cities, and let their people treat him like a king. So he could forget, for as long as it took him to draw his maps, the color of his skin, which was the color of Little's skin, and the color of all the people that he loved.

*   *   *

The next morning, Little sat on his father's lap at the mahogany desk in their hotel room. With a few deft strokes of his lead, his father began his Bird's Eye Map of Lincoln. He had already studied the city's engineering map just to get, as he liked to say, "the lay of things," and now he drew a horizontal line only a whisker from the top of the paper. That, he told Little, was the horizon, the way it would look to a bird in the air. If he drew the horizon in the middle of the page, it would look the way it would to someone who was standing on the ground and staring straight ahead. If he drew it toward the bottom, it would look the way it would to a worm or a snake slithering along on its belly. So the horizon had to be high for this map because everything drawn in relation to it would appear as it would if someone were passing over, perhaps in one of those hot-air balloons he had seen during the war.

He started with the capitol building, sketching in the tall shaft, and its dome, and even the statue of the man atop it, a statue Little had seen out their hotel window. The man held a bag at his side, and his right arm was crooked as he flung seed out into the wind. Little watched his father draw other buildings and streets that disappeared at the high horizon. That was the vanishing point, his father told him, the place where any two lines would meet and disappear. He drew trees and bushes and arc lamps, and even the irises that grew in beds outside their hotel. To Little, it was as if his father were working some magic spell. Soon he was leaning back, pressing the back of his head into his father's chest, looking down at the capitol and all the buildings around it, from a dizzying height.

The secret, his father told him, was perspective, knowing what to make small and what to make smaller, what to make close and what to make far away. It was that and knowing how to use darker and lighter shades to create a trick of the eye, an illusion of space and depth. "I can make something so small," he said, "it almost disappears." He touched his lead to the map, leaving two specks in a window of their hotel.

"What's that?" Little said.

"That's me and you," his father told him. "The two of us, sitting right here, right now. There we are, and no one will ever know."

Little wished he could shrink the distance between himself and home and forget the night before and the way his father had humbled the man with the white gloves and the scarlet jacket so splendid with its golden stripes and fringe. But he couldn't, and the more he tried to put it out of his head, the more miserable he felt, and soon he was crying.

"Here now," his father said. "What's the trouble, little man?"

Little couldn't begin to say because he knew it would hurt too much to say it all. Not only had he been sad for the man, but sad, too, for himself and his mother and all the people—for the first time, he thought of them as his people—all the Negroes his father secretly despised.

"Homesick?" his father said. "Is that the story?" His voice was so sweet and soothing, not sharp and full of venom the way it had been the night before. "There, there," he said. He put his hand on Little's head. "There, there, little man."

Little closed his eyes and felt his father draw him down until his face was resting on his chest, and he didn't say a word. He let his father believe what he wanted to believe. He let him believe in home, if only for that moment, if only then.

Finally, when Little was asleep, Wash Jones carried him to the bed and laid him down and covered him with the quilt. If Wash had been alone, as he usually was, he might have gone down to the hotel lobby to sit on a leather-covered chair and enjoy the feel of the Persian rug beneath his feet and the way the crystal pendants of the chandelier glittered overhead. But now all he wanted was to sit on the edge of the bed and watch his son sleep. He thought the gentle rise and fall of Little's chest was the most elegant motion he could imagine. And he had helped to create it. He had spent years drawing novelty maps, but at least he had made this one thing that mattered—this one child, sleeping now beside him, dreaming, so Wash Jones imagined, of home.

But Little was dreaming instead that his father was lost somewhere in a strange city, and Little had to find him, an impossible task because the buildings were so tall, and the streets were so wide, and Little was so small he could barely see the faces of the people around him.

Then a knock at the door of their room woke him, and he opened his eyes and understood that he had only been dreaming for there was his father rising from the bed, and Little felt such a joy come over him because he knew he wasn't alone.

It was Cook at the door, come to get a look at Wash Jones's map. He stood at the mahogany desk, his hands clasped behind his back, rocking forward on the balls of his feet. "You're a marvel, Jones," he said. "I've been telling a friend about you, a Mr. Morton of Nebraska City. He'd like you to come down and do a Bird's Eye Map of his estate, Arbor Lodge."

"Today?" said Wash Jones.

"Yes, today," said Cook. "I've booked us passage on the noon train."

Little heard his father's voice dim and saw his shoulders slump as he bowed his head. "I was hoping to go home today." In the time he had watched Little sleep, he had begun to long for home where Ruth waited, as she had all these years, for him to return. He had seen in Little's face the two of them, both him and Ruth—her high cheekbones, his flat nose—and now all that seemed important to him was that they all be in the same place, at last a family. He had even begun to imagine that he might give up mapmaking altogether, find some line of work in Denton, and stay there. "I thought I'd finish your map," he told Cook, "and take my son back to Texas."

"Texas," said Cook. "I wouldn't think you'd be in a hurry to get back to that godforsaken place."

"No, sir," said Wash Jones, and Little pushed his head under the quilt.

What he didn't know—what Wash Jones could have told him—was that there were times when it was best to say what white people wanted to hear, all for the sake of an easier ride through the world.

"Noon," said Cook.

"Yes, sir," said Wash Jones. "I'll be ready quicker than you can say 'Jack Robinson.' "

On the train to Nebraska City, Little and his father rode in a private parlor car with Cook. A car for just the three of them. Little, sitting with his father across from Cook, could hardly believe what he saw. The seats were soft and covered with a red woolen fabric; the oak walls of the car were shiny with shellac. A Negro porter wearing a white coat brought them tall glasses of lemonade on a silver tray.

"This is a good place to live no matter what the Populists would have you believe." Cook lifted his glass. "Nebraska." Through the open window, Little could see the fields of young corn, their rows of green shoots rolling off to the horizon. He could see apple orchards, brilliant with white blossoms. He could smell the overwhelming sweetness of lilac, the sharp scent of wild onions. Cook leaned forward and touched his glass to Wash Jones's knee. "We never enslaved the Negroes here. We knew where we stood on that matter. Not like those lunatics down in 'Bleeding Kansas.' "

"I was in the war between the states," said Wash Jones. "I was a soldier in the Union Army."

"Remarkable," said Cook. He moved his glass over to Little's knee. "Your father is a remarkable man."

Little could feel the cold glass, and something about the fact that Cook could touch him in that way and let the damp soak through his legging and seep into his skin made him think that his father deserved every bit of high living his skill as a mapmaker had brought him.

"My daddy doesn't tolerate smart-alecky talk from jackanapes," Little said, and before Wash Jones could stop him, he had told the story of the bellboy.

Cook sat up straight in his chair and looked at Wash Jones the way Little had seen his father look at the bellboy, with anger and disgust. "Well, we better be careful around your father. He might take a notion to give us what for."

"He wouldn't hurt us," said Little, sensing that he had revealed more about his father than he had intended.

"No, I'm sure he wouldn't," said Cook. "After all, we're not jackanapes. Are we, Jones?"

Before Wash Jones could answer, the train clamped on its brakes, and he felt the lurch of the cars tugging at their couplings. The force threw Little back into his seat, and brought Cook forward until he fell to his knees. Wash Jones tried to help him up, but Cook would have none of it. "Here now," he said. "What are you doing? Do you think I'm an invalid, for pity's sake?"

"No, sir," said Wash Jones. "I'm sorry, sir."

Cook was on his feet now. His lemonade glass had fallen from his hand and was rolling down the runnered aisle. The train had come to a stop. Little could hear the locomotive's steam die away with a sigh, could smell the coal smoke from the boiler.

"Stay here," said Cook. "I'll see what sort of snag we've hit."

While Cook was gone, Little finished his lemonade and set the glass on the floor. His father was leaning over him, looking out the window, but all he could see was that the train had stopped on a bridge over a river.

"Did I say wrong?" Little asked him.

"Cook thinks I'm a blackguard now." Wash Jones's voice was sharp, unable to hold the anger he felt toward Little for telling the story of how he had mistreated the bellboy. "Satan himself. A real golliwog."

"So I said wrong?"

"No, you said the truth."

Wash Jones was afraid that if he didn't change Cook's idea of him, he would lose the commission for the Lincoln map and for the one of Arbor Lodge. He wanted to tell Little that he should always keep his mother's good heart, but then Cook was back, dropping down into his seat with a sigh and blotting sweat from his forehead with a handkerchief.

"There's been an incident," he said. "Some trouble on the track. Populists, no doubt, trying to shut down the railroad. They've built a barricade of logs on the river bridge. Luckily, the engineer got the locomotive shut down in time. Now we're just waiting for the porters to move the logs out of the way."

Wash Jones got to his feet and took off his coat. "I'll help them," he said.

Cook folded his handkerchief. "That's decent of you," he said, "but really unnecessary."

"I'm used to hard work," said Wash Jones. "Little, you stay here and take care of my coat."

The coat, across Little's lap, was heavy, and it smelled of his father's shaving soap and of railroad cinders and of cigar smoke and all the aromas that had stuck to it during his travels.

Outside the train, in front of the locomotive, the porters were heaving logs over the bridge and into the river. Wash Jones watched the logs fall, their lengths growing smaller and smaller until they hit the water and were swept along by the strong current.

The porter who had served their lemonade was brushing dirt and scraps of bark from his white coat. "You get on back to the train," he said to Wash Jones. "You don't belong out here."

"I've come to give you a hand," Wash said.

"All right, sir." The porter clapped his hands together. "Latch on to the end of this log, and we'll see what you can do."

Wash Jones balanced on the rail, the soles of his boots slippery on the polished steel. He took the end of the log in both hands.

"Ready?" the porter said, and Wash Jones braced himself. "One, two, three."

Inside the parlor car, Cook had his hands on Little's head. "I can tell your traits and capacities by the shape of your skull." Little could feel Cook's fingers rubbing over bumps, probing indentations. "You'll be a loving man, a good man, but you'll get used to people admiring you. You'll expect it, just like your father. You'll have to be careful that you don't wish too much for yourself."

A conductor in a navy blue uniform came into the car and leaned over to whisper to Cook. He kept his voice low and shielded his lips with his hand, but still Little could hear him.

"That gentleman who was with you," the conductor said. "The Negro gentleman. He's gone."

Cook jerked his head around so he could face the conductor, and the conductor stepped back. "Gone?" Cook said, and his voice was loud. "What do you mean, gone?"

"Into the river, sir." The conductor bent down to whisper again to Cook. "Carried away with the current, sir. Drowned."

The train went on to Nebraska City, and Little did his best to understand that his father had somehow fallen into the river, and the porters had seen him go under and then nothing but the rush of the current. As the train started again and went on across the bridge, Little looked down at the wide band of gray river, thinking he might catch a glimpse of his father, but all he saw were the logs floating and turning with the current.

Cook took out his tin of horehound drops and offered one to Little, and Little, though he was ashamed of himself for wanting a candy just then, took one. He was thinking how this was all so familiar to him, the hollow feeling he had whenever his father was away from him and how he imagined that if he stuck to his best behavior—if he were polite and eager to please—his father would come home and maybe this time or the next time, he might stay.

At the station in Nebraska City, a hansom was waiting to carry Cook and Little to Arbor Lodge. Little carried his father's coat and would not let go of it all the time he was at the Lodge or later when J. Sterling Morton would accompany him on the train back to Denton.

That afternoon, when Little and Cook arrived, and Cook told Morton what had happened on the river bridge, Morton got down on his knee, and he took Little by the shoulders. "I never met your father," he said, "but I've seen his maps. He understood preservation. Such a careful eye for detail. It takes a world of love to pay such close attention to things."

Morton's high forehead and his pointed nose gave him a gruff appearance, but he won Little with his kind voice and his hands, so tender, as they flitted like butterflies to pat Little on the back or stroke his cheek or smooth the lapels of his coat or button the cuff of his shirt.

While Cook arranged for a party of men to begin dragging the river, Morton walked with Little through the grove of tall oak trees that surrounded the lodge. Along gravel pathways, beds of irises were in bloom, and Morton insisted that Little stop and feel the soft beards of the petals, some of them purple, some of them yellow, some of them white.

"I planted nearly every tree you see here," Morton said. "Nearly every flower." He reached out and took Little's hand. "We have to do what we can to make the world lovely."

And Little did think it was beautiful there at Arbor Lodge in the shade of the oak trees, birds singing, his father's coat bundled up in his arms. He glanced back and saw the tall white columns of the three colonnades at the lodge and thought how marvelous it would be to sit there and look out at a world, green and lush, a world he himself had made.

"There is a unity in nature," Morton said. "None of these trees or flowers could have grown without living creatures dying and returning to the earth. Generations of flesh pass away, my lad, and plants and trees take their sustenance from them. So while there is constant change in the world, there is never loss. Never that. For nature permits no waste. Substance lives forever."

They walked through an apple orchard to a grove of catalpa trees, thick with white blossoms.

"Those trees came from Ohio years ago," Morton said. "They were only seeds then from trees on the farm owned by General Harrison who later became our President. Now look at them." Little tipped his head back and looked up into the broad-leafed canopy of the catalpas. "I'm going to give you some seeds to take home with you, and when you get there, I want you to plant them. From a president to you, Little. You may feel lost now, but I have no doubt you'll find your way."

All his life, Little would remember Morton and the way he rode with him on the train back to Texas, hoisted him up, even, and sat him on his lap, told him story after story, said to the other passengers, "What do you think of my boy?"

Wash Jones's body would never be found. He would be forever a wool coat, a case of pens and leads and inks, a valise Cook would send back from the hotel in Lincoln.

Little planted the catalpa seeds in the backyard of his mother's house, which would become his house, and Eugie's and Camellia's. Three trees grew. Then came the Chinese pistachio, and a dogwood, and a mimosa, and the white lilac, the rarest of them all, and with each tree, Little felt his secret take deeper root in him. When he had first known that his father was dead, a small measure of relief had come over him, just a breath, because he had imagined he would never again feel shame in the company of the people he loved best.

"I'm taking you home," Morton had said to him, and to Little, at the time, there could have been no sweeter word. Home to Quakertown where he promised himself he would stay forever.

10

It was early on a Sunday morning when Kizer heard someone knocking on the front door. His father had risen early and gone out to his property east of town. Tibby was sleeping after a night when she had drunk too much and stayed up well past midnight pacing the floors. Kizer hurried to the door, not wanting the knocking to wake her.

At first, when he opened the door and saw Eugie Jones standing there, her gloved fist raised, ready to knock again, he thought perhaps she had come to say she had made everything right between him and Camellia.

But then she said, "You've got my girl in a passel of trouble. What do you aim to do about it?"

Up and down the street, neighbors were starting to come out of their houses, beginning to stroll past the Bells' on their way to church. "Good morning, Kizer," one gentleman said. "Is there trouble?"

Kizer knew it was odd to see a colored woman at the front door on a Sunday morning. "No, there's no trouble," he called out. "It's a beautiful day."

"Well," Eugie said. "What do you have to offer up for yourself?"

"I'd marry your Camellia in a heartbeat," he said, "if she'd have me."

"Marry," Eugie said with a snort. "Now wouldn't that make a fine mess of greens."

"But I love Camellia. And I know she loves me."

"Love? Is that what you call what you did? Took her like you had a right."

"Camellia told you that?"

"Love," Eugie said again. "You think love would be enough to make up for all the trouble you'd be asking for?"

Before he could answer, she told him what she expected. Fifty dollars. That would be enough to pay the doctor. "Fifty dollars," she said, "and then you're done. Then this thing never happened, and Camellia can marry Ike."

"Abortion?" Kizer said. "What you're suggesting is a hundred times worse than anything I ever did with Camellia."

"Are you saying you won't give it up?"

"And have that horrible thing on my head?"

Eugie put her hands on her hips. "If you don't," she said, "I'm set to holler it out to all your neighbors, everything you and Camellia been up to. Holler it to your mama and daddy, too."

"Is this what Camellia wants?"

"It is."

"I need to hear her say that."

Eugie shook her head. "It's best you two keep clear of each other now. Do you love her like you claim?"

"With all my heart."

"Then you ought to be able to see that this is the best thing. Best for Camellia, best for you, best for your mama and daddy. And if Camellia wanted to be with you, do you think she would have sent me here to ask for this?"

"She sent you?"

Eugie held out her hand. "Fifty dollars. Then I'll be on my way."

"It'll be on your soul," Kizer said. "It'll be on both our souls."

"Can't be worried about the afterlife. Got too much trouble here and now."

11

The next morning, after Little had hitched his mule and left for Mr. Andrew Bell's, Eugie and Camellia settled their hats on their heads. Outside, the sky was that endless blue dome Captain Jiggs had always said was the clear eyes of God. "That's how close he is," Eugie had told Camellia as a child. "He's watching everything we do."

Eugie opened the front gate and stepped through it. Camellia followed, stopping to close the gate and latch it. A drop of dew from a white lilac blossom fell onto the back of her hand on the vein that ran from her ring finger to her heart. She watched it stain her skin, such lovely skin, Kizer had told her. "Like brown sugar that's been boiled and pulled so the air gets in and lightens it up. That's you, Camellia, sweet, creamy taffy."

But today it was hard to feel sweet. It was hard to feel anything at all, just a deadweight as if her legs were made of wood.

Dr. L. C. Parrish's office was at the top of two flights of stairs, and halfway up, Eugie could see the transom open above the door. As she and Camellia stepped up onto the landing, they heard Dr. Parrish, inside, talking to the parrot he kept in a cage in the corner of the waiting room. Through the door's frosted glass, they could see his shadow bend over the cage. "Marcus Garvey," he said to the parrot, "who are you, Marcus Garvey?"

The parrot squawked. "I'm a smooth talker."

"That's right," said Dr. Parrish. "You're a smooth talker. And what do you want? What's Marcus Garvey want?"

"Money," said the parrot. "Money, money, money."

Dr. Parrish laughed. His shadow bent back at the waist as he threw up his hands. In her dress pocket, Eugie clutched the envelope that Kizer had given her. Camellia thought about Ike and how he gave money to Marcus Garvey and his Universal Negro Improvement Association. "We're going home to Africa one day," Ike had told her. "Just like Marcus Garvey says."

Africa, she thought. Sakes alive. To her, Africa was a shape on the map that hung in her classroom, a shape shaded red and brown and green. Home was that classroom with the portraits of Lincoln and Washington on the wall, and the smells of chalk dust and paste, and the sounds of pencils scratching in lesson books, and scissors snipping through construction paper, and children squealing as they played tag and blind-man's bluff at recess. Home was the way the shy girls clung to her on the playground, and it was the small frame house where she now slept on a bed, covered with a quilt her Granny Ruth had made. It was the way a blue norther could come up fast in winter and drop the temperature thirty degrees or more, and the way a thunderstorm would hit in summer, the sky turning purple and orange. Home was Quakertown, not Africa. She agreed with Dr. Parrish. "No use trying to run," he had told her once when they had spoken about Marcus Garvey. "No, sir. Better to fix what we got right here."

Camellia opened the door to Dr. Parrish's office and stepped over the threshold. She smelled the aseptic scent of ether and gauze and Mercurochrome, and she knew she had left some good, sweet part of herself on the other side. She could hear the change in her voice, the stern I-mean-business tenor she used when she needed to snap a pupil into shape.

"Dr. Parrish," she announced. "I'm here."

Now it was Eugie who could barely move. So many times she had come into that office, first when she had been big with Camellia. How Dr. Parrish had poked and prodded her, angry because she had come to him, pregnant, after he had warned her that childbirth would be difficult for her, dangerous even, because of her kidney stones. He could take care of it, he told her, offer her relief. And no one would be the wiser. "Oh, don't look at me like I'm the devil," he had said. "I'm a man of medicine. It's my job to keep people well."

Now, what she had been unwilling to imagine for herself she had arranged for Camellia, and she felt something inside of her so coiled and tangled she couldn't for the life of her unravel it. If she had accepted Dr. Parrish's offer all those years ago, she wouldn't be there now with all her sorrow and dread knotted up inside her, but oh, the joy she would have missed, and she would not have missed it for all the world. You try to do the right thing, she told herself, but it's always so hard if you're any kind of person at all.

To let Camellia have this child—Kizer's child—who could say how it would all work out? There had been a moment when Eugie had been tempted to let it go. When she had walked up to the Bells' fine house to demand money, she had allowed herself to imagine that Camellia might even marry Kizer and live in such a home on Oak Street, and Little and Eugie would visit, and she would remember what it had been like when she had lived there as a girl. But she recalled too much of the other part of that time, too much of the ugliness, to imagine this dream for Camellia could ever come true.

So she came into Dr. Parrish's office, and she took the envelope from her dress pocket and offered it to him. He was a tall, thin man with squared shoulders and a straight back. He had yet to slip into his white doctor's coat. Garters kept his shirtsleeves free from his wrists.

The parrot lifted his wings and scraped their tips over the wire cage. Eugie stared straight ahead at the solid oak door that led to the examination room. She heard, from the other side, instruments clinking together, chiming gently, as if they were no more potent than the bone china teacups she had inherited from her mother.

Camellia saw a purple cloche hat hanging from a coat rack near the bird cage, a red ribbon trailing down to the floor.

"My nurse is making ready," Dr. Parrish said. "You know Mavis Brown. Don't worry. She'll keep your secret for you."

When he took the envelope from Eugie, she stared at his beautiful hands, at his long fingers, and she felt an odd mix of consolation—such lovely hands—and horror. Oh, Baby-Girl, she wanted to cry out, what have I done?

12

At Mr. Andrew Bell's, Kizer was upstairs on the sleeping porch, watching Little Jones who was on the front lawn, kneeling beside a pittosporum shrub. At the request of Kizer's father, Little was grooming the pittosporum into the shape of the sphinx. From the picture Mr. Bell had shown him, Little had built a wire mesh frame that duplicated the outline of the body, which was that of a resting lion, and the head, the head of a man, his face framed by the triangular folds of his headdress. All spring, Little had let the pittosporum grow inside the frame, and he had sheared away the stems and leaves that poked through the wire.

Kizer felt sorry for Little, working so patiently there in the heat. He was on his knees, clipping the stems of the pittosporum with small, gentle cuts. The blades of his shears, honed to a sharp edge, gleamed in the sunlight, but he didn't wield them with the reckless abandon such sharpness might have tempted most men to do. He made a few cuts and then stopped to run his hand over the wire mesh, brushing away bits of leaves. It was the slow, loving motion of that hand that overwhelmed Kizer, thinking as he was, of Camellia and how the two of them had made a baby who would never know the world. He had agreed to never speak of it, and he knew Camellia, who was going to marry Ike Mattoon, would never speak of it, and it would be their secret—Kizer's and

Camellia's and Eugie's—and someday, when they were all gone, the fact of it would be lost forever.

Little, as he rubbed his hand over the soft leaves of the pittosporum, remembered how, whenever Camellia had been cranky or upset as a toddler, he had taken her out into their yard and told her to touch the glossy leaves of the cleyera, to trace the bell-shaped flowers of the forsythia, to smell the clove perfume of the moonflowers opening at twilight.

Now here she was, a grown woman, as delicate as her name-sake blossoms, which burned in full sun and needed the shade of filtered light. She was marrying Ike Mattoon, a war veteran, and someday she would have her own children, and she would give them the world as Little had given it to her.

Kizer came out onto the lawn, the tip of his cane sinking down into the damp ground. "You're hard at work," he said to Little.

"Yes, sir, Mr. Kizer." Little pushed the straw hat up on his head and squinted at him. "Doing just like your daddy said to do, make this shrub into this lion-man, this whatever it is."

"Sphinx," said Kizer.

"Yes, sir," said Little. He bowed his head to escape the glare of the sun. "I just do what your daddy says."

Kizer reached out with his cane and flicked it at a stray stem poking through the wire mesh at the lion's chest. "It must seem ridiculous to you. A silly thing, I mean, for someone to want."

"I've made birds, sheep, fish." Little snipped the stray stem. The sphinx's body had filled in, but it would be awhile before the head emerged. "What people want is their business. I figure they got their reasons. It's not my place to judge what's in their hearts. I just give them what they want. It's easy as pie once I've got the wire form in place. Whatever doesn't fit has got to go."

Kizer let his cane fall to the ground; then, as if the weight of all that was inside him was too much to bear, he got down on his knees. He reached out and touched Little on the wrist.

"Mr. Kizer?" Little kept his eyes on the pittosporum. He concentrated on the stray stems that still needed his attention. He tried to ignore the fact that Kizer's hand was resting on his wrist.

"Your daughter," Kizer said.

"Camellia," said Little.

"She and I . . ."

"Yes."

"The fact is . . ."

"You and her."

"Yes." Kizer gripped Little's wrist more tightly. "Exactly."

Little could not have said with any certainty what it had been that had prepared him to intuit what Kizer had been wanting to tell him. Perhaps it had been the way Little had watched the poor boy crumple to his knees and the sight of the thick sole and heel of his left shoe that had reminded him of Camellia and the way she was always quick to show a kind face to the students who, because they were poor or ill-featured or slow to learn, needed her love. Or maybe it had been the fact that Kizer's cane had reminded him of Captain Jiggs who had bought Eugie's mother as a slave and then had taken her as a wife. Whatever the reason, Little had sensed, perhaps in the way Kizer clung so desperately to his wrist, that he and Camellia were in trouble.

"You hadn't ought to tell me this," Little said. "Camellia is going to marry Ike Mattoon."

But Kizer, once he had started, couldn't stop the flow of words. The sound of his voice was, to Little, like the sound his shears made against the pittosporum stems, a sharp whistling keen. "Fifty dollars," Little heard, and then something about Eugie and how right now, this morning, she was with Camellia. "Dr. L. C. Parrish," he heard, and then a word he didn't know.

"Say it plain, please, Mr. Kizer."

"Curettage," said Kizer. "Abortion."

The sun was so fierce Little could feel the heat on his eyeballs. He spoke in the quiet voice he had learned to use in the company of the people who employed him. "I don't know why you told me this. I don't know what you expect me to do."

"Won't you stop it?" Kizer's voice was choked and pleading.

"Stop it?" said Little. "What chance you think I got?"

"She's your daughter."

"She's her mother's daughter," Little said, and Kizer heard the anguish in his voice. "That's plain now."

13

In the examination room, the nurse, Mavis Brown, told Camellia to remove her clothing. "Everything," she said. "I've got a gown for you to put on."

Camellia lifted her hat away from her head and set it on the examination table.

"Not there," said Mavis Brown. She scooped up the hat and tossed it onto a chair. "The table's where we do our business."

Camellia felt the way she knew the shy first graders did each fall, hesitant and afraid to make a mistake, anxious to catch on to the way things were done. And Mavis Brown, unlike Camellia, who always tried to put her students at ease, only set her more on edge. Mavis in her white nurse's dress, with its long white striped apron, and her hair oiled and pulled back into a knot that bobbed up and down beneath her nurse's hat. She wore white stockings and shoes that squeaked on the floor as she moved to the table where the instruments were laid out on a tray, their nickel-plating dull and scratched. "Shake a leg," she told Camellia. "I've got to shave you."

"Shave me?" said Camellia.

"That's right. And then bathe you with bichloride solution. Your privates, I mean. Then you'll be ready for the doctor."

Camellia's fingers were trembling, and she had trouble with the buttons of her dress. The fact that Mavis Brown was standing there, hands on her hips, watching, made undoing the buttons an even more difficult chore. Camellia was ashamed of her plain cotton shift, but even more vexed at the prospect of standing naked before Mavis Brown, who was a voluptuous woman with generous hips and breasts, the healthy sheen of her dark, rich flesh such a contrast to Camellia's own light skin.

Mavis's son, Alvin, had been one of Camellia's pupils, and he had been a handful, always up to something, until finally Camellia had asked Mavis Brown in for a chat. "Your Alvin," she had said. "He's out of control."

"I do what I can," Mavis Brown had said. "Me and no husband."

"I didn't mean . . ."

"Sure you did. You think we're trash."

Of course, Camellia thought now, Mavis Brown had been correct. The remark about Alvin had insinuated that Mavis herself was living a life without decorum or boundaries. Camellia imagined that Mavis was enjoying this moment in Dr. Parrish's office, thinking, probably, that even light-skinned schoolteachers could lose command of their lives.

"These buttons," Camellia said.

"Sugar," said Mavis Brown. "Do you want me to help you?"

Camellia was so frightened, so ashamed, all she could do was drop her arms to her sides and stand there, waiting for Mavis Brown to come to her. As Mavis undid the buttons, she told Camellia there was nothing to worry about. "Honey, this isn't going to be bad at all, not at all." Mavis's tone was the same gentle murmur Camellia used to console a student. "You'd be surprised at how many's had it done, some of them more than once. Blondeanna Sparks, Rayanne Mink, Della Treece." Camellia heard the parrot, Marcus Garvey, squawking in the waiting room. Then the door opened a crack, and she saw Dr. Parrish's hand on the knob. "It'll be all right?" she heard her mother say, and Dr. Parrish said, "Don't worry, Eugenia, I'll get it all. I'll scrape her good."

Mavis Brown took Camellia by the shoulders and pressed against her in a clumsy hug. She whispered in her ear. "I don't know why you don't just keep it, sugar. You and Ike getting married anyway."

Camellia thought, then, of both Ike and Kizer; how much they each needed from her. She could still feel Ike trembling the first night she had given herself to him. She remembered the shy way Kizer had first touched her, hesitant, but needy like a timid pupil wanting to pet her. She thought of the baby she carried. So many lives depending on what she did next. She grabbed the front of her dress and pulled it closed, and she said in a quiet voice, "No."

14

On Oak Street, Kizer was pacing about the dining room table where his mother sat examining a tea service she had purchased recently. His cane knocked against the legs of the table; his steps thumped dully over the Persian rug. Each step made the teapot dome rattle, and finally Tibby said, "Mercy. You're restless. Please, Kizer, won't you stop this pacing and sit down? Why aren't you at the bank today?"

Kizer suddenly stopped and turned to her. "All right, then," he said in a fierce voice. "I'll go. I will."

And he would, he told himself. He would drive into Quakertown to the doctor's office, and he would stop what Camellia meant to happen there.

It had started to rain by the time Kizer got to Quakertown. He drove down Frame Street, hunched over the steering wheel, peering out through the rain-glazed windshield. He almost didn't see Camellia and Eugie leaving Dr. L. C. Parrish's office. They stepped into the rain, their heads bowed, and Kizer knew he was too late. He cursed himself for giving Eugie the fifty dollars that had purchased such a despicable thing.

A few minutes later, at the Farmer's National Bank, he burst into his father's office. "I'm going abroad," he said. "I've booked passage on the next steamer."

He thought of the travelogues and the night he had sat in the balcony with Camellia and their fingers had touched. He thought of Paris; he had dreamed of going there one day with her. Now she was lost to him, and the child they had conceived. But still he could feel the light touch of Camellia's finger. He knew he would feel it always, carry it with him, no matter where he went in the world.

15

Camellia and Eugie stopped under the window awning at Billy Moten's Apothecary and stood there a moment, neither of them saying a word.

"I've heard drinking blueing will do it," Eugie finally said, "or starch or gunpowder or tansy or slippery elm."

Camellia shook her head and placed her hand on her stomach. "No, I've decided. I'm going to have this baby."

"And Kizer Bell?"

"Kizer doesn't want me. He paid you, didn't he?"

"Yes, he paid me." Eugie put her hand on Camellia's back between the wings of her sharp shoulder blades.

"Don't you say 'shoo' to Daddy," Camellia said. "It's our secret."

"Someday we'll have to say something. To your daddy. To Ike."

Maybe this would all work out fine, Camellia thought. Maybe the baby would be Ike's, and everything could go on the way they had meant for it to do. Maybe she could even forget about Kizer Bell, but to think of him now nearly brought her to tears. "I'll say it when I know a way to say it. For now, it's our secret."

"That's what it is," said Eugie. "For better or worse."

That evening, when Little came home, Eugie was waiting for

him on the front porch. "I was just sitting here," she told him, "thinking how glorious." She swept her arm out before her. "The mimosa, the lilac. All because of you, Little."

He sat down on the porch floor, his back against a post, and waited for her to say more, to tell him about Camellia and Kizer Bell and Dr. L. C. Parrish, but all she said was, "Do you remember the night Baby-Girl was born? How you said we had to name her Camellia on account her skin was soft and buttery like a camellia blossom?"

"I remember."

"You wouldn't want a thing to hurt her, would you, Little?"

"Has something happened to Camellia?" He stared at Eugie, trying to will her with his eyes to tell him what had happened at Dr. L. C. Parrish's office, so the calamity would be theirs and not hers alone.

She bit down on her lip and looked away for a moment. When she turned back to Little, she was smiling. "Camellia? Don't you worry, Little. There's not a thing wrong with your Baby-Girl. I'm just talking. Mother of the bride has a right to get soft in the heart."

He was about to come out with it, tell Eugie exactly what he knew, but just then Camellia appeared at the door, and through the screen, he could see that she was wearing her wedding gown, the white satin with the lace bodice sequined with silver beads, and overwhelmed by the sight of her, angelic and pristine, he couldn't bring himself to say the words.

"Papa," she said, "I'm getting married come Sunday. Can you believe it? Quick, tell me I'm beautiful."

He imagined, at that moment, they were sealing the secret between them, between him and Eugie and Camellia, sealing it out of love because it would be less hurtful in silence than it would be if they ever spoke it. But there was shame in his heart, shame now in everything around him—the mimosa and the roses and the Chinese pistachio and the white lilac. All of it seemed such a glitter show now that he knew what he did, that they weren't the people he had always imagined them to be.

"Baby-Girl," he said to Camellia, "I can hardly believe it's you."

16

The Saturday evening before the wedding, Ike locked the door to his barbershop, saw the night's first star piercing the sky, and pulled down the green shade. Grackles were screeching outside. "Trash birds talking," Ike said to Mr. Smoke, who was sitting in the barber chair, a cigarette in his mouth, one long leg folded over the other as he counted a stack of five-dollar bills. "Black bastards," Mr. Smoke said. The cigarette, its ash growing longer, jounced up and down. "Let 'em squawk."

For some time, Ike and Mr. Smoke had been selling bootleg liquor from the back room at Ike's barbershop. Nightly, there would come a series of knocks at the alley door, and Ike or Mr. Smoke would look through the peephole to make sure it wasn't prohibition agents. Sometimes it would be white folks, and sometimes it would be neighbors from Quakertown—Miss Abigail Lou, for example, who liked "a taste of medicine" for her arthritis, or Uncle Me, who had no money and came to beg. Most of the time, Ike sent him packing, but on occasion, he gave in and let him have a bottle. Either way, he felt guilty, not knowing whether it was better to send Uncle Me away with the gin or with the willy bugs that were sure to get him if he didn't.

"You sure that ain't Uncle Me out there screeching." Mr.

Smoke tied a string around the stack of fives. He stretched out his skinny neck and crowed. "Me! Me! Me!"

"Don't talk wicked about Uncle Me." Ike traced a finger over his scar, feeling the ridge where Dr. Parrish had stitched it. "That's asking for bad juju, Smoke."

Through some silent agreement, the people of Quakertown had decided to look after Uncle Me, son of an incest, who was crackbrained and incapable of fending for himself. Some put down pallets for him in their sheds; others left food where he was sure to find it. On particularly cold nights, someone would bring him in to sleep on the floor by the stove, to bathe him even, and to set him up with a warm coat, a pair of shoes, some gloves. On more than one occasion, Ike had cut his hair and shaved him, feeling such an ease when Uncle Me, his face swaddled in hot towels, purred deep in his throat like a cat who just ate the bird, and said, "Hmm boy. Me good."

Mr. Smoke tossed the stack of fives to Ike. "Tell me again how it goes."

"His grandfather is his father." Ike opened the cash drawer and tucked the fives inside. "His mother is his sister. He's his own uncle."

"That's him." Mr. Smoke slapped his leg. "Uncle Me."

Ike had seen plenty of soldiers go buggy in the war. Shell-shocked. He had cut their hair at a field hospital in France. Sometimes he had to do it while they were tied down in bed, their big eyes trying to follow the movement of his scissors. He had felt their fear, had imagined how horrible it would be for a man to lose himself, which was the way he had been feeling since the night the men had cut his face.

On this night, he intended to leave the business to Mr. Smoke and to go to his room at Sibby Long's boardinghouse where he could write a letter to his mother in Tennessee. He would explain to her again that the reason he was marrying Camellia Jones was because she was the type of girl it was easy to love, sweet and right-minded and forgiving to a fault. She had continued to love him, even when he had turned brittle with rage. He knew that poison in him—hated it as much as he hated the white men who had cut his face—but it was so hard to calm himself, to be the sort of man he knew Camellia deserved. Her tolerance filled him with such guilt he had decided to turn the business over to Mr. Smoke and to walk the straight and narrow from there on.

"You go on, boy." Mr. Smoke eased himself up from the barber chair, and the ash from his cigarette tumbled down onto his shirt front. He snapped his fingers. His nails were long and pointed, and the joints of his first and second fingers were stained yellow with nicotine. "You going to be a married man. Mr. Smoke, he ain't got no woman to answer to. Yes, sir. Mr. Smoke, he be doing business now."

Before Ike could leave the shop, he heard a knock on the alley door. "One last customer," he said to Mr. Smoke. "For old time's sake. One for the road."

He parted the green curtains and slipped into the back room, dimly lit with a single bulb in a shade hanging from the ceiling. A narrow aisle ran between the crates of hair tonics and creams and talcum powders, each containing a few bottles of the gin that he and Mr. Smoke brought over each evening from Mr. Smoke's shed. Ike peered through the peephole in the alley door and saw Kizer Bell waiting outside, his shoulders hunched and his head bowed. Ike always enjoyed this picture of Kizer—nervous and ashamed—and he made him wait longer than necessary so he could relish it a bit more, the sight of the banker's son waiting for him, Ike Mattoon, to open a door.

Ike heard footsteps in the alley, and a woman's voice. "That's right. Camellia Jones."

Kizer knocked again, this time with the crook of his cane. He leaned in close to the door, as if he wanted to press himself through it like a ghost. Two women and a boy came up behind him in the alley and slowed their walk. Ike could see that one of the ladies was Mavis Brown in her white nurse's uniform and her purple hat—she was the one who had spoken Camellia's name—and the other woman was Hocie Simms who lived in the room across from his at Sibby Long's. Mavis was holding the hand of her son, Alvin, who was pulling as hard as he could to get away from her. Hocie was carrying a bag of popcorn, bought at the stand outside the RCO Ice Cream Parlor while she waited with Alvin for Mavis to leave Dr. Parrish's office. Now she clutched at Mavis's arm. "Good evening," Hocie said in a bright voice. She was a willowy girl whose husband had died in the war. Sometimes she came to Ike's room and asked him if she could play a record on his phonograph. She played Leadbelly and William C. Handy and Satchmo. "Ladies," Kizer said, and then Mavis Brown and Alvin and Hocie Simms scurried away, the two women giggling behind their hands.

"Glory," Kizer said when Ike finally opened the alley door. "I think you keep me waiting out here on purpose just so I'll be on display."

"Now why would I do that?" said Ike. "You're my best customer, Mr. Bell."

Kizer used the tip of his cane to herd Ike back into the shadows of the room so he could enter. "Not after tonight. Tomorrow, I catch the train for New York, and from there I sail for Europe."

Ike reached into a crate and pulled out a bottle of gin. "Fancy that. Both of us going on a trip tomorrow. You going over the pond. Me going on my honeymoon."

"Your wedding." Kizer felt a surprising tenderness for Ike. They loved the same woman, and the poor fool didn't even know it. "Yes, I've heard about that. You and Camellia Jones. Kiss the bride for me. Will you do that? Tell her it's from Kizer Bell."

He took the bottle from Ike and pushed a wad of bills into his hand. Then another knock came at the alley door, this time more of a scratching as if there were a dog on the other side, whining to be let in.

"It's that halfwit, isn't it?" said Kizer. "That Uncle Me."

"Don't worry about him. We take care of our own here in Quakertown."

Kizer rapped his cane on the floor. "We'll see about that before long."

"See what?"

"Never mind. Ask Little Jones what's afoot. Now open that door so I can leave this miserable place."

When Ike opened the door, Kizer, trying to exit, and Uncle Me, trying to enter, bumped into each other and stood there a moment, face to face.

"You," said Uncle Me. He was walleyed. Both eyes turned outward, the pupils shrinking into the corners and leaving mostly the clouded whites of the corneas showing in the sockets.

"Me?" said Kizer. Because of the walleyes, it was always difficult to tell which direction Uncle Me was looking.

"You," Uncle Me said again. Then he held up his left hand and made a circle by touching the tip of his forefinger to the tip of his thumb. He moved the circle back and forth over the forefinger of his right hand. "Hmmm, good," he said.

"That's vulgar," said Kizer.

He struck Uncle Me about the legs with his cane. Then he pushed his way past and limped off down the alley.

At Sibby Long's boardinghouse, Mavis Brown and Hocie Simms were sitting on the front steps sharing the last of the popcorn when Ike came up the walk.

"Hey, Daddy," said Hocie. She took a single piece of popcorn and slipped it into her mouth.

Ike put one foot up on the wooden step, wedging in between Hocie and Mavis. He could see, in the spaces between the steps, that Alvin was crouched down beneath the porch, eavesdropping. Ike brought his foot back onto the walk. "Daddy?" he said. "Hocie, what kind of nonsense are you talking now?"

"You getting married, ain't you?" Hocie put her hands on the step and leaned back. "Won't be long then. You be a daddy. Ask Mavis. She a nurse. She know about them kind of things."

Alvin crawled out from under the steps. His leggings had drooped down to his ankles, and his shoes were untied. "You my daddy?" he said.

"Alvin," said Mavis. She reached out and tried to swat his behind, but he jumped out of the way.

"No, son. I'm not your daddy."

"I didn't think so." Alvin smacked his hands together and a puff of dust sifted out. "You too ugly to be my daddy. Somebody cut up your face."

This time, Mavis caught Alvin by the belt and swatted him until he started to howl. "I'm sorry, Ike," she said.

"Nothing to be sorry for," he told her. "Your boy just told the truth. I'd rather hear that than a pack of lies any day."

Hocie sat up straight. "You sure about that?"

He crouched down, took her hand, and put it on his face. "You feel that scar?" he said. "That's what a white man can do to you and never have to answer for it. I think we ought to have to face up to the facts of our lives, no matter what color we are, don't you?"

Hocie pulled her hand away, curled her fingers into a fist, and hid it behind her. "I lost my man in the war," she said. "He didn't get to come home like you. Go on, Mavis. Tell him about Camellia."

Mavis swished the end of her hat ribbon at Hocie's face. "Hocie Simms, you're a scandal," she said.

"What about Camellia?" Ike said. "I heard you mention her name in the alley tonight."

"Camellia's a lucky girl." Mavis shook her finger at Alvin. "Stop your squalling, Alvin Raymond Brown, or I'll lay into you again. That's all we were saying, Ike. You're the best fish in this pond, and come tomorrow Camellia is going to reel you in."

After Ike had gone into the rooming house, Hocie whispered to Mavis, "You getting soft. He said he wanted the truth, and you just shut up tight as a drum."

"You felt that scar," said Mavis. "I've felt ones like it when I've helped Dr. Parrish sew someone up. Didn't it feel like every misery you've ever had? Ike's been hurt enough. What good would it do to tell him Camellia came this close to getting rid of his baby?"

"You told me."

"I guess I can't help being jealous."

"I hate that Camellia Jones," Hocie said. "She act like a white girl. I hear she part white. You think there anything to that?"

"Shut up, Hocie. White, black, it don't matter. I suspect she wants the same thing we do. A man to love her so she won't be alone."

17

Ike opened the door to his room and saw the envelope lying on the floor. He recognized his mother's elegant handwriting in the address: *Mr. Isaac Mattoon, c/o Miss Sibby Long, 15 Withers Street, Denton, Texas.* She had taught him to sign his name with the same slants and ovals and spirals, to round the *I*, to let the lines of the *M* roll up and down. A man with a respectable signature, she told him, would always be a man people would respect. "This is your name," she said the first time she wrote it out for him. "You write it like this. That way it will never look ugly."

"Isaac," his father told him once. "We named you after the son that came to Abraham and Sarah when they were old."

Ike's mother and father were much older than the parents of his friends. A spinster schoolteacher and a Baptist minister who found each other and had a son because God, they said, took mercy on their loneliness.

But then Ike left them, first for the war and later for Texas. Every time he saw his mother's handwriting, he felt guilty for leaving home.

Now all it took was the sight of that envelope, and he was overwhelmed with the memory of all he had left behind. He remembered his father's church on Sunday mornings in summer, the window sashes propped up with the sawed-off ends of broomsticks, a breeze stirring the leaves on the oaks in the grove outside. In winter, coal smoke rolled up from the chimney, and horses, hitched outside, shook their harness bells as they waited in the snow. He remembered helping his mother stoke the fire at the schoolhouse and fill the inkwells on the students' desks. Later, he listened to the sound of her handbell starting the day or calling the children in from recess or the noon meal. Faithful as a sentinel, she stood on the steps to the schoolhouse and waved her arm up and down, bidding her children come in the way his father, each Sunday and again on Wednesday nights, invited the lost to come home.

He thought of his mother now, her head gray and her shoulders stooped, still ringing her bell, and his heart ached to see her, to show her the man he had become, about to be a husband, and someday, a daddy. "I know you would love Camellia," he had written his mother. "She's a teacher like you."

He picked up the envelope and tore open the end. He let the folded stationery sheet slide out onto his palm. Then he sat at the library table by the window and switched on the lamp. He could hear a motor sputter to a stop outside on the street, and Hocie Simms say, "Help us, Jesus," but he didn't look out because he was mesmerized by his mother's handwriting, the ink blotted to a shade of blue the color of the sky at twilight, and he was following the flow of her hand, the rise and curve of her words:

My Dearest Isaac,

We have sad news, but not so sad you should let it ruin your wedding day. Your daddy's church has burned, but everyone is safe, praise the Lord. I know your first thought will be, it was white folks who set it, but there's no proof of that, and even if it turns out to be true, there's no accounting for the meanness in some people's souls. As for me, I'd rather go on believing that people are good at

*heart. Even at those times when they're not, it's our job to
keep on living the best way we know how. So we meet, a
few of us when we can, here in our house until we can
build the church again. Like I said, don't worry about us,
and do your best not to always see the worst in people.
Your daddy and I are fine and will be till we see you
again, you and your bride, Camellia, such a lovely name. I
write it here just to see how pretty it looks. Camellia
Mattoon. All happiness to you, my son, my darling Isaac,
joy of my life.*

The tears had come without warning and were running now
down Ike's face, catching the rill of his scar and dripping onto his
chin. All his life, he had wanted to love the way his mother loved,
wholly and without despair, but he had never been able to trust
in God the way she did, not when he knew that so many white
people loathed him. He raised his head and saw, then, two men
cloaked in white robes, their faces covered with hoods, tacking a
sign to the telephone pole at the end of the walk. He saw Mavis
Brown run out into the yard to grab Alvin, who had started
toward the street for a closer look. He heard Hocie Simms running up the stairs, shouting. "The Klux," she said. "The Klux.
Sweet Jesus, the Klux."

18

Mr. Bell stepped into the foyer of his home and heard Tibby upstairs. "Liar! You're a liar! Kizer, why would you say such a horrible thing?"

Kizer tromped over the floor with his rolling hobble, and as always, when Mr. Bell thought of his son's deformity, he ached. Kizer had always been his mother's child. Like her, he was a dreamy noodle, always with his nose stuck in a book or off to the college auditorium to attend a lecture or a travelogue. He had never taken an interest in hunting the way Mr. Bell had hoped, or in the gun collection Mr. Bell proudly displayed in his den. He had tried to show Kizer the intricacies of double-action revolvers, magazine pistols, derringers. He had identified rod-ejectors and breech blocks and bright hammers, but he knew none of it mattered to Kizer.

His voice, when he finally answered his mother, was calm. "It's not a lie. It's a fact. *Fait accompli*. Does it sound any prettier in French? However I say it, it's done, and nothing we can do can make it otherwise. The same as your drinking."

Mr. Bell came halfway up the staircase. A closet door slammed shut, and Kizer's cane thumped the floor. Then Tibby said in a flat voice, "It's all right if you want to take your anger out on me. God knows I've given you enough of a right. But remember, now

you're like me. You've something horrible of your own to live
with. I'll do what I can to help you. I'll let you be as angry as you
want. The truth is, you need me now even if you don't know it.
You need me because I'm the one who knows how easily our lives
can come apart."

At the top of the stairs, Mr. Bell could see that the door to
Kizer's room had been left slightly ajar, and through the thin strip
of light, he could see Tibby sitting in a chair, her face handsome
in the dim lamplight. He could never be sorry for his life with this
sweet girl, his Tibby, whom he saw first as Puck in an Ariel Club
production of *A Midsummer Night's Dream*. It had been 1898,
his first summer with his father at the bank after graduating from
Tulane, and in all the years that had passed—through the misery
of her drinking, and the worry over Kizer's leg—he still remembered her capering about in the stage light and how she closed the
play with her sweet apology:

> *If we shadows have offended,*
> *Think but this—and all is mended—*
> *That you have but slumber'd here*
> *While these visions did appear.*

Often, even now, he woke from sleep, and imagined he had
only dreamed the passing years, convinced himself, for the slightest instant, that Kizer was sound of limb, and Tibby brave of
heart, and he himself a man satisfied with the life he had made.
But the facts were so much different from these. Still he hoped
that somehow they would pull through, and one day be the family he had always desired, a family like Little Jones's—dare he say
he envied a Negro—but there it was, as Kizer said, a fact. And
now the two of them were linked, he and Little Jones—linked for
the sake of this city and for the sake of Quakertown.

"That may be. Yes, Mother. Of course, you're right." Mr. Bell
could see Kizer hanging suits of clothes in his steamer trunk. "I've

grown tired of deceit. I want it all out. Every bit of it. I want you to see how miserable I am."

"Will you tell your father?"

"If he were here, I'd tell him right now. I've already told Little Jones."

Mr. Bell pushed open the door. "Told Little Jones what?"

Kizer wheeled about, tears in his eyes. "I've been such a fool," he said.

Then he told his father the story of Camellia and the baby.

Andrew Bell had been to the home of Little Jones many times in the years he had known him. He came in autumn to see the leaves of the Chinese pistachio turn yellow and red and orange. In the winter, he enjoyed the fire-red nandinas. Come spring, he stopped to take in the white blossoms on the hawthorns, the snowball bush, the pear tree, and in summer there were the purplish-red blooms on the crape myrtles, the crimson azaleas, the blue hydrangeas. He often found an excuse to drive to Quakertown, perhaps to remind Little of a tree that needed pruning at his own home on Oak Street. He was careful to never let Little suspect the real reason he came, to have a few minutes away from his house where Tibby annoyed him by pacing from room to room, often stopping to shout, "This house is so big. When did it get so big?" At Little Jones's house, Camellia often sat at the kitchen table marking lessons for her pupils while Eugie sat nearby with her sewing basket open. He loved them both, truth be told, loved the way Camellia wrote "Good" on her students' lessons with the pinkish-red blush of her marking pencil, adored the way Eugie sighted thread through a needle's eye and mended rips in pants, darned holes in socks, or sewed on buttons. When he was in their company, he felt confident that the world would hold together. This was the renewal he gathered from them, and from Little, whom he loved most of all. He loved him because he was so much in control of the days and seasons he moved through, knowing when to water this plant, when to cut back another, comfortable that he could deter any blight or mold or pest. "All living things get sick," he had told Mr. Bell once when black knot had threatened the plum trees at Oak Street. "But don't fret, sir. What gets sick can get healthy. All I have to do is prune away the fungus." And he had, and the plum trees had survived, and when Mr. Bell had told Little he was a genius, Little had said, "You just leave this all to me. I'll look after it."

So it seemed right, after Mr. Bell had listened to Kizer's story of him and Camellia and the unfortunate event at the office of Dr. L. C. Parrish, that he go to Quakertown, to Little Jones, whom Mr. Bell had come to believe, could remedy anything.

"I want to tell you I'm sorry," he said to Little. "Sorry my son has been so irresponsible. Sorry for all our trouble."

They stood at the gate, Little inside and Mr. Bell outside, the white pickets between them. Little was stiff with rage, but he was afraid to make it known, particularly now that he had seen the poster tacked to the telephone pole on the corner. MARCH FOR RIGHT, it said in large letters. DENTON, TEXAS. SUNDAY, JUNE 21. And then in smaller print at the bottom, "The Ku Klux Klan stands for law and order. It stands for the protection of the sanctity of the home and the purity of young girls."

Little imagined it was no accident that the march was going to take place just before the city started offering to buy up houses in Quakertown. He suspected Mr. Bell had arranged it, and he hated him for that, hated himself, even, for agreeing to be the caretaker of the park and attaching himself to whatever machinery it would take to bring it to pass. He thought of his mother praying each evening before bed, and when he did, he felt the shame that Quakertown held for him now that he carried the secret of Camellia and Kizer Bell and the baby that was gone. He didn't know what he wanted more, to protect the place he had always known as home or to make it disappear.

"Won't you say something, Little?" Mr. Bell said. "You and I, we've always trusted each other. Damn it, Little, what I'm trying to say is I've always thought well of you and your family." Two women stopped to read the poster on the telephone pole, and then called to two others passing by across the street. "Quite a stir," said Mr. Bell. "What's all the fuss about?"

"Klan aims to march tomorrow," Little said, more sharply than he had intended. "Tomorrow when Camellia's getting married."

Mr. Bell was horrified. He knew that someone, Mr. Goody perhaps, had taken it upon himself to bring violence to Quakertown. "Good God. How stupid I've been," he said.

And then he was running. Little watched him race to the corner and tear the poster from the pole. He ripped it to pieces and threw them on the ground. Then he ran back to his motorcar. "I'll do what I can to stop the march," he said to Little, and Little stood there and listened to the sound of Mr. Bell's car moving up and down the streets of Quakertown, stopping, Little learned later, to tear down every Klux poster he could find. The talk spread through Quakertown. The banker, Mr. Andrew Bell, was standing up to the Klux. Everything would be all right. "A man as up in the cotton as that? Shoot, when he say 'boo,' you git."

19

But Camellia would not be pacified. "The Klan marching on my wedding day," she said. "It's a sign."

She was trying to pour tea into one of Eugie's bone china cups, but her hands were trembling, and Eugie had to take the pot and pour it for her.

"No sign of nothing," said Little. Again, he couldn't bring himself to tell Camellia and Eugie that he knew about Kizer Bell and the baby. "Just meanness, that's all."

Camellia was sure that she had invited this trouble because she, a woman engaged to be married, a schoolteacher who punished children when they did something wrong, had become involved with two men and now carried a child who was a mystery to her.

She was trying so hard to do the right thing. "Should we call it off?" she said to Eugie. "Is that what we should do?"

If Little hadn't been there in the kitchen with them, Eugie might have said to Camellia, "And what will you do when it comes time to have this baby? You with no husband?" But what she said was this: "You promised you'd marry Ike. You hold to it. Don't let some wicked white men keep you from your bliss."

"Read the tea leaves, Mama," Camellia said. "Tell me what they know."

Here was Eugie's chance. She could say she saw danger ahead,

dark clouds. She knew Camellia wanted her to give her any reason she could to stop her from marrying Ike, but Eugie saw too
much heartache waiting for her Baby-Girl if she kept hoping that
Kizer Bell might make her his bride.

"Nothing here but happy days," she told Camellia.

"You listen to Moms," Little said. When he had seen Camellia's trembling fingers, his resentment had lifted. How could he
do anything but love her? The anger he had felt toward Eugie and
Camellia for their secret had left him, even the rage he had felt
toward Mr. Andrew Bell. People make mistakes, his mother had
always taught him, but God was still there, waiting. "It's not
what you do that counts the most," she had said. "It's what you
do next."

Camellia was trying to hold the teacup steady. "All right," she
said in a quiet voice. "I'll marry him."

A pounding on the front door startled her, and hot tea sloshed
over the rim of the cup and onto her hand. She dropped the
teacup to the floor, and it shattered. "Oh, Mama." She put her
hand to her mouth. "I've broken one of Granny Jiggs's teacups.
You see what a mess this all is."

"Spilt milk," Eugie said, though inside it broke her heart to see
the bone china in pieces and to think of how her mother had
saved it from the fire. "Nothing I can't clean up. Little, go on and
see who's trying to knock our front door off the hinges."

It was Ike, and Little could tell right away he was in a state.
Sweat was beaded up on his forehead, and his suspenders were
hanging off his shoulders. "Have you heard?" The scar on his
cheek quivered when he spoke. He held up one of the Klan's
posters. "Tomorrow."

"Mr. Bell says he's going to stop it," Little said.

Ike shook his head back and forth. "You believe that if you
want. Mr. Bell's been sucking you dry for years now. All the ex-
tras you do for him."

"Is that what you came here for? To treat me nasty?"

"I'm sorry, Papa Jones. It's just this." He shook the poster. "They burned my daddy's church in Tennessee. My mother wrote me a letter."

"I'm sorry for that," said Little.

"White man's always watching." Ike remembered how quickly the razor had slashed through his face. "Just waiting for his chance."

Eugie came from the kitchen into the living room. "You go on home, Ike." She shooed at him with her hands. "I mean it. It's bad luck if you see your bride tonight."

"I don't believe in luck," he said. "I want to see Camellia. In fact, if you don't let me see her right now, I might not marry her. What would you think about that?"

Eugie poked him in the chest with her finger. "Maybe she won't marry you, Mr. Sasspot. Then, you'll be a sorry sight."

Camellia was in the kitchen listening to Ike's voice rise in volume. "Mama Jones," he said, "don't be your old grumpy self. I fought the Germans in the Kaiser's war. I figure I can handle you." *Kizer*. There was his name, and at the most inappropriate time. "I *will* see her," Ike said, and something inside Camellia thrilled to the way he refused to back down, superstition be damned. He was someone to count on, unlike Kizer Bell who had paid her fifty dollars and let her go to Dr. L. C. Parrish.

Ike stomped into the kitchen. He got down on his knees, right there on the jagged pieces of china, and he said, "Camellia, I'm here to confess the wrong I've been doing." Mercy, she thought. She didn't want anything to do with confessions. Let secrets be secrets. He frightened her with the urgent pleading in his eyes, the way his voice trembled. "I'm a bootlegger, Camellia." His mother's letter, her good, true words, had convinced him to go to his wedding day with nothing to hide. "But that's all over now. I wouldn't want to shame a respectable lady like you. I'm asking you to forgive me."

Her face was on fire, knowing now how Ike loved her enough

to say the worst thing there was to say about him. Of course, she had known about Ike and Mr. Smoke all along, knew even that Kizer bought liquor there for his mother, but it hadn't mattered, not then, caught up in her own shameful ways. What could she offer Ike now in return? Not the most secret part of herself, not just yet. Then it came to her that if she chose, here was her chance. She had a reason now to turn him out. She had every reason in the world. A schoolteacher marry a bootlegger? The idea! She still ached for Kizer. She couldn't deny that. But here was Ike, and she had made up her mind.

She reached out and laid her hand on his face. Then, with no thought of it, she idly ran her finger along the ridge of his scar, and he pulled his face away from her and waited as if someone were holding a knife to his throat—waiting for pardon or death—and it was then that she knew she could never leave him.

20

The wedding took place at two o'clock on the front lawn that Little Washington Jones had groomed into the showcase of Quakertown. Though the catalpa trees had lost their white blossoms, the mimosas were still pink and feathery, and the white lilac near the front gate was still handsome enough to make the arriving guests stop and admire it. The women still wore their church dresses, and the men wore their ties and their freshly brushed hats. Some of them reached up to touch the white blossoms, to sniff their fragrance. They stepped into the cool shade of Little's lawn and felt what they always did when they passed it, a certain awe that in their worst moments easily turned to envy.

"Look here," someone said. "A dead leaf on his pear tree. I'm surprised he'd allow it."

"I just hope he puts out a good feed," said another guest. "Can't have him forgetting he's got hungry neighbors."

Bat Suggs, Mr. and Mrs. Oat Sparks, Griff Lane, Poot Mackey, Billy Moten, Hocie Simms, Mavis Brown and her son Alvin. These were the first of the guests. Then came Nib Colter, Miss Abigail Lou, Dr. L. C. Parrish, followed by Sibby Long, Mr. and Mrs. Henry Treece, Celia Dorrough, Grandma Sue Moore, Mr. and Mrs. Tilman Monk, W. L. Briggs. There were ladies who knew Eugie from the Heroines of Jericho, and young girls who had gone to school with Camellia at Bishop College in Dallas. The organist (they had borrowed the Wurlitzer from Willie Mack's Mortuary and set it up on the porch), at least so the rumor went, was going to be Miss Portia Washington Pittman. "Yes," someone whispered, "that's Booker T. Washington's daughter. She lives in Dallas. Camellia got to rubbing elbows with her when she went to school down there." "Goodness," said someone else. "Them Jones moving up in the world."

They had borrowed chairs from Willie Mack's as well, and Willie Mack himself had arranged them in rows on the lawn, the walkway serving as an aisle between the two sides. Little had cut the grass and even raked the clippings so no one would find a blade stuck to a shoe sole and complain in the days to come that walking over his lawn, because he had waited so long to mow, had been like tromping through a hay field.

At exactly two o'clock, the organist began to play. And yes, it was Miss Portia Washington Pittman, Hocie Simms confirmed, though whether she really knew was anyone's guess. The music was something slow and dreamy, the sort that Milly Menthol played at the Palace Theater whenever Mary Pickford fell in love.

"What a snooze," Hocie said to Mavis Brown. Nothing like when Sippie Wallace went to town on "I'm a Mighty Tight Woman." Hocie was wearing a sleeveless dress, one strap threatening to slide off her shoulder, and a fresh marcel from Miss Abigail Lou's, the spit curls plastered to her cheeks with pomade. "Look at that." She nudged Mavis in the side. "That Miss Pittman, she wearing a necktie. You ever see such a getup like that?"

Mavis waved a wasp away from her face. Alvin was trying to stand up in his chair. "Get down." She grabbed him by the cross of his suspenders and yanked. "You behave yourself. Stop showing your behind."

The front door of the house opened, and the groom's party came down onto the walk: Ike Mattoon and his best man, Mr.

Smoke, and the Reverend Franklin Dubose, who just that morning at the AME Church had tried to calm the anxiety everyone felt because of the Klan marching. "This is a glorious day," he had said. "God's glorious day. And sometimes God puts the ugly next to the beautiful just so we can tell the difference. Hate march and the wedding march. We know which one God will be attending."

Hocie and Mavis, and who knew how many other women, single and married, sitting there on Willie Mack's chairs, were remembering exactly what Reverend Dubose had said as they looked at Ike, so handsome in his suit, the double-breasted jacket pinched in at the waist, the creases in his trousers razor sharp. He wore a single rosebud pinned to his lapel, and he stood with the regal bearing, chin lifted and shoulders back, he had learned in the army.

For a moment, the single women imagined they were marrying Ike Mattoon, and the married ones remembered how grand their own husbands had been on their wedding day. Then the gate to the right of the house opened, and a small boy and girl, two of Camellia's pupils, came through it. The boy was wearing long pants, perhaps the first he had ever worn. The collar of his white shirt was stiff with starch. He held a satin-covered pillow at his waist and kept his eyes fixed on the rings that lay there. The girl wore a simple knee-length shift, the shade of a peach when it first starts to color. A dainty wicker basket dangled from her arm, and as she walked, she dipped her hand into it and scattered rose petals on the lawn.

Such beautiful children, the guests thought. Even Mavis Brown thought it, though her Alvin had not been chosen. Someday, she believed, he would grow out of his wildness and marry, and who knew how many generations of Browns would live there in Quakertown.

Eugie was the next person to come through the gate, and she, too, was wearing a peach-colored dress, and holding three pink daisies, tied together with a length of lace left over from Camellia's gown.

"Her mama's the maid of honor," Hocie whispered to Mavis. "Now that's proud. Don't pay to be too proud. Break your neck, get your nose too high up in the air."

The organ music swelled, those glorious chords that announced the bride, and everyone stood, their eyes on the gate through which the children and Eugie had just passed, but Camellia wasn't there. She was behind them at the front gate—how had they managed that trick?—and Little Jones was escorting her up the walk. She was carrying a bouquet of red roses Little had cut for her himself, and her feet, the white leather shoes just visible below the hem of her dress, were taking small, cautious steps.

She was thinking how carefully she and her mother had tatted the lace and sewn the beads to the bodice. "Patience," Eugie had told her. "Don't get in a hurry. That way you won't make a mistake."

Ike turned and watched Camellia coming toward him. He wished that his mother and father could be there to see her, his lovely bride, but they had all agreed, given their age and the conditions they would face if they traveled by train, it would be wiser if they stayed in Tennessee. He didn't know where to lay the blame: on the Jim Crow laws that would have made the trip such a burden or on himself because he had strayed so far from home.

But then Camellia was beside him, and he knew he would have traveled around the world and back on the slightest chance he might find her.

21

A few blocks away, on the courthouse lawn, Mr. Bell tried to stop the Klan from marching into Quakertown. He carried the Rider revolver in his coat pocket, not knowing whether he would have to use it or even have the nerve. Men were slipping into white robes, men he had known most of his life, men from the Chamber of Commerce, the Rotarians, the board of trustees at the college. They were draping sashes over their shoulders, settling hoods on their heads. The hoods came up to peaks and pieces of cloth dropped over the men's faces so only their eyes showed through the holes cut in the masks.

"They're having a wedding there," Mr. Bell said to the police chief, Harold Sumner. "Is there any need of ruining that?"

"You want to scare some niggers?" Harold Sumner crossed his arms over his chest. "You got to go where the niggers are."

"I don't want these men going there. If we're going to move Quakertown, let's do it peacefully and by the law. We've agreed to a plan."

"You can't stop these men now, Mr. Bell. They've got a permit. Just like you said. Everything's being done legal and on the up-and-up."

At the train depot, Kizer checked his pocket watch, then stepped out onto the platform where his steamer trunk sat on a cart. Across the tracks, he could see Oakland Street, which ran along the edge of Quakertown and on up the hill to the college. He kept looking up the street instead of down the tracks to see whether his train was coming.

"I hear they're going to move Quakertown," the depot master said to him. "Move the whole goddamn mess."

"Makes no difference to me. I'm going abroad."

"Across the pond?" The depot master took a bandanna out of his hip pocket and wiped his brow. "If you stay gone too long, things sure be different when you get back."

"I'm counting on it," said Kizer. "If I ever come back at all."

"Oh, you got to come back," said the depot master. "One thing I know in the railroad business. Sooner or later, everyone comes home."

22

The Klansmen came down the street, four abreast, carrying American flags, and the wedding guests, hearing the feet tramping over the packed dirt and the robes swishing about the marchers' legs, turned a moment toward the commotion and then jerked their heads back around and sat still.

Only Alvin Brown seemed to be unconcerned. He leapt out into the aisle and started making his way to the wedding party. He bent over at the waist, stuck his rear end up into the air, and placed his knuckles on the ground. He stopped from time to time to scratch at his armpits, and afraid to move, everyone, even his mother, sat there and let him do it.

"Would you look at that?" a voice from the passing marchers called out. "Charlie Darwin just about got it right. It's the niggers who come from monkeys."

All through the ceremony, and on into the reception—coconut cake and sweet tea served there on the lawn—that voice echoed in people's heads. Although the marchers had gone by without further incident, they had thrown a somber mood over the celebration and a rage was simmering in Ike. At the reception, he heard Mr. Smoke talking to Nib Colter and Tilman Monk by the white lilac tree. "The city going to buy up Quakertown," Mr.

Smoke said. His cigarette was dancing in his mouth. "I tell you gents, that the truth."

"That's what all this Klan business was about?" Ike said.

"Running us out," said Mr. Smoke. "The ones of us what might not wants to sell."

Ike crossed his arms over his chest. "Not me. I'm a grown man. I go where I want."

Nib Colter winked at Tilman Monk. "What about the café at the Litz Hotel? You ever eat there, Ike? Or the fountain outside the courthouse? The one marked WHITES ONLY. You ever drink out of that?"

"Or try on clothes at Neiman's Department Store?" said Tilman Monk.

"I wouldn't drink after a white man." Ike spit into the lilac tree. "Too risky."

Mr. Smoke tossed his cigarette butt over the fence. "That what I'm telling you. We go where they tells us to go. They wants us gone, we be gone."

"Too risky," said Ike with a grin, "on account those people got germs."

When it came time for the customary wedding train, the parade through Quakertown to show off the bride and groom, Ike and Camellia rode in a surrey loaned to them by Dr. L. C. Parrish. Mr. Smoke took the reins and led those who wanted to follow, either in their own buggies and wagons or on foot, up and down the streets. They went up the long hill to the college and turned down Oakland Street. When they reached the end, Ike leaned over the front seat and tapped Mr. Smoke on the shoulder. "Go on," Ike said. "Take us downtown, around the square."

"You sure about that?" said Mr. Smoke. "No one I know ever took a wedding train downtown."

"They come into our place," said Ike, "we'll go into theirs."

As they turned down Locust Street and headed toward the square, people in the train began to fall back, remembering the

Klansmen who had marched by the wedding and not wanting to be anywhere near a white person just yet. All except Alvin Brown, who was dissatisfied to let the train go on without him. He broke away from his mother, slipped into an alley, and started to run.

"Ike, don't do anything stupid," Camellia said. The beads on her wedding gown sparkled in the sun. "It's not the time to be stubborn."

"Just going for a ride, Mrs. Mattoon. You just relax and enjoy the view."

By the time the surrey crossed the tracks and made it to the square, only Little and Eugie were following in Little's buckboard, and Alvin Brown, who came out of the alley, relieved to find himself in the clear.

"I don't know where they think they're going," said Little. "But I don't like it."

"That Ike's always been bullheaded," said Eugie. "You know how he got himself cut. I hope he's not looking for trouble."

There were men lingering in the shade of the courthouse lawn, white robes folded over the backs of benches. They were men Little recognized—Mr. Neiman, Mr. Goody, Mr. Alexander—men whose lawns and gardens he tended. And Mr. Andrew Bell was there, causing some sort of commotion. He was shaking his fist in the faces of the men, and one of them, Mr. Goody, poked Mr. Bell in the chest with his finger. "Back off now," Mr. Goody said.

Ike knew these men, too, at least some of them, the ones who bought bootleg liquor from him and Mr. Smoke. But Ike knew if he were to call to them, "Hidee-ho, gents," they would act like he was a cur dog strayed too far from home.

"Stop up here," he said to Mr. Smoke.

"Stop?" said Camellia. "Why do you want to stop?"

Said Ike, "I'm thirsty. Reckon a fella could get a drink around here, Mr. Smoke?"

"I'm going to turn this rig around." Mr. Smoke pulled hard on the reins. "I'm going to take you on home. Goose don't put his neck on the chopping block of his own mind."

When the surrey slowed, Ike jumped down and started moving across the courthouse lawn.

"Ike," Camellia called to him. She was gathering the hem of her dress, and in the time it took her to crawl down from the surrey, Eugie was on her way across the courthouse lawn, as was Little and Mr. Smoke.

Camellia stepped onto the grass; then she noticed, up the street, Kizer standing on the platform at the train depot. He had planted his cane squarely in front of him, and he was leaning on it with both hands. He was bent slightly at the waist, and his shoulders were slumped. Like an old man, Camellia thought, an old man waiting for a traveling companion to join him. She knew that would be the image she would carry with her always, the sight of him looking so forlorn on the depot platform, and for an instant, she wanted to go to him, to stop him from getting on whatever train he was waiting for, and going away from her. Then she heard one of the white men say in a sharp voice, "Hey, boy. Come on over here."

Ike was in the shade of the elm trees, at the stone fountain reserved for whites, and he was bent over it, drinking long and deep.

"No trouble," said Mr. Andrew Bell, and it wasn't clear to Camellia whether he was giving the warning to Ike or to Mr. Goody, who was standing there in the shade, his arm raised, one finger pointed at Ike.

She wanted to shake her finger at Ike herself. How dare he pull such a stunt? She couldn't imagine Kizer doing anything as foolhardy as that; then she thought how risky it had been for him to seek her out, to fall in love with her. She looked down at the wedding band on her finger. She held it up so the gold caught the sun, and she had no choice but to admit that the ring was real.

Mr. Goody took a step toward the fountain. Mr. Bell grabbed

him by the shoulders, but Mr. Goody shook him off. He spun around on his heel, and with the back of his hand, he struck Mr. Bell across the face.

"I'm tired of you, Bell." Mr. Bell was sprawled on the ground, and Mr. Goody was standing over him, his fists clenched. "I'm tired of this whole nigger mess."

Alvin Brown dashed by Camellia, running straight toward the fountain where, so it seemed to him, a great bit of horseplay was taking place. Eugie and Little and Mr. Smoke were trying to pull Ike away from the fountain, and Mr. Goody was kicking at Mr. Bell's legs. Mr. Bell scrambled backward on the seat of his pants, and when he was far enough away to cause Mr. Goody to lose interest, he got to his feet. The other white men were keeping their distance. Mr. Neiman and Mr. Alexander had drifted off to their automobiles.

Camellia heard the conductor at the train depot calling, "All aboard," and for an instant she wanted to turn and run.

Then Mr. Goody pulled Ike away from the fountain. He held him by the lapels of that beautiful, double-breasted coat. "Have you ever seen me before, boy?" Ike's lips were pressed together, and he was staring at Mr. Goody. "Have you?" The lapels of his coat were up around Ike's ears. Mr. Goody yanked on the lapels and brought Ike closer to him. "I'm talking to you, boy. Ever see me in your barbershop? Ever see me buying illegal liquor from you or your partner?"

"We never seen you," said Mr. Smoke.

"I'm waiting for this nigger to answer." Mr. Goody's chin bumped against Ike's as he spoke. "Think you can get away with this, don't you, boy, because you're a big bootlegger? Maybe some folks here are willing to look the other way when you put your big nigger lips on that fountain because they depend on you for their liquor, but I've never had that nasty habit myself. You've never seen me, have you, boy? I've got nothing to lose if you don't wake up tomorrow."

Camellia was at the fountain now, holding onto Alvin Brown. "Tell him, Ike," she said in an even voice, the voice she used in school when she was trying to encourage a pupil. "Tell him what he wants to hear."

Ike leaned his head back as if he were trying to hear what Camellia was saying to him. Then, with a nod, he spit a mouthful of water into Mr. Goody's face.

There was no movement for a while, everyone frozen the way people were in the slides at the travelogues. The only sound was the water dripping from Mr. Goody's face onto the stones. He let his hands drop away from Ike. He took a handkerchief out of his pocket and wiped water from his red moustache.

That's when Mr. Bell came around in front of Mr. Goody and pointed his revolver at him.

"What do you think you'll do with that?" said Mr. Goody. "A fool like you."

Blood was leaking from the corner of Mr. Bell's mouth, and his hand was shaking. He saw Ike reach inside his suit coat, take out a straight razor, and open it.

"We don't want trouble here," Mr. Bell said. He took a couple of steps back so he could keep an eye on both Ike and Mr. Goody. "I know I don't. I don't think anyone wants to do anything that might ruin them or this city. Think of what happened down in Waco. Let's just walk away, all of us. Let's go back to our homes and remember we're decent people with families."

"You call this decent?" Mr. Goody wiped his face again. "Nigger spit in my face. Now he's pulled out a razor."

"A mistake," said Mr. Bell. "We've all made our share. Tell him you're sorry, Ike."

"No mistake to it," said Ike. "I meant to do it."

Fool, Mr. Bell wanted to shout at him. Here I am giving you a chance, and you won't take it. I'm on your side. I'm looking out for you. Trying to save your skin. You don't even know what I could tell you about your bride.

"You goddamn goon," said Mr. Goody. "You nigger-faced go-rilla."

Ike lunged at Mr. Goody with the razor, and Mr. Goody jumped out of the way. Mr. Bell drew the hammer back on his revolver.

At that moment, Mavis Brown appeared on the courthouse lawn, calling out, "Alvin. Alvin Raymond Brown."

Alvin broke free from Camellia. He tried to run, but he bumped into Mr. Bell and the revolver fired.

By this time, Kizer was closing his eyes on the train, calling back the image of Camellia lifting her hand on the courthouse lawn. From the depot platform, he had seen the glint of light from her ring, and still he could imagine that she had been waving to him, though from his distance, he hadn't been sure. It would be days before he would reach New York and find waiting at his hotel a telegram from his mother. "Father in dire straits. Come home. All is lost."

Two

23

At first, when the shot rang out, Little wasn't sure whether anyone had been hit. There was a tremendous ringing in his ears, and the sun, breaking through the elm trees, was blinding him. Then he heard Camellia cry out, "Mama," and he turned and saw Eugie slumped over the fountain, one foot scrabbling against the stones as if she were trying very hard to push herself up. Little gathered her in his arms and lifted her back from the fountain. That's when he saw the bullet hole in her chest.

Mr. Bell went on and on about how he never meant to fire the revolver. He dropped it, and it clattered across the paving stones around the fountain. The police chief, Harold Sumner, who had arrived on the scene, picked up the revolver and emptied the remaining bullets into his palm.

"I saw exactly what happened," he said. "Plain as day. Mr. Bell, you and I should step over to the jail and have a chat."

"What about that nigger?" said Mr. Goody.

"Give me that razor, boy," Harold Sumner said to Ike. "You ain't doing any cutting now."

Ike closed the razor and handed it to Harold Sumner. Then he tried to say something to Little, but his words were all mushed up because he was sobbing.

"What can you say," Little said to him, "that will ever matter?"

"Uncle's right," said Mr. Goody in a strained voice, tight with fear and disgust. "Talk ain't nothing now."

Tibby paced about the drawing room, a gin rickey in her hand, as she recited lines she remembered from the numerous theatrical productions she had taken part in as a young woman. It was something she often did when she was alone, and the quiet of the large house overwhelmed her.

" ' 'Tis his own blame,' " she said. " 'Hath put himself from rest, and must needs taste his folly.' "

She generally, as was the case at that moment, failed to recall the characters she had assumed or the plays in which she had spoken particular lines. She only knew the sounds of the words and the familiar tempos of her deliveries. All it took was a certain rhythm or stress or inflection to remind her that once she had enjoyed the luxury of becoming other women, all of them pleasing to her precisely because they weren't her. Now it was as if those women lived in her, but only in bits and pieces, never enough for her to resurrect them completely.

On this afternoon, like a stage cue gone awry, an unexpected knock came on the front door. Tibby slipped into the foyer and saw a shadow on the door's etched glass. She hid what was left of her gin rickey behind the vase of lilies on the table beside the staircase. She checked her face in the mirror, pinching her cheeks to bring out a blush the way her mother had taught her to do before entertaining a suitor. Then she opened the door and found Mr. Neiman standing before her, his hat in his hands. She looked at the red tips of his ears.

"Mrs. Bell," he said. He bowed his head. "I'm very sorry to disturb you, but there's been some trouble." Tibby noticed the ill-fit of his shirt collar, too large, and she thought what an indignity it must be to own a clothing shop and be such a poor advertisement for its lines. Mr. Neiman raised his head and looked at her for the first time. "It's your husband. It's Mr. Bell."

She felt a flutter in her chest. "Something's happened to Mr. Bell?"

Mr. Neiman hesitated. Then he told her, again with his head bowed as if all his attention was on the creased crown of his hat, that Mr. Bell had shot and killed a colored woman, Eugie Jones, the sewing woman who did alterations for his store.

"Murder? Will they charge him with murder?"

"I really can't say, Mrs. Bell. I only came to bring you the news, and to offer to drive you down to the jail so you can see your husband."

"Yes, of course. Let me find my handbag." She could barely think straight. Eugie Jones dead. Andrew in jail. Though she tried to deny it, she felt something rising up through her regret and sorrow, some quickening of the heart. For once, it was Andrew who needed *her*, and Kizer, once he got the news, would come home to them. "I want to go to the telegraph office," she said to Mr. Neiman. "Is it open on Sunday? It has to be. I have to get word to my son."

It was not a sight one would have expected to see on the courthouse lawn on that Sunday afternoon. Three men—Little, and Ike, and Mr. Smoke, their white shirts gleaming, their foreheads shiny—carrying a woman across the grass, the pale peach of her dress spattered with blood. Camellia followed behind with Mavis Brown and Alvin.

"Oh, Lord, Camellia," Mavis said. "My Alvin. He never meant to cause harm."

But Camellia couldn't answer. Her rage was so great she could find no words for it. She watched the men as they laid Eugie on the bed of Little's buckboard.

"Take her to Doc Parrish's," Ike begged, hoping still that someone could save her.

"No." Little's voice was low-pitched but firm. He kneeled beside Eugie, unable to tolerate the idea of L. C. Parrish. "Mavis, you're a nurse," he said. "Step up here."

He held out his hand to Mavis Brown and helped her up onto the buckboard. She got down on her knees and pressed her fingertips to the carotid artery in Eugie's neck. For several seconds, there was no sound but the rustle of the elm leaves and the groan and creak as the mule strained against its traces. Then Mavis Brown let her fingers drop away from Eugie, and she said, in the calm voice tinged with regret she had learned from Dr. Parrish, "Mr. Jones, I'm sorry. She's gone."

"I'll take her to Willie Mack's?" Little said, and he said it with a rise in his voice as if he were asking a question.

By this time, Ike was squatting on the grass, his head hanging down, his hands over his ears. His shoulders were heaving, and the sound coming from his mouth was a wail that seemed to those who heard it to be the noise of every sorrow the world had ever known. The cicadas were chirring in the elm trees, a drone that would linger throughout the summer.

Camellia, at that moment, wanted to go to Ike and hold him, so she could remember what it had been like back in the winter, before Kizer, before her visit to Dr. L. C. Parrish, before Mr. Andrew Bell's revolver had fired. Back to when she had told Eugie, "Mama, Mama. Ike asked me to marry him." But there was another part of her that wanted to be far, far away from him now.

"Yes, we'll go to Willie Mack's." She climbed up into the bed of the buckboard, not caring if she soiled her wedding dress. "I'll ride back here," she said, "with Mama."

Mr. Bell's right hand was shaking. "My God," he said to Harold Sumner. "Look at me."

They were sitting across from each other at Harold Sumner's desk in the basement of the courthouse.

"Mr. Bell, you've got to get yourself together." Harold Sumner clicked the chamber shut on the revolver and laid it on his desk on top of a stack of "Wanted" posters. "You're an important man in this town."

"I killed Eugie Jones."

Mr. Bell closed his left hand over his right to keep it from trembling and to stop himself from saying how much he loved Eugie and Camellia and Little. He was certain that a man like Harold Sumner would never understand how he could feel genuine affection for a family of Negroes.

"Yes, sir," said Harold Sumner. "That woman is dead, but from where I stand, the blame doesn't fall on you."

"Goody's hotheaded," said Mr. Bell. "But still."

"It's not Goody I'm talking about." Harold Sumner tossed Ike's razor out onto the desk. "Everyone saw what that nigger did. Seems to me you were only trying to keep someone from getting cut up or worse. I'm certain you meant to fire your revolver up into the air, just to stop things from getting out of hand, but then that boy run into you. Isn't that the way it played out?"

The door to the office opened, and there stood Tibby.

"Well, Mr. Bell?" said Harold Sumner.

"Yes," said Mr. Bell. "You're right. It was all a terrible mistake."

Bert Gleason, who had gotten word of the mishap, was just getting out of his automobile when Tibby and Mr. Bell left the basement of the courthouse. He hurried across the lawn to meet them. "I came right away." His shirtsleeves were rolled to his elbows, and he hadn't taken time to button his collar. "I heard you killed someone."

"It was an accident," said Tibby. She clung to Andrew's arm. "A horrid accident. Ask Harold Sumner. Everything's going to be all right."

Mr. Bell hurried past Bert Gleason, bumping him with his

shoulder. All he wanted was to be home, away from the court-house lawn where the horrible thing had happened.

"It wasn't your fault." Tibby clutched his arm more tightly. She glanced back at Bert Gleason and spoke loudly enough for him to hear her. "It was rabble-rousers. Thank goodness someone was there to control them or who knows what might have gone on."

"Bell," Bert Gleason shouted, and Mr. Bell stopped and turned back to him. "Who was it, Bell? Who did you kill?"

It was too much for Mr. Bell to speak the name.

"Eugie Jones," Tibby finally said. "That poor woman. God rest her soul."

Bert Gleason wanted to make sure he had heard the name correctly. He strode across the lawn until he was standing face to face with Mr. Bell. "Eugie Jones? You shot Eugenia Jones?" He was remembering, years before, when she had lived across from him in the rented house on Oak Street, and the first time he had kissed her in the old carriage house. Her lips had tasted of something sweet she had eaten—strawberries, he had decided—and her skin had smelled of talcum. She had been so young. They had both been so young. And though he had gone to Cuba and come home determined to live a decent life, he had never told Eugenia Jiggs how sorry he was that he had caused her to suffer. How simple it would have been, sometime in the years that had passed, for him to have gone to Quakertown and found her.

All of Quakertown, that night, was quiet. There was no shivaree for Camellia and Ike. No one came to Sibby Long's boardinghouse to roust the newlyweds from their room. No one fired shotguns into the air, or banged dishpans together, or pounded on washtubs.

"I'll stay in the house with you tonight," Camellia said to Little when darkness had come and she switched on the lamp by the window where she had sat all those nights ago, tatting lace for the wedding dress she still wore, bloodstained now from where she had held Eugie to her as the buckboard carried them to Willie Mack's. What had she heard Eugie say to Little that night when he had been bragging about his lawn? ("You're putting on the swank, Little Jones. You're as proud as Lucifer.")

When Camellia turned on the lamp, Little, sitting in the rocking chair Camellia herself had occupied the night she had been tatting the lace, shaded his eyes with his hand. "No, you go on," he said.

Though he wanted nothing more than for her to stay, he suspected that in some secret consultation beyond his presence, Eugie had determined that Camellia would link her life to Ike Mattoon's, and to do anything now that might prevent it, Little felt, would be to diminish Eugie herself and what she must have anguished over the last months of her life.

He didn't blame Andrew Bell—he had only been trying to protect them—or Alvin Brown, who was just a boy and couldn't be held accountable, or even Mr. Goody, whose reaction was one any Negro could have expected and headed off with a little sense. Even Wash Jones, who never tolerated smart-alecky talk from jackanapes, would have known that. Little didn't even blame the Klan, only felt contempt for them. Blame was a different matter. Blame required a single face—not a hooded, marching Klan—but one person he could look in the eyes and hold responsible, and that person, for better or worse, was Ike Mattoon.

"The two of us have got different lives now," Little said to Camellia. "Your place isn't here anymore. I wish it wasn't true, but it is."

Ike scrambled to his feet when Camellia came out the door. He had picked a moonflower from her father's arbor and was offering the large, white blossom to her the way a shy pupil might make her a gift of a valentine.

"They only bloom at night," she said.

He took a step back from her. "Did I do wrong to pick it then?"

"It smells like cloves." She held it up to his face. "Sweet."

He came to her and tried to hold her. "Camellia."

She pushed him away. "We'll go now," she said. Then she stepped down from the porch and walked to the gate, reversing the path she had taken earlier that afternoon when she had come to him on the arm of her father. Ike did the only thing he could. He followed.

As the two of them made their way to Sibby Long's, neighbors gathered on porches and in yards, watched them pass. Already, in kitchens, women were busy cooking food that they would carry in to Little Jones. They were opening jars of okra, chowchow, tomato preserves. They were baking sweet potato pies, and peach cobblers, and caramel layer cakes the way they had a few weeks earlier for the Juneteenth holiday, the celebration that marked the end of slavery in Texas. But now there was no talk of parades, or picnics, or fireworks shows. There was little talk at all, save a comment from time to time about their progress—"Thickening's on the boil"—or a muttered, "Lord, Lord, Lord," half-prayer, half-lament.

It was the men who were doing the earnest talking. They were saying, "Listen here. If this thing can happen once, it can happen twice. Ain't no one safe." "They want to buy us out and move us? Maybe that ain't a bad thing." "Nothing good here now. Not with the Klux. Not after they shot Eugie Jones dead."

Then there was the group sitting on crates in the back room of Ike's barbershop. They were passing around a bottle and listening to Mr. Smoke. Nib Colter was there and Tilman Monk, Griff Lane, and Poot Mackey, and Bat Suggs. Dr. L. C. Parrish was tapping a tongue depressor against the back of his hand. When the bottle came to him, he laid the depressor flat over the mouth, tipped up the bottle as if he were soaking a swab with ether, and then stuck the depressor into his mouth.

Mr. Smoke scratched a match over the top of a crate, and the men, in the sudden flare of light, glanced around and took note of their grim faces. Mr. Smoke's gaunt cheeks caved in as he drew on his cigarette, the paper and tobacco crackling as it caught the flame.

"And that why we got to go back to Africa." Mr. Smoke blew out his match, and the room returned to darkness. "That the only place we be safe."

Dr. Parrish took the tongue depressor from his mouth, and the scent of the liquor-soaked wood drifted out into the room. "That's Ike talking, Mr. Smoke. That's his Marcus Garvey flim-flam. What makes you think we'd be safe in Africa? White man found us once. I suggest, gentlemen, he could find us again."

"Sure found us today," said Poot Mackey.

"Yes, sir," said Griff Lane. "Found us something fierce."

"It was Mr. Andrew Bell." The fire in Mr. Smoke's cigarette burned more brightly for a moment. "He the one what did the shooting."

"I heard it was all an accident," said Tilman Monk. His voice, the bass in the AME Church choir, was a low rumble. "That's what Mavis Brown told the missus."

"Maybe so," said Mr. Smoke. "But Mr. Bell, he the one what ought to have to answer."

"Won't be no answering." Bat Suggs tipped up the bottle and drank. "Ain't never no answering white to colored."

"You got that from here to Sunday," said Nib Colter. "I heard they let Mr. Bell go. Story is it was all Ike's doing—what happened to Eugie—all his fault."

"What he do?" said Mr. Smoke. " 'Cept want a drink of water. Since when that a crime?"

The voices had been rising in the small room, growing more fierce with anger.

"Gentlemen," Dr. Parrish said. "I would advise restraint."

He raised his arms and turned his palms out as if bracing him-self against a coming force, but it was dark in the room, the only light the ember of Mr. Smoke's cigarette, and no one could see him.

*   *   *

Just before Camellia and Ike reached Sibby Long's, Uncle Me came out of the shadow of an alley and started following them. He had picked up a Jew's harp somewhere, and he plucked it in tempo with the steps they took. Each time a foot came down, the harp twanged, that single, irritating sound that made Camellia want to stop and slap it away from his mouth.

"Does he have to follow us?" she said to Ike. "Does he have to play that idiotic thing? Tonight of all nights?"

"Don't blame him," Ike said. "He doesn't understand what's happened."

Camellia stopped beneath a streetlamp and turned back to Uncle Me. Of course, he didn't understand. She knew that, but compassion, usually her long suit, was hard-won tonight. She reached up and yanked the harp out of Uncle Me's mouth.

He howled. He threw back his head and wailed. His lip was bleeding, and when the blood ran down onto his tongue, he touched his finger to his mouth.

"You've cut him," said Ike, and Camellia bristled at the accusation in his voice.

"Now you're concerned?" she said. "For an imbecile? But you gave no thought at all to someone getting hurt this afternoon."

"I'd change it all if I could, Camellia."

"Well, you can't."

"But I can be different, kinder. You'll see."

"That's talk, Ike Mattoon. Just like your Marcus Garvey talk. See what that's got us?"

Ike scraped the toe of his shoe through the dirt. "I'm done with that. We'll stay here in Quakertown. This is our home."

"Too late," said Camellia. "Too late for Mama."

"There's nothing I can say to bring her back. That's true, Camellia. But I can live right, day by day. You'll see how much I can love you."

For a moment, she wanted to believe him, wanted to think that she could tell him about the child she carried and how she wasn't sure who the father was—tell him about Kizer Bell—but then, for just an instant, a feeling of relief filled her—*Mama, forgive me*—because now she was the only one who knew her secret. She had let Eugie believe the baby was Kizer's because she had thought it the best thing to do in the face of uncertainty—why take the chance when she and Ike could have other babies? She had regretted letting Eugie believe the lie until Kizer had given her the fifty dollars, but now the secret was hers to tell or hide as she saw fit.

Uncle Me reached out and touched his finger to the bloodstain on the bodice of her dress.

"Here now." She knocked his arm away. "Don't touch me. Ike, don't let him touch me."

"He's only showing you the blood," Ike said, and his voice was barely a whisper. "Maybe that's how we find each other. We all got blood at the root."

"I'm nothing like him." Camellia stamped her foot at Uncle Me, and he ran back into the shadows. He was howling again, and all through Quakertown, dogs began to growl and bark and strain against their chains.

Bert Gleason remembered well the care Little Jones had once taken with the courtyard in front of their home on Oak Street, so it was a simple matter for him to find the house he was looking for in Quakertown. He simply drove up and down the streets until he saw the house with the white lilac tree by the front gate. He could remember the Sunday when Little had carried that tree down Oak Street in his buckboard and Bert's mother had said, "A white lilac. I swan. And Little Jones making sure everyone on Oak Street gets a gander." At the time, Bert had thought, What a smug nigger, but that had been a different Bert from the one who stood now at the gate to Little's house, inhaling the sweet fragrance of the lilac tree, thinking if he had found something so exotic and grand, he, too, would have put it on display.

The house was dark, but Bert Gleason, peering through the screen door, could hear the slow creak of a rocking chair, and he knew someone was inside.

"Little Jones," he said. He shaded his eyes with his hand and pressed his forehead to the screen. He tried to make out some shape or movement, but all he saw was the impenetrable dark. "Are you in there, Little Jones?"

The creak of the rocking chair went on and on, and a tired voice spoke from the darkness.

"If you come to kill me, go on. Get it done."

"I didn't come to kill anyone." Bert Gleason felt the old shame return to him, the shame that had filled him after he had set fire to the rented house on Oak Street. "I'm Bert Gleason. You used to tend my father's place. I've come to say I've heard about your trouble, and I'm sorry for it."

It seemed to Bert that Little would never answer him, but then the rocker stopped, and Little said, "You lived on Oak Street across from Eugie and her mother."

That was all, and when it became clear to Bert that Little wouldn't say the rest of it, wouldn't say, "You burned them out," he felt an immense gratitude toward the man who sat now in the dark, mourning, and he made it up in his mind that he would do whatever he could to make this all easier for Little Jones in a way he had been unable to make things easier for Eugie.

"I understand you've agreed to this scheme of Andrew Bell's to move Quakertown and build a park here." Bert faltered, then, having spoken Bell's name, afraid that Little would now turn him away, but no protest came, so Bert went on. "But I expect you feel differently now."

"The Klan? They don't scare me none."

"I wasn't talking about the Klan." Somehow Bert understood that he was not to open the screen and step into the house. He recalled all the times Little Jones had come to his father's back door and waited there on the steps, straw hat in his hands, for someone to bring him his pay. "I just meant maybe it would be best to keep Quakertown where it is."

Little studied it over, sitting there in the dark, and what came to him was this. No matter what happened with Mr. Andrew Bell, someone would find a way to move Quakertown. The Klan's march had made it plain that there were any number of men—and maybe Bert Gleason was one of them—who would see to it that the plan was carried out. If Little didn't go along with it, if he didn't agree to be the caretaker of the park, they would have to move him, too. All those years, he had lived there with Eugie. Her clothes still hung in the wardrobe, and her sewing basket sat on the floor by her chair. Already that night, he had seen her at her sewing machine, in the bedroom brushing her hair, outside at the arbor admiring the moonflowers. He couldn't imagine her spirit going with him to a new place. This was their home, and he would do whatever he had to do to keep it. "Best we build that park," he said.

"If you're sure you still want this to happen, I'll do what I can to make it work out."

"I'm sure of it," Little said.

Tibby sat near the bed and watched her husband sleep. He was curled up on his side, his face half-hidden by the pillow, and from time to time, he ground his teeth together and muttered and grumbled, chewing some bitter dream to death.

"Dear Tibby," he had said to her when they had entered their home and closed the door behind them. "I imagine Kizer loved that girl, perhaps the only girl who will ever love him, and he thought he couldn't have her because she was colored. He thought he would shame us. We must have made him believe that."

"Colored or white, Andrew. The fact is he wasn't decent with her."

"And now her mother's dead. By my hand. God have mercy on me and Kizer both."

Yes, mercy, Tibby was thinking now as she reached out and laid her hand on her husband's cheek, hoping her touch might calm his dreams. But he woke with a start and grabbed her by the wrist. "Tibby," he said. "Oh, Tibby."

Once she had played the fool in the Ariel Club's *King Lear,* and it was one of those lines that came to her. " 'This cold night will turn us all into fools and madmen,' " she said, and Andrew nodded, unaware that the words weren't hers, listening only to the compassion in her soothing voice.

"Yes," he said, stroking her hand. "You understand it so well, Tibby. Fools and madmen, the world is full of them both. Dear Tibby, don't leave me."

Where would she go, she was thinking, even if she had a mind to leave? She and Andrew had lived so long together, she could barely imagine a life apart.

"You've always been kind to me," she said, and now the words were hers, and she felt them more deeply than anything she had ever uttered onstage. "You could have given up on me long ago. You had every right. Maybe you would have found a better wife. But you stayed, and so will I. Don't worry. If anyone tries to slander you, I'll tell them, 'Andrew Bell is a good and decent man.' "

Downstairs, someone was knocking on the front door.

It was Bert Gleason, demanding to see Andrew, telling Tibby he must, at once, before the mob arrived.

"Mob?" She opened the door wider to let him enter. "What mob? Mercy, have you gone mad?"

"It's not me who's mad." He glanced behind him as Tibby closed the door. He peered out through the oval glass. "It's those folks down in Quakertown. I just came from there, and I ran into a gang of them over at Little Jones's. They're coming here now for Andrew."

"Well, they won't have him," Tibby said. "Not as long as I'm in this house."

"They're carrying torches and kerosene. I hate to have to tell you this, Mrs. Bell, but they aim to burn the place. I must see Andrew now."

"Let them come." Mr. Bell's voice rang out from the top of the stairs. "I deserve whatever ill they intend to bring me."

He looked, to Tibby, like an invalid roused from his bed, and for a moment, she felt the same anger and pity she imagined must have been his all those nights when she had drunk too much and spent the night roaming the house—such a big, quiet house. He was trying now to sash his robe about him, his fingers fumbling, and she started to go up the stairs to help him. But then he gave up and let the robe hang open, and the sight of his white nightshirt and his pale, hairless shins stopped her. His hair was mussed, and his feet were bare, and she wished he had taken the time to step into his slippers.

At that moment, Mr. Bell noticed a glow in the oval glass of the front door and heard men's angry voices on his lawn. An instant later, a brickbat crashed through the door, and bits of glass sprinkled Tibby's hair.

"Stay here," said Bert Gleason. "Let me go out and see what I can do."

Mr. Smoke and Tilman Monk had just stepped up on the porch when Bert Gleason came out of the house. Tilman Monk was carrying a five-gallon can of kerosene, and Mr. Smoke was holding a pine knot torch high above his head.

"We wants Mr. Andrew Bell," Mr. Smoke said. "You know that why we here."

"It looks like you're after trouble." Bert Gleason could see the men gathered on the lawn, their torches burning. Some of them carried ax handles. One man had noosed a rope. They had come in mule-drawn wagons the way Little Jones came to tend the lawns and gardens of Oak Street. "Do you think this town needs anymore ugliness tonight?"

"It's only what you all started." Tilman Monk's bass voice surprised Bert Gleason, as calm and as steady as the giant iron rollers at his mill. "Started with the Klan. We come to finish it."

"I saw you there at Little Jones's just a while ago." Bert Gleason could smell the tar burning on the torches and the fumes from the kerosene can. "What does he say about all this?"

"What you expect him to say?" Mr. Smoke dipped the torch, and Bert Gleason felt its heat on his face. "After that man kill his Eugie?"

"So he would have it?" Bert Gleason couldn't believe that Little would give the mob his blessing.

"He did not say us no," said Tilman Monk, and his voice was as somber as if he had been speaking in church.

Inside the house, Tibby helped Mr. Bell dress. She buttoned his shirt while he fastened his suspenders. He reached to the bed for his vest, but she grabbed his arm. "There isn't time," she told him.

"Tibby," he said, "I'm scared to death."

"Hurry." She tugged on his arm. "We'll be all right."

Tilman Monk was pouring kerosene on the planks of the porch, and it sloshed up onto the legs of Bert Gleason's trousers.

"I be moving if I be you," said Mr. Smoke. He waved the torch around. "Things about to get a might hot."

Another wagon was coming down the street, and Tilman Monk, hearing the mule's shoes on the cobblestones, stopped his work to see who was coming. Mr. Smoke turned, too. "It Little Jones," he said to Bert Gleason. "Now you can ask him yourself what he think."

Little got down from his wagon, and the men on the lawn moved aside so he could come up the walkway past the pittosporum shrub he was pruning into the shape of the sphinx, past the fountain grass just starting to bloom, and the yellow flowers of the hypericum. He knew, even in the dark, every plant and flower and tree in that yard because he had been the one who had planted them. The mountain laurel, the Italian jasmine, the Russian olive tree, the Mexican plum. He imagined the hot flames of the men's torches, the heat from the burning house, searing leaves and flowers, peeling bark. He pictured, come morning, the charred trunks and limbs of trees, the sooty ash of the flower beds, and the wire frame of the pittosporum sphinx melted and twisted into a tangle no one would be able to identify.

He stepped up on the porch. "I've worked this lawn for years," he said in a voice he meant to carry out to the men standing there with their torches. He was thinking of the day his own father had died and Mr. Morton of Nebraska City had walked with him around the grounds at Arbor Lodge and told him there was never loss in the world, only flesh returning to earth to sustain some other living thing. "I can tell you, more than most maybe, how what we plant grows the way we tend it. Go home. Leave this man alone. My wife is dead. My Eugie." Here his voice broke, and he had to fight to steady it. "Come judgment," he said. "No one needs blood on his soul."

"Is that the way you want it, then?" Tilman Monk said.

"That's what you can do for me," said Little. "That's all I'm asking."

Mr. Smoke shook his head. "You a fool, Little Jones."

Little came down from the porch, and Tilman Monk followed. On the lawn, the mob watched Little move to the Bells' front door and study the hole the brickbat had left. As he spread his hand over the jagged hole, they cringed, afraid that he might cut himself. Then, it seemed to them that he was trying to cover the hole so the ugliness they had brought couldn't get into the house. Shame filled them, and they turned and got into their wagons and started back to Quakertown.

"I'll find something to patch that," Little said to Bert Gleason.

"No, you go on home," Bert Gleason said. "I'll take care of it."

He watched Little climb up onto his buckboard's seat. "Little," he called. "There will be better days, Little. You'll see."

Little only waved and then gave the reins a shake. The mule started back up Oak Street, and Bert Gleason stood on the porch, amazed at how quiet the night had become, only the sound of the mule's shoes and the creak of the traces. Then a loud explosion rang out, and dogs started to bark, and at first he thought it was a gun shot. Then another explosion came, and he realized it was only the sound of an automobile backfiring at the crank. He went into the house, calling out, "Bell, Bell. You're safe now."

But no answer came, and it took Bert Gleason only a quick check of the rooms to understand that he was alone.

24

Not long after Eugie's funeral, the blossoms on the white lilac tree shriveled and burned in the hot sun. The leaves withered and dropped to the ground. Little knew that the tree had gone into shock and dropped its leaves to keep water in the roots and give it a chance to save itself. He couldn't help but think it sweet that the lilac would choose that particular time to shed its leaves as if mourning Eugie's death. There was, surprisingly, sweetness all around him in the days after her passing. There were kind words and embraces and neighbors dropping by with food. People invited him into their homes, and he went. The talk was always of moving Quakertown and the new homes on the land farther east.

"That Mr. Bell, he skedaddled," Oat Sparks said one night.

"That's right," said Mrs. Sparks. "Now Mr. Gleason running the show."

For a while, Little kept the lawn at Mr. Bell's, simply because he couldn't bear to see it go to ruin. Then one morning, when he arrived, a man wearing a straw boater was bent over hammering the stake of a FOR SALE sign into the marigold bed at the foot of the driveway. Little recognized him as Mr. Armor Heath, the real estate man.

"Mr. Heath, why in the world would you want to mess up that flower bed?" Little said to him.

"Don't tell me how to do my business." He pointed the hammer at Little. "Is that what you're trying to do?"

"No, sir. It's just that I take care of the flowers and whatnot for Mr. Bell."

"Mr. Bell's gone, and he's not coming back."

"Gone for good?"

"Didn't I just say that?"

It all seemed to Little a cowardly thing to do, and after what he had done for Mr. Bell the night all those rabble-rousers had wanted to burn down his house and who knows what all. So when he came to Oak Street to see to his other houses, he made sure he drove by the Bells' to watch the trees and shrubs and flowers do whatever it was they would do without his hand to intervene. Caterpillars spun webs in the catalpa trees, red spiders infested the marigolds, cutworms ate away at the rosebuds. Each time he passed, he noted some new development, and he felt a kindly allowance for the imperfections of everything left living on the earth. He tolerated the destruction, the first time he had ever left the workings of nature undisturbed, and hoped his patience, his willingness to let decay come, might teach him how to forgive.

From time to time, Ike and Camellia came to visit, but Little never spoke to Ike. It was the one knot he couldn't prune from his heart; out of all the people involved in Eugie's death, Ike was the one he blamed above all the others because he had brought them to the place where disaster had been possible.

"He's my husband," Camellia said to Little one afternoon. "You can't go on pretending he doesn't exist."

They were in the kitchen, and she was trimming Little's hair, a chore she had taken on since he refused to go to Ike's barbershop. She had tied an old bed sheet around his neck, and was working on the woolly hair that fringed his bald head.

"Have you forgiven him?" Little said. "Can you tell me that?"

"I've made room for him. We have a life together."

"But have you forgiven him?"

Camellia stepped back from Little and tapped the points of the scissors against her stomach. "I'm going to have a baby, Papa." She felt relieved to have that much of her secret out; she intended it as proof that she and Ike, as much as was possible in the wake of Eugie's death, were living a regular life.

"A baby?" Little tipped his head back and squinted at her. "Ike's baby?"

"Well, of course, Ike's baby," she said. "Papa, don't torment me."

The night of Eugie's death, when they had finally found themselves alone in his room at Sibby Long's, Ike sat on the bed and wept. Camellia's heart went out to him. She couldn't help herself. Angry as she was, she felt her old love for him awakening. She held him, rocked him against her. She kissed his scar as if her touch could take it away, and he let her. They both wept because they felt such a tangle of love and sorrow, joy and regret. In the days that followed, his kindness left her feeling muddleheaded. At times, it made her love him all the more, but at other times, it made it seem that he had turned into Kizer, and then she ached for the man she had let go away from her.

But Kizer was in Paris. He had reached the Waldorf Astoria in New York and found two telegrams waiting for him. The first, from his mother, asking him to return home, had alarmed him. But the second, from his father, was comforting, if a bit mysterious. "All is well. *Bon voyage*. If we make it, Bert Gleason will know where we are. Happy Days. Godspeed."

Once Kizer was settled in his room, he put a call through to Bert Gleason. "My parents," he said. "Are they all right?"

"They're in Hot Springs," Bert Gleason said.

"On vacation?"

"No, to live there for good. Things got crazy here after you left."

Out the window, Kizer watched the cabs making their way

along the street, the lighted TAXI signs on their roofs glowing in the dusk. He thought of how quickly and secretly he had driven away with Camellia that first night, never suspecting, until the moment he smelled the lovely aroma of peaches, tasted the juice on her skin, that he would be unable to drive back to his home on Oak Street, step back into that house the same man he had been when he had left it.

"Is my father in trouble?" he said to Bert Gleason.

"It was touch-and-go for a while. He shot a woman. Killed her. All by accident, of course."

"Killed who?"

"Eugenia Jiggs." For a moment, the name didn't mean anything to Kizer. Then Bert Gleason said, "You probably knew her as Eugie Jones."

Kizer could not have said, then, exactly what the news meant to him. At first, he felt a small measure of vindication because this woman who had engineered Camellia's abortion was dead, but it was only a passing thought that immediately shamed him. His more pressing concern was with Camellia. Poor sweet Camellia.

"Her daughter," he said. "I believe her name is Camellia."

"Married that day," said Bert Gleason. "Can you imagine it?"

Kizer closed his eyes. "How did it happen?"

"There was trouble on the courthouse lawn. All that Klan nonsense. Your father tried to stop it, and things got out of hand. He never meant to hurt anyone. I believe that. Least of all, Eugenia."

Only after he had hung up the telephone did Kizer realize that when he had asked his question, he hadn't been thinking of Eugie Jones or his father at all. He had been thinking of Camellia and what a fool he had been, such a coward, to let her go.

Mr. Bell had sent the telegram from a Western Union office in Texarkana.

"Traveling late," the clerk had said to him.

"Eloping," he had answered with a wink.

It was the joke he and Tibby had made once they had left Denton and knew they had put the mob behind them. Lovers stealing off in the night. Not even a suitcase with them. Just the clothes on their backs, and the money in their pockets to last them until they could reach Hot Springs and put a call through to Bert Gleason. Sell the lots to the city, Mr. Bell had decided. Turn everything over to Bert. Resign from the bank. Sell the house. Light out for the piney woods around Hot Springs. He and Tibby. Jesus, they were a pair. They had driven out the alley while the mob had gathered out front, had slipped through Denton and out to the highway, and once they had headed east, it had been so easy to keep going.

Outside the Western Union office, Tibby stood in the middle of the street, one foot in Texas, one in Arkansas. It was well after midnight, and she was still giddy with their escape. "Look at me," she called to Mr. Bell when he came out of the office. "I'm in two states at the same time."

Mr. Bell closed his arms around her waist. "Do you want to change your mind?" he said. "Should we turn around and go back?"

"No," she said. "I don't want to go back."

They reached Hot Springs at dawn just as the sun was breaking through the pine trees. They shaded their eyes with their hands, squinting now to see through the windshield, blinking furiously as if they had awakened in a place other than the one where they had gone to sleep. They checked into the Arlington Hotel, and the desk clerk, a heavy-faced man with gold-rimmed spectacles, didn't even raise an eyebrow when it became clear they had no luggage. He had obviously learned, Mr. Bell thought, to ask no questions, learned from the gangsters and bootleggers and gamblers who came into town. Even Al Capone, Mr. Bell had heard, came to take the waters.

"That clerk must think we're desperadoes," Tibby said when they were finally alone in their room.

The heavy brocade drapes were closed, and the room was dark. Mr. and Mrs. Bell stood in the middle of the room, not sure what to do next. They were both weary and frightened, and far, far from the place they had always known as home. For a moment, all the spirit went out of them.

"Aren't we?" Mr. Bell said.

"Yes," said Tibby in a glum tone. "I suppose we are."

"Don't worry, Tibby, pet." Mr. Bell held her to him. "I'll get in touch with Bert Gleason quick as a wink. I'll put us back on our feet."

In the weeks that followed Eugie's death and the Bells' escape, Bert Gleason was the talk of Quakertown. The word spread that he was making sure that land went cheap to anyone who wanted to buy it. And on top of that, no one was going to have to give up a house. Bert Gleason was going to see that the houses in Quakertown were moved. Imagine that. Jacked up onto runners atop huge rollers and pulled away by teams of horses.

Little Jones verified that this was all true. Whenever anyone wanted information, he was the one they asked. And when they asked, he felt some measure of love return to him, some dignity he had lost when Eugie and Camellia had decided, alone, what to do about the baby. Here were people who needed him, people who asked his advice, and, when he heard the hope in their voices, he couldn't refuse them.

Is it good land? they wanted to know.

He told them, Yes.

High land?

Yes.

Drainage?

Yes.

And all of this was true. The land east of town was higher, rising up from the flood plain of the creek that ran along the edge of Quakertown. No longer would folks have to worry about the spring rains that pushed the creek over its banks and brought it into their yards, turned their streets to mud, crept over their thresholds from time to time.

Is it what they should do? they asked Little, and he told them, Yes.

They listened because he was Little Washington Jones, and they had watched him for years grow nearly anything he wanted out of that gumbo clay. If he said they could grow a neighborhood, a better one than Quakertown, who were they to disagree? He had the touch. Some sort of magic mojo in those hands, and if he would touch them, they reasoned, touch their homes, surely they would prosper.

So they brought him into their houses, invited him to sit at their tables, eat their food, all for the touch of his hand when he knocked upon their doors, the touch they believed would bless them.

And the white people sought his favor, too:

You got to sell this idea, Little.

I can sell it, he said.

Can't have anyone dragging their feet.

I'll set them to marching, he said.

Find something white folks value, his father had told him. Do it well, and your life will be as smooth as silk.

One day, Mr. Neiman, of Neiman's Department Store, presented Little with a new fedora hat, shipped in straight from New York City. A cream-colored hat with a maroon band made of satin.

"A token of our appreciation," Mr. Neiman said, "for everything you're doing for the city."

The hat was a half-size too large, a fact Mr. Neiman didn't seem to notice. Little didn't mind. He liked to push the hat up and wear it high on the crown of his head so people could see his face. That way, he thought, he'd look more friendly. He put on a smile, gave everyone the glad hand. And if, from time to time, he put a strut into his walk—if he paraded down Frame Street just so people could stop him and ask for the lowdown—who could blame him? It was the only time, when he was out and about—Mr. High-Hat, Mr. Man-About-Town—that he felt any relief from the sorrow and malice, the tremendous loneliness, that had filled him since Eugie had died.

What he never said to the people in Quakertown, who were excited now about moving—what he kept quiet within himself—was the fact that he wasn't going with them.

They started to call the land east of town Rhodie Hill because they had heard so many of their ancestors tell the story of a slave named Rhodie who ran away to freedom in Mexico by sprinkling black pepper in her socks and running without her shoes so the hounds that chased after her would start to sneeze and lose her scent.

When we get to Rhodie Hill, folks said, we'll be in high cotton.

And Little said, Yes, yes, yes.

But still there were those who grumbled about the move. They were too old, they said, to be pulling up stakes.

"I'm root-bound here," Sibby Long said to Little one morning when they were both shopping in Nib Colter's grocery.

"Root-bound means you can't breathe," Little told her. "Can't grow. Too cramped together in too little space. Just like all the ones you got living in your boardinghouse." He couldn't bring himself to name Camellia or Ike. "Sometimes we got to thin things out a touch."

"What if I won't go?"

"No one says you got to go. Henry Treece and his wife are talking about going to Los Angeles to be near their son, and Grandma Sue Moore has a daughter in Kansas City."

"I mean what if I won't sell."

"They'll condemn you, Sibby." How easy it was to toss that lie into the mix.

"Condemn me? Little Jones, you know I run a clean house."

"City's got codes," Little said. "They're going to stop looking the other way now they've got a reason to use them."

Soon, that word was making its way along the streets. Little Jones says you might as well sell. If you get muleheaded, the city's going to condemn your house, and then you might end up without a pot to piss in.

And that, Little told them, when they asked, was one hundred percent, call Heaven to witness, true.

Camellia worried about the children getting to school.

"Going to build a new one," Little told her. "Out there at Rhodie Hill. Might not be ready this fall, but it won't be long."

Camellia carried the news home to Ike. "A new school," she said. She was so excited she held her arms out to her sides and twirled around in the middle of the room the way she saw girls do sometimes on the playground, spinning until they got so dizzy they fell into each other and dropped to the ground in a giggling clump. She fell back on the bed.

Ike was sitting at the desk writing a letter to his mother. He had written once, after Eugie's death, telling the story, and his mother had answered: "Love people and they'll love you. Believe in forgiveness."

"I'm going to go out there tomorrow," he said. "Going to have a look around."

"Choose a lot for us," said Camellia. She had grown so tired of Sibby Long's. Cooking meals on a hot plate, being surprised in the privy by some other boarder, having Hocie Simms come to their room to play records on Ike's phonograph. "Make it a good one, and we'll build a house."

"Is that what you want, Camellia?"

"Our own house," she said. "With flower boxes at the windows and a swing from a tree in the yard."

"A swing?" Ike laughed. "What in the world you want with a swing?"

"Baby got to have a swing," she said. The news of the new school had made her believe in fresh beginnings. And maybe it was true; maybe the child she carried was Ike's.

"Baby?" He got to his feet and went to the bed. "You mean?"

She took his hand and laid it on her stomach. "That's what I'm saying, Ike."

Her hand was trembling, and she hoped, if he noticed, he would imagine she was shaking with joy. She was relieved to have the secret out of her even though she was scared now, scared to death.

The next day was Sunday, and after church, Ike walked out to Rhodie Hill.

Camellia cooked dinner for her father and spent the afternoon sorting through her mother's clothes.

"I might be able to wear some of these dresses," she said. "As the baby comes along."

Little closed the doors to the wardrobe. "You just stay away from those dresses. Those were Moms'. I like keeping them here."

"You don't have to get uppity about it." Camellia folded her arms over her chest and turned her face away from him with a sniff. "Mama was right. You are a high-hat nigger."

"Don't you be proud with me." He cupped her chin with his hand and twisted her face around so she would have to look at him. "If you ask me, you shouldn't be the one judging anyone."

"What's that supposed to mean?"

"It means I know." He had seen her on Frame Street the night before, telling everyone she met that she was expecting. She had been so giddy about this baby, as if it was her first, no regard for the other child, the one she had conceived in shame and then given over to Dr. Parrish's means. What right did she think she had to happiness, Little thought, when every night he sat alone in the dark house and ached for his Eugie. "I know about you and Kizer Bell and the baby that you killed. He told me how it all played out."

Camellia's eyes opened wide for an instant as if someone had grabbed her by the throat. Then she looked down at the floor, and Little, ashamed himself now of how sharp he had been, let his hand drop from her face.

"If you knew," she finally said, "why didn't you say something?"

"You and Moms had decided. It wasn't for me to say anything. If either of you had wanted to hear from me, you would have asked."

"So you've stopped loving me?"

Little thought of the delicate camellia flower, how it took such care. "Still love you," he said. "Still love Moms. You're just different to me. That's all. Whole world's different to me now. Sort of strange."

Camellia braced herself by pressing her hand against the wardrobe, letting her fingers trace the scrollwork at the doors' edges. She couldn't bring herself to tell him that she hadn't been able to go through with the abortion that day at Dr. Parrish's office because then Little would know that the child she carried might be Kizer's. She feared that such knowledge would only wound her father more, and he might turn away from her forever. So she lay her face against her arm. "I suppose you'll tell Ike."

Little shook his head. "Not my secret to tell. Your life is yours, and mine is mine. You thought you could get along all right without me from the git-go. Don't expect me to jump into the game now."

"I had Mama then," Camellia cried.

"Baby-Girl," said Little, "so did I."

When Ike came back to Sibby Long's, Camellia was sleeping. He sat on the bed and saw tears leaking out from the corners of her eyes. She was crying in her sleep, and he bent over and kissed her tears.

"Camellia," he said. "Wake up. You're dreaming bad juju."

She opened her eyes and blotted them with the heels of her hands. "Crazy dreams," she said. "Where you been so long?"

"Out to Rhodie Hill. Remember? It's good land just like your father says. High land. Good place for a baby."

"I don't want to live out there," Camellia said.

"What happened to those flower boxes? That swing in the tree?"

"I don't trust Bert Gleason."

She sat up in bed and told Ike about the night Bert had burned her mother's house.

"I can hardly believe it," Ike said.

Not too long ago, Camellia thought, he would have been out-raged, would have been talking about the devil white man and Marcus Garvey and going home to Africa. But now here he was shaking his head and pointing out how Bert Gleason was looking out for their best interests.

"I'm not doubting your story, but people change, Camellia."

"I wish we could go away," she said. She feared her father would tell her secret. "Africa, even. Anywhere a long way from here."

Bert Gleason brought the circus to town and bought tickets for anyone in Quakertown who wanted to go. A big canvas tent, with an American flag flying from its peak, went up on the athletic field at the college, and for once, the maids and porters who worked there walked up the long hill, decked out in bright shirts and dresses, and sat in the bleachers under the canvas tent, sat next to the girls they served, mingled with the merchants who wouldn't let them eat in their cafés or try on clothes in their department stores. No white person uttered a word of protest because it was clear that Bert Gleason was running the show. Hocie Simms offered Mr. Neiman a sip from her lemon shake-up, and he politely declined. Mr. Smoke spread his handkerchief on the bleacher so a young lady from the college wouldn't dirty her dress, and since the bleachers were nearly full by this time, she had no choice but to accept his kindness.

At the entrance to the tent, Bert Gleason scanned the crowd and saw black faces next to white. The calliope piped out "Wait Till the Clouds Roll By, Jennie," and vendors circulated through the crowd hawking popcorn, roasted peanuts, palm-leaf fans, toy balloons, chewing gum, soda water.

Camellia and Ike sat in front of Mavis and Alvin Brown, who were next to Hocie Simms. From time to time, Alvin placed his hands on Camellia's shoulders and pressed down, trying to hoist himself up for a better look at what was going on in the ring. At one point, Camellia tired of the jostling. She spun around and grabbed Alvin by his wrist. "Stop it," she said with a snap.

Alvin howled, and Camellia let him go. Mavis Brown glared at her. She gathered Alvin up onto her lap and whispered to Hocie Simms, "Think she'll be so nasty with her own?"

Little Jones didn't go to the circus. Instead, he drove his wagon out to Rhodie Hill, and there, under the hot sun, he walked the perimeter of the thirty-five acres, saw the red flags marking off the lots, and stared off toward Quakertown. He could hear the faint music of the calliope, and at that distance, it seemed a sad and mournful sound.

But to those under the big top, it was gay and rollicking. The clowns were out now in their baggy pants and enormous shoes. They had painted their faces with exaggerated smiles and stuck big red bulbs on the ends of their noses.

One clown in a tattered Prince Albert suit, a frown painted on his face, carried a camera on a tripod and brought people down from the bleachers and posed them for photographs. Who could refuse the shy tramp of a clown with his sad face? He brought whoever was sitting in a group, unconcerned that some of the people were black and some were white. He posed Nib Colter with his hand on C. K. Alexander's shoulder, and Sibby Long snuggled in close to Armor Heath. The clown got behind the camera, stuck his head under the black cloth, and lifted the rubber bulb that tripped the shutter.

"Smile," he told them.

"Smile," some people in the bleachers said.

"One," he said.

"Two," said voices from the crowd.

Then, before he could say three, he came out from under the cloth and shook his head. He paced and muttered and fretted, and a giant "ah" of sympathy rose up from the crowd. Then he stopped his pacing, snapped his fingers, and rearranged his models. He repeated the process two more times, and finally, never satisfied with the poses, he picked up his camera and walked away, leaving his subjects frozen a moment the way he had last arranged them. Everyone in the bleachers laughed at the poor fools, suckered in by the sad little clown.

Soon there were elephants and tigers and lions, acrobats and flyers, high-wire acts and stunt riders.

Alvin Brown jumped up and down behind Camellia, jarring her.

One of the elephants reared up on his hind legs and trumpeted an angry call. The handler, a bare-chested man wearing a turban, tried to bring him down by hooking his long pole over the elephant's ear. The elephant came down, and for a moment, it looked as if everything was under control. The handler turned and bowed to the audience, and the audience cheered. That's when the elephant swung his head around, caught the handler on its tusks, and tossed the man up into the air. He landed on the ground with a thud as if a sack of potatoes or chicken feed had been dropped there.

Several handlers appeared then. They calmed the elephant and led the whole bunch out of the ring. Another group of men carried the fallen handler away on a stretcher.

"You think that man's dead?" Alvin Brown asked his mother. "The way Miss Eugie was dead?"

Camellia stood up and turned around. She bent over and shook her finger in Alvin Brown's face. "You are a wicked boy," she said. Then she took Ike by the arm, and they left the tent.

*   *   *

At Rhodie Hill, Little stood at the highest point and looked back to Denton. He saw it the way he imagined his father had when he had drawn the Bird's Eye Map that still hung in what had once been Mr. Bell's bank. Little could see the clock tower on the courthouse rising up, and beyond it, the houses of Quakertown, and then up the long hill, the college and the peaks of the canvas tent on the athletic field. He remembered the tricks his father could pull to make people believe they were looking at something from a great height. "There has to be two kinds of people for any piece of magic to work," he had told Little once. "Those who want to be tricked, and those who want to do the tricking."

Now Little knew which he was. What he had known all along was how far the distance from Rhodie Hill would be for the ones who had to walk to the college to work or who wanted to go to the businesses left at the edge of Quakertown on Saturdays to shop. In the fear left by the Klan's march and the excitement about moving to higher ground that he himself had helped fuel, no one had thought about the extra hardship and what it might mean.

When the calliope started to play "The Stars and Stripes Forever," the crowd went out of the tent to the midway where there were games of chance and sideshow attractions. One of them was a group of women brought out of French West Africa, promoted as "The Ubangi Saucer-Lipped Women."

Hocie Simms and Mavis Brown paid their dimes and went into a small tent, Alvin in tow, though once they were inside, Mavis regretted having him with her.

The women were bare-breasted. They had colorful cloths wrapped around their waists and beaded necklaces looped around their necks. Their lips stretched out a good six inches from their chins.

The Ubangi, a barker announced, gauged the beauty of their women by the length of their lips. When they were babies, tribesmen slit their lips and inserted small disks, increasing the size of the disks as the girls grew. "Consider the Queen Guetika," the barker said. "The loveliest of them all."

The women were foul-smelling, and they sat in front of grass huts, gobbling raw fish and unpeeled bananas.

Mavis Brown had seen all manner of deformity and injury in her years as a nurse, but nothing had ever offended her as much as this. In fact, all the Negroes from Quakertown who had come to see the Ubangi were quiet now, shifting about in their seats, staring down at their hands, at each other, anywhere but straight ahead.

"Them women's showing their titties," Alvin said, and Mavis grabbed him and hurried out of the tent.

On the midway, Camellia was buying balloons for a group of children.

"Run on," Mavis told Alvin. "Make sure Miss Camellia knows you want a balloon."

The children were jumping up to grab the balloons that stuck straight up in the air at the end of their strings. Camellia stooped down and patiently tied the strings to the children's wrists, so the balloons wouldn't fly away. Alvin crowded into the back of the group, inching forward as each child peeled away with his or her balloon. Ike stood next to Camellia and patted the children on their heads.

"Practicing up to be a mommy and daddy," Hocie Simms said.

Finally, all the children had run off, squealing with their balloons, and Alvin stepped forward, holding out his arm. Camellia took Ike's hand, turned, and strolled off down the midway, leaving Alvin there to stare at the balloon vendor, who had started to search out other customers.

"Hold on a minute." Bert Gleason came up behind Mavis and Hocie and rushed to the balloon man. "You forgot someone." He gave the vendor a dime, selected a bright red balloon, and tied it around Alvin's wrist. "There you go, little man."

Alvin turned back to his mother. "Mommy, see? See my balloon?"

"That's sweet, what you did," Mavis said to Bert Gleason. Inside, she was burning with rage. She had kept Camellia's secret only to be treated like this.

"Camellia must have not seen your boy." Bert Gleason put his hand on Alvin's head and ushered him back to his mother. "You know how it is? Newlyweds only have eyes for each other."

"I don't know why she lets on she so head-over-heels for that fool," Hocie Simms said.

"What do you mean?" asked Bert Gleason.

"Go on, Mavis. Tell him."

The image of Alvin turning back to her, his lips quivering, as if he held the weight of a thousand saucers in them, while Camellia walked away from him, was still fresh in Mavis's mind. Who did that girl think she was anyway? "The truth is," she told Bert Gleason. "Well, I really shouldn't tell you this, but the fact is, that Camellia, she came this close to giving up Ike's baby."

"Giving it up," said Bert Gleason.

"Yes, sir," said Mavis. "You know what I mean. Abortion."

Bert Gleason scratched his head. "That's a fantastic story. Why tell it to me?"

"I don't want to make trouble for Camellia," Mavis said. "That was never my plan, but I guess I couldn't stand the way she treated my boy."

On his way back from Rhodie Hill, Little Jones met a group of men leading an elephant, chains around his legs. One length stretched from each front leg to a tusk so he couldn't raise them. There were even chains wrapped around his trunk.

Little stopped his wagon and watched as the men, there in the clearing, chained the elephant to three trees, his front legs to two mesquite, one rear leg to a live oak. Little noticed, then, that some of the men were carrying rifles.

"What in the world's going on?" he said to a man standing off from the others. He was wearing a short necktie and a fedora hat.

"That's Black Diamond," the man said. "He near killed a man today."

"So you've brought him out here?"

"Have too. Once they turn on you, you can't never trust them again. Believe me, you got no choice but to put them down."

Little started his wagon moving. Then he heard the first volley of rifle shots. He didn't turn around, not wanting to see what it took to kill something so large, or to imagine, even, the way the elephant must have looked at the men with his sad, weary eyes, trying to understand why they had brought him to this place.

25

The bond referendum to acquire Quakertown passed, and soon horses came at night, and the men with sleds and rollers, and they took the houses away. Little sat on his porch, one of Eugie's shawls over his legs, because the nights had cooled now, and one morning there would be frost, and the begonias would wilt, and the nandinas would turn as red as blood. He listened to the groan of timber, the men's cries of "gee" or "haw" as they commanded the teams to veer right or left. The lantern lights swung as the men worked, and the horses strained in their harnesses. The sled runners screeched over the rollers and the men hurried ahead to reposition the cylinders. Such hard, frantic work. The men cried out in the night: "Easy." "Slow up there." "Goddamn it, whoa." Such a slow chore. Fifty-eight houses moved from Quakertown to Rhodie Hill.

One night, Bert Gleason came to Little's house. A man was with him, a tall man in a white linen suit, gold cufflinks sparkling at his wrists.

"This is Mr. Comstock." Bert Gleason stepped up onto Little's porch. "He's a horticulturist from Dallas. He'll be asking your help with the planning of the park."

"I understand you're something of a whiz." Mr. Comstock scraped his foot through the flower bed where the last of the begonias were hanging on. "A hobbyist of sorts."

"Oh, Little knows his business, all right," Bert Gleason said.

"You might want to give up on these begonias." Mr. Comstock lifted his foot, and with a dainty turn of his ankle, shook a scrap of pine mulch from his shoe. "They're a hot-weather flower. Try some hearty pansies instead."

"I reckon these begonias got some days left," Little said.

The sleeves of Mr. Comstock's suit coat were too short for his long arms, and he tugged at the ends, which only called attention to his gold cufflinks, a maneuver Little suspected he had practiced time and time again until it pleased him. "Mr. Jones." He nodded toward Little. "I'm sure we'll be speaking again soon. Perhaps before the frost puts your poor begonias out of their misery. I believe I'll walk around a bit now, Bert. Get a feel for the natural contours of this space."

When Mr. Comstock had slipped off into the darkness, Bert Gleason said to Little, "It's all going according to plan, isn't it?"

"It is that," said Little. "Couldn't stop it now, if we wanted to."

"Why would we want to?" Bert Gleason sat down on a chair next to Little's. "It's the way you wanted things, isn't it?"

"Yes, sir," said Little. "It's the way I want it."

"Good. That's good." Bert Gleason put his hands behind his head and looked up at the sky, at the brilliant points of stars. "Everything's looking up. I brought Mr. Comstock to meet you, Little, because I'm planning to go away for a while."

"Taking a trip, are you?"

"That's right."

"I hope it's somewhere you want to go."

Bert Gleason laughed. "Well, of course it is. I wouldn't go if it wasn't. Haven't you ever thought about traveling? Maybe seeing something you never thought you'd see? I'm going to Europe."

"I went on a trip once with my father." Little remembered the hotel in Lincoln and the map his father had drawn. How long ago it seemed. "I was glad to get back to Quakertown."

Somewhere up the street, a man was shouting above the squeal of the sleds, "Haw, haw. Goddamn it, drive that team."

"Well, now you've got it," Bert Gleason said. "It won't be long before you'll have the place to yourself."

All that autumn, Camellia's schoolroom was half empty, the children who had already moved to Rhodie Hill electing to stay home on the days they would have to walk the two miles through rain and mud. Camellia herself was often absent, sick now in the mornings with the child she carried. One morning, she woke and found spots of blood on her nightdress and went right away to Dr. Parrish.

"Spotting on the cervix," he told her. "Probably doesn't mean a thing, but for a while I want you to stay in bed."

"All day?"

"For a few weeks. Just to make sure everything's all right."

She agreed to let her friend, Portia Washington Pittman—yes, she had been the one who had played the organ at Camellia's wedding—send a girl to replace her in the classroom, a girl named Minnie Lee Wright, who had just earned her certificate from Bishop College.

"Well, I'm no good now," Camellia said one morning to Ike as she lay in bed. "I'm just an old sack of potatoes."

The truth was she loved the fact that Dr. Parrish had made her an invalid. She liked to believe that time stopped as she lay in her bed and that as long as she stayed there the baby wouldn't come.

"You rest up," Ike told her. "I'll take care of you."

It was a sweet time for both of them. Several times a day, he came home from the barbershop to see how she was doing. He brought her gifts from Billy Moten's Apothecary: rock candy, a comb for her hair, an emery board, a *Reader's Digest* magazine. Evenings, he laid a checkerboard on the bed, and they played until she tired of the games, the constant moves and chase, and how often the games ended in stalemates.

"You got to have a little pluck," Ike told her once. "Give up something to get something better back. Trouble with you is you want to hold on to everything you got."

She barely slept that night, knowing that what Ike had told her was true. She had been afraid to let him go when she fell in love with Kizer; she had been unable to give up the baby, and now, even after Kizer had gone from her life, she still found herself daydreaming about him, remembering how sweet they had been together.

Ike's kindly attention brought back all the honor Kizer had paid her, all the moments she had spent with him. She started to feel a genuine affection for Ike, so sweet he was with his attention. Perhaps, it wasn't love, she thought, but at least something close, some comfort that now, when others had left her, he was near.

One evening, Minnie Lee Wright came by to bring Camellia a stack of cards her students had made for her with crayons and construction paper. Minnie Lee was a chatty girl who had a habit of making exaggerated faces when she talked. She smirked and frowned, crossed her eyes, twisted up her mouth or let it hang open. Her hands were like birds, fluttering here and there as she sat on the edge of Camellia's bed and showed her the cards. She told her everything was apple pie, hunky-dory at school. "Besides these cards, we've made jack-o'-lanterns out of orange construction paper." Here she stuck her fingers in her mouth and stretched her lips wide. "And next week I'm taking the children to Dallas so they can see Bishop College." She pressed her lips together in a pout and let her cheeks go slack. "That is, if it's all right with you."

Camellia was sitting up in bed, a pillow behind her back. "All right? Why wouldn't it be all right? It would be a marvelous experience for the children. Riding the train are you?"

"Yes, indeedy Bob," Minnie Lee said.

"Who's paying the fares?"

"Why, Mrs. Mattoon, I expect I can afford a few dimes."

"That's very generous. I'm sure the children adore you."

"Yes, ma'am," Minnie Lee said with a wide grin. Then she clapped her hand over her mouth with a loud smack. "Excuse me for being so proud," she said. "It's the first time I ever taught for real."

Camellia could remember the first time she had stepped in front of her class. How badly she had wanted the children to love her. She had wanted them to understand that they weren't alone in the world, that whatever they did would ripple out and touch someone else.

But who was she to have such grand notions now? After the mess she had made of things. How could she ever expect to teach children to consider one another's feelings when she had been so selfish? What right would she have? The words would be razors in her mouth. How she wished that she was once again innocent and hopeful like Minnie Lee Wright.

"She's a real go-getter," Camellia said that night to Ike as they lay in bed, the moonlight washing over them. "I could disappear—poof!—and that school would get on fine without me."

"Disappear?" said Ike. He was lying close to her, his head nestled against her shoulder. She could feel the ridge of his scar on her arm. "And where do you think you'd go?"

"Nowhere I guess. I suspect I'm stuck right here."

"It's not a bad place, Camellia. It's your home."

"The way Papa treats me, I feel like a stranger."

Even though Ike had gone to Little and told him that Dr. Parrish had ordered Camellia to bed, Little hadn't come to see her. "Doc say she'll be all right?" he had asked Ike, the first words he had said to him since the night Eugie had died, and Ike had told him, yes, Doc Parrish had said she'd be fine. "Mighty busy these days," Little had said to Ike. "What with them moving Quakertown and me helping them plan the park. I'll get over there soon as I can."

"He's just mad," Ike said to Camellia. "Mad at me. Can't say

I blame him. Maybe we'd all be better off if I was to go some-where else."

Camellia felt a panic rise up in her. "Don't talk crazy," she said. Without Ike, she would feel so alone. "How would I get along if I didn't have you?"

"I'm not going anywhere," Ike said. "I'm here with you, and one day this baby will be with us. Good Lord, that'll be the day. I can hardly imagine it. Your daddy will come around when he sees his grandbaby." Ike laid his hand on Camellia's stomach and rubbed a slow circle. "This child will heal all our hurt. You'll see. I think that's why God sends us babies. So we don't forget how fresh we once were. Bright as new pennies."

The houses around Sibby Long's disappeared one by one. Each morning, Ike stepped outside and saw another empty lot, a patch of raw earth, mangled and scarred where the horses had pulled a house away. Evenings, he sat on the steps with Sibby Long and Hocie Simms and Mavis Brown and watched the men with their lanterns and teams of horses.

"You better make ready," the foreman said to them one night. He was a thick-chested man, and when he gave an order, he hooked his thumbs into the galluses of his overalls and pushed his chest out even more.

"Can't move this house," said Sibby Long. "Got a mother to be laying in here. Doctor's orders."

"I'm the one giving the orders around here," said the foreman. "She'll have to do her laying in somewhere else."

"Where that be?" said Hocie Simms. "You done moved most of Quakertown."

"Not my problem." The foreman rocked back on his heels. "Find her a place or we'll move the house with her in it."

"You go tell Little Jones that," said Sibby Long.

When Ike went back to their room, Camellia was sitting up in bed. "They're going to move us," she said. "I heard that man."

"Don't worry," he told her. "I'll get your daddy to stop them."
Camellia shook her head. "I don't think Papa cares a lick
about me anymore."

"Blood calls to blood, Camellia. Deep down at the root. Can't
wash it away, no matter how hard you try."

So Ike went to Little Jones and he told him that the men with
their horses were coming for Sibby Long's and Camellia still not
supposed to leave her bed. "What will you do about it?"

"She's your wife," Little said. "You're the man who's supposed
to look after her."

"Yes, but you're the one who's in on this park-building scheme.
I'm just a hell-raising nigger. Why would any white man listen to
me? You're the one who fell in their honey pot. Besides, it would
mean a lot to Camellia right now if you were the one who spoke
up for her."

A few nights later, the foreman came over to the steps where
Ike and Sibby and Hocie and Mavis were sitting, and he swung
the lantern up so it lit their faces. "Tomorrow night," he said
from the shadows. "We're moving this house come hell or high
water."

"We see about that," said Hocie Simms. "Here come Little
Jones now."

Little came up the walk. The cuffs of his white shirt gleamed in
the lantern light. The cream-colored fedora was bright on his
head. "I'm Little Jones," he told the foreman. "Mr. Little Washington Jones. My daughter is in this house. Doctor says she can't
be rousted."

"Uncle, I don't care if Jesus Christ is in there turning water into
wine." The foreman laughed. "We're going to move this house.
The city bought the land it sits on." He swung the lantern toward
Sibby Long. "You sold it, granny, and now it's time for you to get
shed of it."

Little put his hand on the foreman's arm and felt the heat from
the lantern's flame. He tried to pull the arm down so the kerosene

smoke would stop trailing off into the faces of Sibby Long, and Mavis, and Hocie, and Ike. But the foreman was strong, and the arm wouldn't budge.

"No need to choke these folks," Little said.

He could see the foreman's jaw muscles tighten. "Uncle, you better let go of me now."

Little let his hand drop away from the foreman's arm. "Yes, sir, but you see, sir, like I said, I'm Little Jones. I'm the one the city chose to be the caretaker of the new park. Now there are folks, important folks, who would be willing to listen to me."

"Bert Gleason?" The foreman spit on the sidewalk at Little's feet. "He's gone to Europe. La-di-da. This ain't his show now."

"Whose show is it then?" said Sibby Long. "Sure looks like it ain't yours, Little Jones."

The foreman puffed out his big chest. "I'm the one with the horses and sleds. The big shots like Bert Gleason can think what they want. When you get down to it, I'm the one who makes things go." He reached out and pulled Little's fedora down so the brim squashed his ears and hung over his eyes. "Uncle, this house is good as gone."

So the word got out, traveled among the ones still left in Quakertown, spread on out to Rhodie Hill where the others were setting up housekeeping. Little Jones didn't have as much steam as everyone had thought, couldn't even stop the city from throwing his daughter out on the street. People also knew now that he wasn't moving to Rhodie Hill, that he would be able to keep his house right there in Quakertown, that he was going to be the caretaker of the new city park. He had sold them out, people grumbled. Little Jones.

"Baby-Girl," he said to Camellia the next morning when he came to tell her, yes, indeed, it was true, he had been unable to stop the move. He had talked to Mr. Armor Heath, and the best Mr. Heath had been able to do had been to offer to send a mo-

torcar to carry Camellia from Sibby Long's to either Little's house
or to Rhodie Hill. "It'll take most of the night to move this house.
You'd be better off back in your old room. I'm saying you can
have it, if you want, for as long as you need it."

The morning sun was shining in Camellia's eyes, and it was difficult for her to look at Little, who stood at the side of the window, half-turned to her, his fedora in his hands. She slouched
down in bed and held a *Life* magazine up in front of her face.
"And Ike?" she said.

"I'm inviting you," Little told her. "Not him."

She lowered the magazine and stared directly into the bright
sunlight. "Your heart is still that hard?"

"Cuss me if you want, but that man will never spend a single
night in the house your mother called home."

"So to accept your offer I have to forsake my husband."

"Call it that if you want. It shouldn't be too hard for you."

"People make mistakes, Papa."

He looked at her then. "Are you sorry for what you did with
Kizer Bell?" She bit her lip and looked away from him. "Say it,
and I'll let the both of you come stay with me, you and Ike."

"I won't say anything you try to make me say. Papa, you have
no idea what's in my heart."

"Wickedness," said Little. "Deceit. That's what I see there."

When the men came with their horses to move Sibby Long's,
Ike carried Camellia, wrapped in a quilt, down the stairs and out
into the cold night. He laid her in the back seat of Mr. Heath's
motorcar.

"Where shall I drive you?" Mr. Heath asked. "Your father's?"

"No," said Camellia. "Rhodie Hill."

"Is there someone out there who'll take you in until the boardinghouse arrives?"

"Mr. Oat Sparks," Ike said. "We're all going to stay there. The
others have gone on ahead."

Hocie Simms and Mavis Brown and the others had left before

supper, and for a few hours, Ike and Camellia had been alone in the house. "Someday we'll have a house this big," Ike had said. "Fill it up with young'uns. Always be someone laughing, or crying, maybe. Well, that's the way life goes."

The boardinghouse was the only two-story home in Quakertown, and when it was finally up on the sled, the horses couldn't pull it onto the rollers. The drivers laid into them with whips, but the horses stumbled. Their eyes grew wide, and they snorted ragged breaths that fogged the air with the steam of their efforts. A white lather broke out on their chests. Veins trembled in their necks. They tried to rear up on their hind legs and break free from their harness, and the drivers had to settle them, holding them by the straps of their bridles, stroking their necks, and cooing to them, "Whoa, whoa, here now, whoa."

"Goddamn it," the foreman said. "We need more teams."

"It'll take a while to find them," one of the drivers said. "Night's getting on."

"All right, goddamn it." The foreman kicked at the ground. "Unhook the horses. Jack the damn thing off the sled, and let's get on to the next one."

"Sibby said you couldn't move this house," Ike told the foreman.

"If we can't move it," the foreman said, "we'll tear it down."

But it sat there for days while all the houses around it disappeared, sat there long enough for Dr. L. C. Parrish to come to examine Camellia and pronounce her fit. "Get on out of this bed," he told her. "Vacation's over. You just needed a little rest while that baby got itself settled. Now, young lady, you're going back to school."

The first thing she did, after Ike had helped her to her feet, was stand at the window and look out across what had once been Quakertown. When she had taken to her bed, there had still been houses, and picket fences, and laundry flapping on clotheslines. There had been coal smoke curling from chimneys, and chickens and guineas strutting about the yards. Now what she saw was the ground—the ugly, muddy clay—and the ruts the sleds had left. A tangle of wire, what was left from a fence, sagged from a post that had been dragged nearly level to the ground. There were scraps of corrugated tin, brickbats, tar paper, shingles. There were concrete walks that now led up to nothing.

The sight reminded her of the photographs of battlefields in France that Ike kept in a cigar box in his closet. In one, he stood in a crater a shell had left, the furl of earth rimming his waist. "Me," he had written on the back of the photo, "on my way to China." There were photos of the Argonne Forest during General Pershing's offensive, the woods littered with barbed wire and ravines. Quakertown had this same look of devastation, and though Camellia could see her father's house across the way, the shiny white pickets of its fence, the yellow and red chrysanthemums in their gay beds, the distance felt great to her, and she knew what she imagined the war orphans in France had learned—home was never safe or forever.

She heard something scrape across the floor behind her, and when she turned, she saw Ike stooping down to pick up an envelope that was lying just inside the doorway.

He saw the large, sloppy scrawl of the address, and he knew the letter was from his father, only the second the Reverend Heddy Mattoon had ever written his son, the first being a note he had sent during the war, encouraging Ike to remain true to God no matter how ugly the world got. "There is a plan," he had written. "It's not for us to know it. All things happen for a reason that may only become clear on the Day of Judgment or perhaps never."

"You open it." Ike brought the envelope to Camellia. "I'm afraid to."

"Afraid?" Camellia took the envelope and looked at the return address written across the flap. "It's from your father."

"That's right," Ike said. "I've never known him to write just to shoot the breeze."

*   *   *

Little was sitting at the kitchen table, studying Mr. Comstock's layout of the park, when he heard the meek tapping at his door. At first, he thought it was the wind rattling the screen door against the frame, but then the knocking came again, this time with more force. He slipped off his spectacles and laid them on Mr. Comstock's drawing. When Little had first seen it at the home of Mr. Andrew Bell, he had admired the neat strokes of color that had re-created the bushes and trees and flowers and pools, but now so much of it seemed wrong—a bald cypress that would one day be drowned by shade as the nearby red oaks grew to tower over it, a boggy patch by the creek that would better be covered with houttuynia than the Asian jasmine Mr. Comstock had planned, a slope where the strong roots of lavender or thrift would offer a more vigorous carpet than the low-growing and more delicate lamium.

It was all a matter of putting the right plant in the right spot, Little was thinking he would tell Comstock. Then he opened the front door and saw Camellia standing there on the porch, her hands in the pockets of her wool coat.

"So you're up and around," he said. "You're all right. That's good."

"I've come to tell you we're going away," Camellia told him. "Ike and me."

"Out to Rhodie Hill? I tried my best to stop them from moving Sibby Long's."

"No." Camellia shook her head. "To Tennessee. We're going to live with Ike's folks."

"Live away from here?" It had always been Eugie's fear, and Little felt now that he had made it come true because he had helped arrange the move of Quakertown. "Moms would have never wanted that."

"I don't know that it would matter to Mama now. She's gone away, too. But Ike's mother, poor soul, she's been struck down with apoplexy. Someone's got to look after her."

"Tennessee," said Little. "That's a good piece away. Feels far just standing here saying it. What about your school?"

"The girl who came up from Dallas is going to stay and take my place."

"Won't you miss it?" What Little really wanted to ask was, *Won't you miss me?*

"It's not the same here," Camellia said. "Not since they moved Quakertown. Ike's shop isn't doing hardly any business now that folks live so far away. He's already sold his chair and clippers and whatnot to a barber he knows in Aubrey. That money will get us to Tennessee. And I want to go. It's my chance to do something good. Maybe prove to you I'm not as wicked as you think I am."

Little thought of how his father had drowned in the river. "Shouldn't get too far from home," he said to Camellia. "Trouble comes and the folks who care the most about you aren't there to help."

"It's already decided. We're taking the train tomorrow. You come with us, Papa. Ike said it's all right."

"I don't need his permission to come and go. Besides, I got work to do here."

"Flowers and trees," Camellia said. "They mean more to you than your daughter."

"Treat a flower or a tree right, and it makes your life pretty. I loved you as hard as I could, always tried to show you the right way, and you ended up making everything as ugly as sin. I reckon you can try to find your own way now."

Camellia stamped her foot on the porch. "Stubborn, that's what you are. Nothing like Ike's mother and father. They're good Christian people. They believe in love, forgiveness." She took a scrap of paper from her pocket and flung it at Little. "There. That's their address. In case you ever want to find me."

She turned and hurried down the steps. Little opened the screen door and shouted after her. "You better hope they believe in forgiveness, if the truth ever comes out about you and Kizer Bell."

A few nights later, a blue norther came screaming in, and Little lay awake, listening to the windowpanes rattling, and the timbers of his house groaning. For a moment, he imagined the city had made a mistake and had sent the men with their horses and sleds to drag his house away, but it was only the wind. He got up and stoked the fire. He draped a quilt over his shoulders and sat next to the stove.

Sometime after midnight, the wind died down, and it was so quiet then. Little looked out his window and saw, in the moonlight, a lone figure come up from the trees along the creek and go running across the frozen ruts of the open land, helter-skelter, running first one way and then another, stumbling over the ruts, coming to rest, finally, at Little's gate. A call rose up in the cold night, and Little realized he was the only living soul in Quakertown to hear it: "Me, me, me!"

Such a mournful wail. Little couldn't help weeping for Eugie, and for Camellia, and for himself, the only one left who could open his door, and say to the idiot, Uncle Me, "Please, come in."

26

The temperature of the water, the bathhouse matron told Tibby, was one hundred degrees, cooled from one hundred and forty-three as it came from the springs. Thermal waters bubbling up from the rocks. Healing waters to cure arthritis, bursitis, neuralgia. Tibby lay back in the porcelain tub, the water lapping at her chin. She imagined that the heat was drawing out the poison of the years and years of liquor. Above her, a mosaic of stained glass spread out across the ceiling. Nude swimmers curled and stretched around the circle of pale blue. The women's hair flowed down past their hips. Tibby thought of Botticelli's painting, *The Three Graces,* in which the women in their diaphanous gowns came out at night to join hands and dance in a dark wood, daisies in bloom at their bare feet. Such a delicate, tender dance, full of mercy. One of the dancers laid her head to the side and gazed at another with such love, such yearning, as if she wanted something for her very badly and didn't know how to give it. Tibby imagined the swimmers in the stained glass watching over her, inviting her to give herself to the water, to rise from it healthy and whole.

Since she had arrived in Hot Springs, there had been only one ugly incident. One day, when Mr. Bell had gone to the Reno to try his luck at the slots, she had started to feel sorry for the two of them, the exiles, and she had paid a bellboy a handsome price to go across the street to the Southern Club, a discreet gambling house above a cigar store, for a bottle of gin. It was the same bellboy who, a few hours later, led her back to her room after she had tried to play the drum set left on the lobby bandstand. How silly she had been, she had told Mr. Bell when he had returned. His silly, silly Tibby. "There, there," he had told her. "We're only just getting started here. A little slip. Don't worry, you'll get back on track."

She took the baths at the Imperial, which featured the only private dressing rooms; the Buckstaff, with its Tuscan columns; the Superior, with its marble and brass. She adored the sun porches at the Ozark, the Quapaw, and the Maurice. After a bath and a massage, she liked nothing more than to sit on one of the porches in the warm glow of the afternoon sun, and to watch steam misting up from the fountains along the street.

Often, that summer, Mr. Bell joined her on the sun porch of the Maurice to listen to the racing results from Saratoga or Pimlico broadcast over the loudspeakers. He had sold the house in Denton and all the furnishings, going back only once to retrieve some photographs and keepsakes—the program from the Ariel Club's production of *A Midsummer Night's Dream,* which Tibby had autographed for him, an ivory-backed hand mirror he had given her for their first wedding anniversary, the clothing and personal items Kizer had left behind. Everything else Mr. Bell had let go— the paintings, the linens, the china, the silver, even his collection of guns and Kizer's Hudson speedster. He had come back to Hot Springs and said to Tibby, "We're rid of it now."

"Does it make you sad?" she asked.

"Not for a minute." He held her hand in the air between them and gently twirled her around. "Now that you're on the mend."

There had been such ugliness: the night she ran down the street in her nightgown, shouting, "Save me, save me," because for some reason she had assumed Andrew meant her harm; the day she tossed her clothes onto the lawn, every piece she owned, because she had suddenly been overwhelmed with the matter of choosing something to wear; the day she stood over Kizer, sleeping in his crib, after it was clear that he was lame, and felt the nearly irresistible urge to place a pillow over his face to save them both from misery.

She wanted that all out of her, every memory of it, so when she soaked in the porcelain tubs, she kept her eyes on the swimmers in the glass above her, thinking only of the motion of gliding and reaching and traveling back to the innocent girl she had once been.

One afternoon, as she sat with Mr. Bell on the sun porch of the Maurice, drinking Coca-Colas, she took note of the people coming to the fountain on the plaza to fill containers with the spring water. They brought glass jars, coffee cans, masonry crocks. Some of the people were crippled—the elderly with hands gnarled so badly from arthritis that they could barely grip their containers, blind children whose parents sprinkled water on their faces out of some hope that it would bring back sight.

"Look at them," she said to Mr. Bell. "I wonder how far they've traveled to reach these heavenly springs."

"Heavenly springs," he said with a sigh.

There were times when the incident with Eugie Jones seemed to belong to another world, one that had held him for a while and then let him go, but at odd moments, it seemed that it had reclaimed him, as now, when he saw the Negro woman at the fringe of the crowd, waiting for her turn at the fountain. She wore a long skirt and a pair of brogans. A man's slouch hat sat on her head. She kept her hands clasped in front of her, shyly bowed her head, and waited. But even when the crowd had thinned, she hesitated to go to the fountain. There was no sign that said WHITES ONLY, but it was obvious to Mr. Bell that the girl was either afraid or embarrassed because, unlike the others who had come, she had no container in which to catch the water.

"That poor girl," he said to Tibby. "Skittish as a deer. It breaks my heart. She puts me in mind of Camellia Jones."

Tibby poured the rest of her Coca-Cola into her glass and set the bottle down on the table. "Don't talk about that girl. It breaks my heart to think what she did to her baby. How does she live with that?"

"How do any of us live with the horrible things we've done? We find someone to love us, to make us feel human again. We believe in mercy."

The Negro woman had finally gone to the fountain. She was bent over, drinking from her cupped hands.

"It must have been what Kizer loved in her," Mr. Bell went on, talking softly, as if Tibby weren't there and he was talking to himself. "He must have seen some heartache, some sadness."

"I do believe in mercy," Tibby said, and her voice quavered. "I do." She edged her empty Coca-Cola bottle toward Andrew. "Take this bottle out to that girl. I can't bear to watch her slurping from her hands anymore."

Mr. Bell held up the bottle and studied it. "A bottle," he said. "Yes, that's what she needs, isn't it? A bottle to catch the water from the heavenly springs." He stood up from the table and started down the steps of the sun porch. Then he turned back to Tibby, and he said, "Don't be too hard on yourself," and suddenly she was overwhelmed with shame. She imagined that he understood what had remained unspoken between them: she couldn't yet forgive Camellia because she was still unable to forgive herself for the times she had watched Kizer sleeping as a baby and had wished him dead.

27

That autumn in Paris, Kizer kept company with a Mme. Blanchet. She lived in the rooms next to his at the Hôtel du Camélia—how could he have chosen any other?—in the Sixth Arrondissement. She was from Lyons and was seeing Paris, she said, during its crazy years, *les années folles,* after the war. Her husband, an army officer, had died fighting the Germans at Belleau Wood. "It was you," she said to Kizer when they first met. "You brave Americans who stopped the slaughter. And here you are with your wounded leg. Come, I will show you *la ville lumière,* the City of Light."

But they spent most of their days in the museums and their evenings in the crowded and dingy cafés, where Mme. Blanchet enjoyed the calvados, the marc, and the cognac. One night, toward the end of August, as they were riding in a taxi, she kissed Kizer, and immediately she turned her face away from him and touched the back of her hand to the glass in the taxi's door.

"You weren't in the war, were you?" she said. "The Great War?"

"My leg," he told her.

"It's not an injury from battle as you said?"

"I never said that."

"No, but you let me believe it," said Mme. Blanchet. "That was wicked of you."

Not long after that night, she began spending her days at a home for war orphans, telling Kizer he would now have to see the city on his own. She was busy attending to her little messieurs and mademoiselles. "My husband and I," she said, "we were never able to have little ones of our own."

Kizer, free then to choose his own diversions, began to take note of the fact that Paris was a paradise for children. It was clear from the parks and the steam-driven carousels, the pony rides and the puppet plays, that this was a city that cherished its young. After the summer months spent in dimly lit cafés and somber museums, at the insistence of Mme. Blanchet, Kizer was glad to be out in the open.

One afternoon, he left the Guignol puppet play on the Champs Elysées and glanced back at the man who was following him. He had noticed the man at other Guignols—in the Jardin des Tuileries, only yesterday, and before that, in Parc Montsouris and at the Jardin du Luxembourg. The man wore a woolen cap and a pair of gray overalls stained at the knees. He was a pleasant-looking man with a neatly trimmed moustache and creases at the corners of his eyes that deepened when he smiled, which he had done often whenever Kizer had happened to look his way.

The two of them had made a noticeable pair at the puppet plays, usually the only adults there who had come alone. They sat in the back rows, several seats between them, politely leaving the front rows to the parents who had brought their boys and girls to laugh at the little Guignol and his battles with his wife, Madelon, and his friend, the rascal, Gnaufron. Kizer came to watch the children, to thrill to their bright faces and their squealing laughs.

The man in the stained coveralls caught up with him when he stumbled, trying to get out of the way of a cart filled with children being pulled by an ostrich beneath the yellow canopy of the chestnut trees. A man in navy blue trousers and jacket walked alongside the ostrich and tapped its long neck with a stick if the bird hesitated. A light mist had settled over the avenue, and the cart passed so close to Kizer he could smell the ostrich's wet feathers.

"Monsieur." The man in the stained coveralls took Kizer by the elbow and held him out of the cart's path. The rim of one high wheel brushed his sleeve. "Be careful, monsieur. You would not want to end up in a battle like our dear friend Guignol."

Kizer anchored himself by leaning on his cane. "No," he said. "Of course not. *Merci.*"

"The pleasure is mine." The man released Kizer's arm. He removed his woolen cap and swept it in front of him as he bowed. "I am Etienne. You enjoy the little puppets, *oui?*"

"I like the children," Kizer said.

"As I thought." Etienne clapped his hands together. His coveralls smelled of gasoline fumes. "I could bring one to you. A little boy or a little girl, whichever you would like."

For a moment, Kizer didn't understand. Then Etienne winked and said in a hushed voice, "All very discreet, of course, monsieur," and Kizer knew Etienne had assumed he was a pedophile. Etienne reached into the breast pocket of his coveralls. "I have photographs, monsieur."

Kizer stopped him by raising his cane and pressing it against Etienne's hand, keeping whatever photographs were in his pocket hidden. "You've made a mistake," Kizer said. "A terrible mistake."

Etienne tilted his head to the side and studied Kizer with a puzzled look. "You do not like the children?"

Kizer was so flustered, so afraid someone passing might overhear their conversation, that he said, in a whisper that came out sounding desperate and lurid—not what he had intended at all—"Yes, I adore the children."

He turned then, and started walking toward the Place de la Concorde. But Etienne's voice, suddenly loud and sharp, stopped him. "I know where you are staying, monsieur. The Hôtel du Camélia, *oui*? Perhaps I will bring you something there soon."

Kizer spun around, but already, Etienne had disappeared into the crowd.

The next day, Kizer left his hotel at noon, planning another trip to the Marais, a quarter he had stumbled upon once when he had wandered off the Boulevard Beaumarchais. He had never felt so out of place, and yet so linked in spirit to the Poles in the Rue de Jouy, the Arabs in the Rue François-Miron, the Jews in the Rue des Rosiers. The Marais was home to Turks and Lebanese, to Chinese and Russians, to all manner of exiles who knew, as Kizer did, what it was to flee their homelands.

When he stepped from his hotel onto the Rue de Seine, he saw Etienne across the street, still in his stained coveralls. With him was a young girl, perhaps no more than twelve. She was wearing a pair of clogs, her socks folded at her ankles. Her legs were bare, despite the chilly day, her knees red just below the hem of her coat, a dark wool with some sort of fur around the collar and cuffs. She was looking down at her clogs, mesmerized, as if they were the most exotic shoes she had ever worn. She had a woolen hat pulled down over her ears, but Kizer could see the way her bangs fell over her forehead and came dangerously close to her eyes. Etienne was holding her by the elbow, and he must have pressed his thumb into the hard bone because she lifted her head and overwhelmed Kizer with her cool stare, so much like the nude with the fan of peacock feathers glancing back over her shoulder in the *Odalisque* he had seen with Mme. Blanchet in the Louvre. It was the face of Camellia the first time he touched her, put his hand on the sleek skin of her cheek. She stared at him with a calm acceptance of what was about to happen, and like then, as he stood there in the Rue de Seine, he was unable to look away.

Etienne waved, and then, his hand still holding the girl's elbow, he ushered her across the street. *"Bonjour,"* he said. He took the girl by the shoulders and placed her in front of Kizer. "As I promised, *oui*? This is Jeanne."

Jeanne d'Arc, Kizer thought. The Maid of Orleans. The martyred saint France had burned at the stake. He thought of Camellia. How her touch had thrilled him.

"How much?" he asked Etienne. He started to take his wallet from his coat.

"Please, monsieur." Etienne held up his hand. "Let us not discuss payment here."

"Where then?"

"Ahead in the alleyway beside the print shop."

When they were safely hidden in the dark alleyway, Etienne said, "Let me offer you this bit of money." He showed Kizer the note he had folded in his hand. "Now you may open your wallet as if you were offering me change."

Kizer held his wallet open and watched Etienne slip his note inside and remove two others. "For one hour, *oui*?"

"No," Kizer said. His hands were trembling. "The afternoon."

Etienne lifted an eyebrow and then smiled his pleasant smile. "As you wish," he said. Then he removed a larger note from Kizer's wallet. "I will return at five o'clock. I will wait across from your hotel." He slipped the notes into his coveralls and held his pocket open so Kizer could see the snub-nosed revolver nestled there. "You will abide by the terms of our agreement, monsieur. Otherwise, you will force me to find you. Now if you will wait here a few moments while I take my leave, you and Jeanne can then go on with your day."

Etienne turned and walked out of the alleyway and left Kizer and Jeanne alone. Kizer tried to brush her bangs away from her eyes. She cupped her hand and pressed it into his crotch.

He took her hand and held it gently. He started to raise it to his lips to kiss it, but then he stopped, horrified. Jeanne had lifted her face to look at him, and now, so it seemed to Kizer, there was judgment in her eyes. "Come," he told her, and then clutching her hand more tightly, he led her out of the alleyway.

They went first to the Petit Saint-Benoît where Kizer ordered two cassoulets and a bowl of plums for the girl. Jeanne kept her woolen hat on while she ate despite Kizer's best efforts to coax her to remove it. She kept her head bowed over her cassoulet and ate it slowly, sneaking glances at the white-aproned waiters passing their table with one steaming dish after another. When she had finished, her lips were stained purple with the juice of the plums. She grabbed a roll and stuffed it into the pocket of her coat.

After their luncheon, they walked to the Jardin du Luxembourg and strolled about the graveled walks and through the apple and pear orchards, stopping from time to time so Jeanne could toss pieces of the roll to the pigeons. Kizer persuaded her to ride in a pony cart, and when it was finally time for the Guignol, they made their way to the puppet theater and took their seats in the second row of benches. Schoolchildren were filling the benches around them, boys and girls in the company of parents or nursemaids. The little girls wore starched cotton frocks and long white socks that came to their knees. Their slippers were patent leather with dainty straps crisscrossing over the tops of their feet. Jeanne bit her lower lip and kept glancing about, pushing her feet back under the bench as if to hide the plain clogs. Kizer imagined that they must have seemed as unsophisticated and dour to her then as an old Dutch woman's wooden shoes.

He told Jeanne he had a pastille in one of his pockets and then made a game of her trying to find it. He twitched and giggled whenever she dipped her fingers into his vest pocket, his shirt pocket, as if she were tickling him, and she laughed and covered her mouth with her hand. When she finally found the pastille in the pocket of his coat, she refused to keep it for herself, insisting that he have it. He let her lay the lozenge on his tongue and her fingers lingered there.

The Guignol started then, and Jeanne sat with her hands on her bare knees. She leaned forward, enchanted with the puppets and the play, *La Boîte de Dragées*. She joined the other children in shouting out answers to the puppets' questions and squealed with delight as she watched their antics. It was only when Guignol and Gnaufron began to hit each other with sticks, arguing over the last pieces in the box of candy from the play's title, that she fell quiet. She folded her hands in her lap, sat back, and bowed her head.

When the play was over and they rose to leave, she reached out and took Kizer's hand.

It had been, to Kizer's way of thinking, the most marvelous day he had spent in Paris. But now, as they walked back to his hotel, he felt the sadness of each step. He knew, from the way Jeanne tightened her hold on his hand, that she felt it, too. It was nearly five o'clock, and Etienne would be waiting. Kizer would turn Jeanne back to him. What choice did he have? He could run now to the nearest police and tell Jeanne's unfortunate story, but Etienne knew his hotel. It came to Kizer, then, that just as he had lacked the courage to stop Camellia from going to Dr. L. C. Parrish, he would let Jeanne return to Etienne.

But five o'clock came and went, and the gaslights flared on in front of the Hôtel du Camélia, and Etienne was nowhere to be seen.

A wind had come up, and the air had more of a bite. Jeanne crossed her arms over her chest, hunched her shoulders, and stamped her feet.

Finally, at half-past five, Kizer took her into the hotel, up the stairs, to Mme. Blanchet's, where he knocked on the door.

Mme. Blanchet, when she answered, was in a silk dressing gown, a towel wrapped around her head like a turban. She took one look at Kizer and Jeanne standing there in the doorway, his hands resting on the girl's shoulders, and she shook her finger at him. "I knew I should have kept my eye on you. You've spoken so fondly of the children at the Guignols, and now you've stolen one."

He felt the heat come into his face. Even Mme. Blanchet had noticed how desperately he yearned for the children. He was embarrassed to tell her the story of his arrangement with Etienne. Jeanne sat on the bed while he told it all to Mme. Blanchet in a whisper.

When he was through, Mme. Blanchet went to Jeanne. She kneeled by the bed and took the girl's hands. Jeanne began to weep, and Mme. Blanchet pressed her to her bosom.

"This man, this Etienne," Kizer told Mme. Blanchet. "He has a gun. I'm afraid he'll come here intending to use it on me."

Still holding Jeanne, Mme. Blanchet turned her head so she could look at Kizer. He had never seen such a hard look on her face. "So because you're afraid, you're willing to give this child over to him?" Mme. Blanchet narrowed her eyes. "It's good you have your bad leg," she said. "Even whole, you would have been useless in the war."

"What would you have us do, then?" Kizer said.

"I'll take this girl to the orphans' home. Tonight. Now."

"And what about me? That gun?"

"Are you so miserable, so much a coward, that you cannot save one child?"

Jeanne lifted her face away from Mme. Blanchet and looked at Kizer, her cheeks shiny with tears.

"All right," he finally said, and he was overcome with love and fear, and disgust with himself for hesitating. "Yes. By all means. Take her."

A few minutes later, the three of them stood on the sidewalk in front of the hotel, waiting for a taxi. There were lights all along the Rue de Seine—bluish halos around the gaslights, soft yellow glows in the windows of the cafés.

"I won't go with you," Kizer said to Mme. Blanchet. "I imagine it would break my heart to see all those orphans. I'll see you get in the taxi safely, and then . . ."

His voice fell away, and he looked off down the street, imagining how lonely he would feel once Jeanne was gone. But it was the right thing. At least he would do this one good thing in his life.

Mme. Blanchet gave Jeanne a nudge and told her to say au revoir to M. Bell.

When Jeanne came to him, he couldn't keep himself from hugging her. He wrapped his arms around her slight shoulders and pressed her to him. He held her, thinking how he would have loved his own child—his and Camellia's—had circumstances been different. He held Jeanne until he felt her squirming in his arms, straining to get free, and it only made him hold her all the more tightly.

It was then, over the tops of passing motorcars, that he saw Etienne across the street, hands in his pockets, rising up on the balls of his feet as he waited for his chance to cross over to their side.

"It's him," Kizer said to Mme. Blanchet. "There across the street."

The taxi was pulling to the curb. Kizer bowed his head, intending to kiss Jeanne good-bye on her cheek, but she squirmed again in his arms; she twisted her head, and his lips found hers. They tasted of plums. He could feel her warm breath. Instead of pulling away, he kissed her the way he had kissed Camellia the first time, the way Mme. Blanchet had kissed him that summer— with hunger.

Later, if anyone were to ask, he would explain that the kiss had happened by accident, but he knew, even as he was making the story up in his head, it would be a lie. There had been a moment when he could have stopped himself, but he hadn't.

Then Jeanne broke free. She ran down the street and disappeared into the alleyway by the print shop.

Etienne darted out into the traffic and chased after her.

Kizer tried to follow and then realized how hopeless it was with his cane and his hobbling gait. He threw the cane into the alleyway. It clattered over the cobblestones. He leaned against the wall of the print shop, cursing.

Then he felt Mme. Blanchet's arm slip around his waist. "Don't blame yourself." She pressed herself against him. "There is evil in the world." Her voice was soft, intimate, breathless with pity and desire. "Evil," she said again. "We do what we can."

Kizer returned to his room and found a letter from his father, telling him not to worry about money. "You stay on," his father had written on light blue stationery bearing the watermark of the Arlington Hotel in Hot Springs. "Now that your mother and I are in the pink, there's no need for you to worry about the expense."

Mr. Bell had bought the DeSoto Valley Water Company and had begun distributing the mineral water across the country. He had changed the name to Heavenly Springs, and it was going great guns. The bottle labels, one of which he enclosed with his letter, bore a likeness of Tibby in a flowing white gown, angel's wings, a glow of light about her head. She was rising up from a clear pool of water, a saintly smile on her face.

According to the letter, she spent her days rehearsing an amateur theatrical group that performed musical revues at the Hot Springs hotels. "Your mother's a teetotaler now," Mr. Bell had written. "Thank God."

They were building a house in the mountains where they would be able to look down over the city that had saved them. "A house built on water," Mr. Bell joked. "Come home when you've gotten everything out of your system. Stay until spring if you like. Everyone should see Paris in the spring."

Kizer folded the letter and stuffed it back into its envelope. He wasn't sure how to feel about his parents' good fortune. He was thankful, of course, that his mother had righted the ship, and he was even happy for his father, who had explained in a previous letter the unfortunate circumstances that had led to his shooting of Eugie Jones. Kizer forgave him that, knowing as he did how little it took to spin a life out of control. The only thing that bothered him, the one tension he couldn't resolve, was the fact that one part of him longed to be in Hot Springs to share the resurrection his parents were experiencing there, while another part of him detested their renewal because it threatened to obscure everything that had preceded it, the largest part being that he had loved Camellia, had fathered a child with her, and then stood by, silent, losing first the child to Dr. L. C. Parrish's curette and then Camellia to Ike Mattoon.

Kizer went out into the night and found himself, with a crowd of others, in the Place Denfert-Rochereau, passing through the wooden gate that led to the catacombs, the ossuary where bones from the parochial cemeteries, beginning with the Cemetery of the Innocents, had been stacked at the end of the eighteenth century. The disinterments took place at night, the bones transported via covered wagons for the poor and funeral chariots and catafalques for the rich. Too many corpses had been buried in shared trenches. One grave digger, François Pontrain, claimed to have buried ninety thousand bodies in thirty-five years, in ditches only five meters deep. When the stench became too much, and milk and wine began to spoil, and people began to fall ill, the State Council ordered the Cemetery of the Innocents destroyed and the bones moved to the underground rock quarries.

Kizer tried to buy a candle from a man at the gate, a war veteran with a crutch under his arm, one trouser leg folded up and pinned above the knee of his stump, but the man wouldn't take the money. He lit the candle for Kizer, winking at him, as if they were comrades.

A trail of candle flames went down a set of spiral stairs, and

Kizer followed it, feeling his way with the tip of his cane. Finally, he came to a narrow tunnel and felt his shoulder rub the pebbled surface of the stone wall to his right. Behind him, he heard a woman giggle, and a man speaking angrily. Then he heard someone breathing behind him and felt something press into the small of his back.

"Turn around slowly, you scoundrel," the voice behind him said, and when he did, he saw Bert Gleason standing there, a candle in one hand, a shard of rock in the other.

"Mr. Gleason?" Kizer hadn't realized how homesick he had become until he found a familiar face before him.

Bert Gleason tossed down the rock and laughed. "Did I scare you, son?"

"Yes," said Kizer. "You scared me to death."

As they crept through the tunnel, Bert Gleason told Kizer that he had come to Paris after he had arranged the move of Quakertown. "I thought I owed it to myself to come across the pond and see gay Paree. I spotted you as you were going through the gate, but it took me a while to work my way through the crowd to you. Imagine! The two of us here."

The tunnel opened up into a gallery where the walls were lined with skulls and bones. The pattern was the same, alternating rows of skulls and thigh bones. Kizer heard someone remark that the remains of Rabelais, Madame de Pompadour, and Marat were mixed up there with the bones of those massacred in the Revolution.

"Between seven and eight million skeletons," a man with a British accent said. "That's history."

Kizer and Bert Gleason were both quiet, passing between the walls of bones. Only when they came out of the ossuary to the Passage Darceau off the Avenue de Parc Montsouris did they speak.

"That was a damned sight," Bert Gleason said. "Gloomy as hell. I don't know what I was thinking going down there tonight. Gay Paree? Not hardly."

The ossuary had left Kizer aching for home where his mother and father were living well. It was drizzling, a fine rain falling over the avenue. Kizer could feel winter coming to Paris. Soon the cold rains would strip the trees bare and there would be fog and snow. The glorious city would turn gray in the dim light, and the dusk would fall too soon. He thought of the warm baths of Hot Springs, the well-lit lobbies of the hotels.

"We live so poorly," he said to Bert Gleason. "Making choices willy-nilly. Always thinking, if we do this, if we do that, we'll finally be happy."

"If you ask me," Bert Gleason said, "we all have one moment we'd change if we could, but listen to us, prattling on like fools. I suppose those bones did this to us. God, it's good to see you, Kizer. I don't mind saying, ever since I've been here, I've felt like a stranger."

They began walking up the Avenue de Parc Montsouris, and for a good while neither of them spoke. It felt good to Kizer, after being away from home so long, to be in the company of someone he knew.

"So what's your moment?" he finally said to Bert Gleason. "The one you'd change if you could?"

"I'd say what I should have said one night years ago." Bert Gleason answered without hesitation, and Kizer could tell he had been hoping to have the chance to say what he had been thinking while they had been walking in silence. "I'd say, 'Yes, yes. It's true. I love her.' God, is this what Paris does to a man? Fills him with regrets?"

"Who was she?" Kizer could tell Bert Gleason wanted the opportunity to speak her name. "The woman you lost?"

"Eugenia Jiggs. As you can imagine, it was a delicate matter. I didn't have the courage to make my love for her public knowledge so I did something stupid and drove her away."

"Eugie Jones?" Kizer said.

"I'm sorry," said Bert Gleason. "I shouldn't have mentioned her and made you think of that nasty business with your father."

But that wasn't what Kizer was thinking at all. He was thinking instead that somehow the fates had sent Bert Gleason to Paris and that the two of them had gone down into the catacombs so they could rise and face this moment when Kizer knew he would tell Bert Gleason his own secret and that Bert Gleason, unlike his mother or father or Little Jones, would understand exactly what had burdened him all these months.

Kizer touched Bert Gleason's arm, and they stopped by a gaslight. "My moment involves a woman, too. In fact, you're going to find this hard to believe." And then, before he could stop himself, he told Bert Gleason about him and Camellia and the aborted child. "You see what a wretch I am?" he said. "All the ruined lives on my hands?"

Later, crossing the Atlantic on the S.S. *Europa*, he would recall the tender look in Bert Gleason's eyes, the way he wiped at his face and said it was the rain pooling in the hollows above his cheeks. "Dear boy," Bert Gleason said, "Camellia didn't abort the baby."

Kizer would stand at the deck and feel the salt spray sting his eyes and remember how he had said to Bert Gleason, "How do you know anything about this?"

"It was that woman, that nurse of Dr. Parrish's. She told me Camellia changed her mind."

"This nurse, does she know I'm the father?"

"No. She thinks it's Ike Mattoon, of course."

"You're sure Camellia didn't have the abortion?"

"That woman, Mavis Brown, I believe her name is. She was the attending nurse. Wouldn't she know?"

All the miles of ocean, with nothing to do but recall Bert Gleason's last words to him there in the rain of Paris. "You see how we're all connected. All part of it, whatever this living is. Go find her. Go home as soon as you can. Go. You'll always be sorry if you don't." All those miles to remember Jeanne, dear Jeanne, and how her escape from him and Mme. Blanchet had sent him down into the catacombs of the dead and saved him.

28

Each morning that winter, Little found his boots freshly shined, warming by the stove. Uncle Me slept in the bed where Camellia had slept before she had married and gone. He rose early, before dawn, and shined the boots. Then he treated himself to a nip from the bottle he kept in a drawer in the chifforobe in the bedroom Little Jones had let him have. There was a red velvet ribbon in the drawer, and Uncle Me liked to rub it against his face. There was a silver locket, turning gray with tarnish. Inside was a picture of Camellia and one of the white man he had seen with her one night in the country. To these trinkets, Uncle Me added a handful of seashells—the thin wafers of sand dollars, the scalloped fans of oysters, the beehives of snails—and a Prince Albert tobacco tin full of white sand.

Little bought a bottle for Uncle Me each Friday from Mr. Smoke who had moved his bootlegging operation to Rhodie Hill.

"I wouldn't think you be the kind to cozy up with bootleggers," Mr. Smoke said to him the first time he came and asked for a bottle. "Besides, I expect if you want a snort, you can get it with the whiteys. The way I hear it, you their monkey boy."

"It's not for me," Little said in a quiet voice. "It's for a friend."

Mr. Smoke tipped back his head and squinted through the blue haze of his cigarette smoke. "What friend that be? Didn't know there was a soul left in Quakertown."

"Uncle Me."

"Lands, no one seen him so long, we thought the Klux done got him."

"No, he was gone a while," Little said. "Now he's back."

Back in the summer, Uncle Me had jumped a freight train and had ridden all the way to Biloxi, Mississippi. There, he slept out on the beach, swam in the ocean, begged food from the crab houses, then got a job washing glasses at a speakeasy. When he rode a boxcar back to Denton, he found that Quakertown, except for the row of businesses on Frame Street and Little's house, was gone.

When Little asked him why he had gone to Biloxi, Uncle Me could manage no definite answer, only some vague rambling about the day the Klux had come and how he had decided to go off and try to find his mother.

"She walk out on you quite a good little bit ago, did she?" Little said to him.

"Gived me the mitten," Uncle Me said. His walleyes seemed to stare off to opposite corners of the room.

"Don't say it that way," Little told him. "That's what you say when a sweetheart starts making time with another fella. Say it like this. Say, 'She threw dust in my eyes and gave me the go-by.'"

"That what she did." Uncle Me blinked hard. "Throwed dust in my eyes."

Little bought the liquor for him because he wanted Uncle Me to stay. Otherwise, Little had too much quiet and too many unpleasant thoughts to fill it. Thoughts of Eugie and Camellia, all the things he should have said, and now both of them gone.

In the evenings, Uncle Me played his Jew's harp, and Little danced. Uncle Me sat on the floor, his knees up to his chest, his hands cupped around the harp. Little paced off the steps to whatever tune he could find in the twanging.

"You play that harp good," Little said one night.

"It was my daddy's," said Uncle Me.

"Your daddy dead now?"

"Yes, sir. He dead 'fore I bornt."

"Who told you that?"

"No one. That just what I figure."

Little knew the lies and shame that could fill a family. "My daddy's gone, too," he said. "You and me, we're on our own now."

"That right," said Uncle Me. "On our own."

When he drank, he laughed, a high-pitched giggle—*Hee-hee-hee. Hee-hee-hee*—and Little didn't mind it at all, welcomed it, even, the most joyous sound he had heard in his home for quite some time. Then, in an instant, Uncle Me would stop laughing. His eyes would close, and he would fall asleep. All night, his giggles echoed in Little's ears, even though he tried to shut them out, hearing them as laughs of ridicule, taunting him, the fool, his life reduced to dancing jigs for idiots twanging away on a Jew's harp, bribing him with liquor, the way folks would feed a dog to keep him faithful.

So one morning, when he went downtown to meet with Mr. Comstock at the City Commissioners' Office in the courthouse, Little was in no mood for the horticulturist's flashy gold cuff links, or his crisp linen suit, or the habit he had of shifting his eyes to the right or left of Little, just past his ears, as if Little were so slight, he couldn't quite locate him.

Commissioner Armor Heath, the real estate agent, was in attendance. He sat in the high-backed leather chair across the desk from Little and listened to Mr. Comstock explain his plans to cover the east slope of the park with lamium.

"That's asking for trouble," Little said.

Armor Heath was tapping a ruler against the edge of the desk, and when Little spoke, he stopped. He leaned forward, and the leather of the chair creaked. "What did he say, Comstock?"

Mr. Comstock tugged at his shirt cuffs. "I believe Mr. Jones is insinuating that lamium would be a poor choice for this locale."

"Is that right?" Mr. Heath said to Little. "Do you think you know something Mr. Comstock doesn't? Do you believe he's made an error?"

"It's the roots of that lamium," Little said. "They don't grow deep, not like lavender or thrift. On a slope like that? I'm afraid lamium would wash away."

Mr. Heath reached his ruler across the desk and struck the wood only inches from Little's hand. "So you do believe you have some special insight into this situation. Have you ever seen the botanical gardens in Dallas?"

"No, sir. I've never had the opportunity."

"Well, I can tell you they are a treasure to behold, and I can tell you that Mr. Comstock here is the one the fine people of Dallas have to thank for it. I'd say he must know a good deal about his business, wouldn't you?"

Little moved his hands from the desk and folded them in his lap. "I don't mean to question Mr. Comstock," he said.

"Of course you do," said Mr. Heath. "That's exactly what you're doing. You're saying Mr. Comstock, one of the finest horticulturists in these parts—hell, in the whole damned country for that matter—doesn't know his asshole from his elbow when it comes to what to plant on this slope. Unless, of course, I heard you wrong. That could very well be it. Is it, Little Jones? Did I misunderstand what you said?"

It was clear to Little, then, that without Bert Gleason there to back him, his word would amount to nothing when it came to the planning of the park. He understood that Mr. Heath was giving him a chance to retreat. He turned his head to the right and looked out the window. He could see the fountain where Eugie had died. How she would have loved this park, lamium or lavender or thrift. But he knew what he knew. The lamium was all wrong, and he had too much pride to let it pass, to someday have a bare slope and to hear people say, "That Little Jones. What a fool. Planted lamium there and it all washed away."

"No, sir," he said, in a firm voice. "You didn't hear wrong."

Mr. Heath shook his head. "You disappoint me, Little Jones."

"I'm just telling you the truth the way I know it."

"I assure you," Mr. Comstock said to Mr. Heath. "Lamium will have no problem thriving on that slope."

"You don't have to sell me." Mr. Heath pointed his ruler at Little. "Now here's the truth the way I know it. It's not too late to move your ass out to Rhodie Hill."

"Mr. Gleason wouldn't be partial to that."

"Well, Mr. Gleason's not here, is he?"

"No, sir."

"That's right. Now we're going to plant lamium on that slope just the way Mr. Comstock says, and it's going to be your place to see it survives. You got that?"

"Yes, sir," said Little. "I got it."

When Little left the Commissioners' Office, he drove his wagon out to Rhodie Hill. It was one of those fall days in Texas when the sun gets so bright and hot it seems that winter might never come. Meadowlarks, their yellow chests full and gleaming, perched on fence posts, only to rise up with a flutter as Little's wagon passed.

"Scaring everything off, Mr. Mule," Little said. "Don't hardly anyone want anything to do with Little Jones right now."

The red oaks with their fiery leaves shaded him for a while, but soon they gave way to open land, the hills dotted with scrawny mesquite. In the full glare of the sun, Little thought of the long walk from Rhodie Hill to the College for Industrial Arts, and he imagined his former neighbors, the folks he had convinced to leave Quakertown, cussed his name with every step they took because they believed he was living high on the hog in the company of white men like Mr. Comstock and Mr. Heath.

When Little's wagon reached the crest of the hill and he saw the houses spread out in the scrub of what had once been a cow pasture, their unpainted clapboards scaling and peeling in the heat of the sun, he realized that he had no idea now where he belonged in the world. The people who knew him best had left him. Eugie was dead, and Camellia was in Tennessee, and he had driven his friends from Quakertown away to this hill where there were no trees, only the endless sky and the white glare of the sun.

Mr. Smoke was tending the still he kept in a shed he had built from scrap lumber. He was stoking the fire burning beneath the boiler, poking at the logs with a pitchfork. Little listened to the flames crackle, watched the sparks fly up in a glittery haze. Finally, Mr. Smoke straightened up and leaned on his pitchfork. "So it's you again," he said to Little. "Come out to see what you missing out here? Wanting to get you some of the good life? Well, you come on a good day. Cessie got her skirt up. Step outside and get you a good whiff."

Little knew Mr. Smoke was making reference to the open sewage trench and the foul odor that hung over Rhodie Hill. On one of his visits, he had watched Sibby Long, whose boarding-house had finally been moved, burn black flies off her screen door with a match. "Didn't have flies like this back in Quakertown," she had told him with a sneer. "And the skeeters so bad they like to eat you alive."

"I come for another bottle." Little took his coin purse from his hip pocket and found two one-dollar bills. "I guess the price is the same as usual."

Mr. Smoke shook his head. "I got nothing for sale."

"What about those bottles there?" Little pointed to a crate sitting along one wall of the shed.

"Them bottles?" Mr. Smoke smiled at Little. "Them bottles for my special customers."

"I buy from you every week," Little said.

"Not no more you don't." Mr. Smoke jabbed the tines of the pitchfork into the dirt floor. "You starting to cost me business. Folks don't like seeing you around here. Just between you and me, I believe they people out here just as soon do you harm."

"Don't have to worry about floods out here," Little said. It was the only advantage he could see for the folks living on Rhodie Hill.

"Folks got a long way to go to their jobs at the college," Mr. Smoke said. "Me? I had to up and quit. Don't got no automobile, don't got no wagon, too old to make that walk. And it too far to walk to do business down in old Quaker. Can't stop in at RCO's for an ice cream, can't go to Billy Moten's for something when we puny. Got to do all our business on the square with the whiteys. You sold us out, Little Jones. You go on home now, and remember I'm doing you a favor telling you all this. Best lay low for a time. Folks mad here, and you the one they mad at."

"It was Mr. Bell's idea first," Little said, "and then Mr. Gleason's."

"You the one talked it up," Mr. Smoke said. "Besides, can't do nothing against the whiteys. Tried to the night they killed your Eugie and you the one what put a stop to it. Probably a good thing, too, but folks don't think about that now. All they know is they in a misery out here, and you the one easy to blame. Kill a white man, you end up lynched. Nigger kill a nigger? Whitey don't care about that."

Uncle Me had enough left in his last bottle to please him that night. The next morning, Little sat on his porch and waited for the folks from Rhodie Hill to pass on their way to the college. In the still air, he heard the faint echo of their voices, the bright music of their laughter, and he didn't know which pained him more, to be so far away from whatever joy they had found, or to watch them fall silent when they finally came into view and saw him. He didn't call out to them, as he had done back in the summer, and they kept staring straight ahead, refusing to acknowledge him or to recognize the naked land where their homes had once stood.

When Little was sure that everyone had passed, he started walking to Rhodie Hill. He knew that if he didn't get a new bottle, Uncle Me would fly into the heebie-jeebies and then who knew what might happen.

At Rhodie Hill, Little left the dirt road and circled through a pasture to the rear of Mr. Smoke's shed. He crouched behind a mesquite tree and watched a white wisp rise up through the vent Mr. Smoke had cut in the shed's roof. Little knew the still was in operation, and he waited until he saw Mr. Smoke come out of his shed and go into his privy. Then Little made his way through the pasture, slipped into the shed, and grabbed a bottle. He left two one-dollar bills on top of the crate.

He was on his way back across the pasture when he heard Mr. Smoke calling after him, "I see you, Little Jones. Ain't you took enough from me? I tried to warn you. I told you to stay clear of this place."

Little was running, then, afraid the next thing he heard would be a shotgun blast, but the only sounds were the weeds whipping against the legs of his overalls, and the pounding of his own heart, a heart that beat with loneliness and shame.

"You better be grateful for that," he told Uncle Me when he got back to his house and showed him the bottle. "I had to put my neck on the line to get it."

Uncle Me pulled the cork from the bottle with his teeth. Then, he took the cork from his mouth and offered the open bottle to Little.

"No," Little said. "That's for you. I won't be taking none."

"You good to me." Uncle Me took a drink from the bottle and wiped his mouth with the back of his hand. "All the others run out, but you stayed."

"That's right. I stayed." Little turned to the window and saw a man walking up the hill, a white man with a cane and a crooked walk, and Little knew it was Kizer Bell. "For better or worse, I stayed. Go on and put your bottle away. Go on now. Looks like we got company."

Uncle Me jammed the cork back into the bottle's mouth and carried it back to his bedroom. Little opened the door and stepped out onto the porch to meet Kizer Bell.

29

Kizer had walked from the train station, going over and over in his head exactly what he would say to Camellia. He would tell her it wasn't too late for them. "I know you're going to have the baby," he would say. "Our baby. Doesn't that mean something? Doesn't that mean you still feel something for me?" He would tell her what Bert Gleason had told him in Paris, that they were all connected. That no matter if she turned him away, he would always be with her. "Might as well give in to it," he would say. "Just accept what's always been meant to be."

But when he was finally there, it was Little Jones standing before him, the front door open just a crack, and what Kizer said was, "Mr. Jones, I've come to talk to Camellia." He took off his fedora and waved it in front of his face. "I've walked all the way from the train station."

"Camellia's not here." Little came across the porch, and Kizer had no choice but to retreat to the steps. "Not much of anything here anymore. Look around."

Kizer was in an awkward position, his left foot up on the top step, his right foot two steps lower. He had nowhere in front of him to go, so he moved back down the steps and stared up at Little Jones.

"I'd like you to tell me, please, where I might find Camellia."

Kizer shaded his eyes with his hat. "I've come a very long way to speak with her. All the way from Paris."

"Can't tell you where Camellia is," Little said.

"Can't or won't?"

"Won't," said Little. "You go on back to Paris or wherever it is you have to go. Let Camellia be."

Kizer squinted up at Little. "Did she ever tell you the truth about the baby?"

"She's having Ike's baby."

"No," said Kizer. "It's my baby. That's what I've found out. She didn't go through with the abortion like I thought."

"You expect me to cozy up to that?" Little said. "White man tell a colored man any kind of lie."

"I swear it's the truth," said Kizer.

Little shook his head. "I've had enough trouble to last me, trouble you and your father caused. Camellia has, too. What good could come if I told you where she was?"

"I'll do whatever she says. If she tells me to go away, I will."

"That's what I'm telling you," Little said. "Telling you for the last time. Leave me and my family alone."

Kizer put his hat back on his head. "I won't give up easy on this." He leaned heavily on his cane. "I love Camellia."

"Too late for love now," Little told him. "There's been too much heartache for that."

30

Kizer's train from Denton arrived in Hot Springs a little past four that afternoon. He stored his steamer trunk at the station and started walking to the Arlington Hotel. As he passed the Fordyce, he heard a woman singing, and he knew it was his mother. He heard applause rise up, and then a man's voice boomed out, "Bravo, Tibby. Bravo." Kizer started up the walkway to the Fordyce and was surprised to see his father hurrying toward him, his arm uplifted, the tails of his overcoat flapping around his legs.

"Kizer, my word." Mr. Bell grabbed his hand and gave it a vigorous shake. "Aren't you one for surprises? What are you doing here?"

"I was listening to Mother sing," Kizer said.

The people on the third story of the Fordyce were still clapping and calling out for Tibby to sing an encore. Mr. Bell glanced up at the open doorway. "Your mother," he said. "She's a peach. I swear, Kizer. You wouldn't know her now. Did you get the bottle label I sent to Paris? Your mother's the angel of Hot Springs."

"I never knew she could sing like that."

"There's so much you've never known about your mother. My word, I'm glad you've come back. Let's go on up to the music room and let her know you're here."

By the time they had ridden the elevator to the third floor of the Fordyce and walked into the music room, Tibby was singing "Daisy." She was standing by the piano, her hands clasped demurely in front of her, and her voice was light and sweet, the way it must have been, Kizer thought, when she was a girl. He stood with his father, just inside the door, watching his mother—how young she looked—in the warm glow of lamplight.

"Look at her," Mr. Bell whispered. "Didn't I tell you she turned herself around. For the first time in years, I think she's really happy."

The people in the audience were swaying with the tempo of the music. Some of them had closed their eyes and were humming along.

Kizer leaned in close to his father. "I want you to help me. That's why I've come here."

"Help you?" said Mr. Bell. "Well, of course I'll help you. Anything you want."

"It's Camellia Jones. I've learned something surprising. She's kept the baby. My baby. She didn't abort it like we thought."

Mr. Bell took in a deep breath. He nodded his head toward the doorway, and they went out onto the landing. "You've seen her?" he said. "You know this to be true?"

"I haven't seen her. No. But I've heard the news."

"Gossip," said Mr. Bell. "You know how people talk."

"It came from the doctor's nurse. Why would it be a lie? I've been to Denton, but she doesn't live there anymore."

"Denton," Mr. Bell said in a grim voice.

"I've come here to ask you to help me. I intend to find her. No one in Denton would tell me anything, not even her father. You must know someone, someone in the Klan, who could get Little Jones to talk."

"You're asking me to bring more misery to that man?"

"I wouldn't want him hurt. Just persuaded, I guess you'd say."

Inside the music room, the piano was playing gaily and people were singing along with Tibby.

"That ugly life is behind us," Mr. Bell said with a hard edge to his voice. Then he smiled and patted Kizer on the back. "Nothing but blue skies here. Why stir it all up? Quick, put a smile on. Here comes your mother now."

At first, Tibby was shy around him. "Kizer," she said. "Why, Kizer. Here you are."

"I was listening to you sing," he said. "Marvelous. I kept thinking, She's found herself. You have, haven't you, Mother? You've found the girl you were that night at Wright's Opera House . . ."

Tibby put a finger to his lips. "Shh," she said. "Let's not talk about sad things now. I've had enough to last me."

"I'm sorry I've been part of it, your sadness." Kizer tapped his lame leg with his cane. "I suppose I'll always remind you of that part of your life you've come here to escape."

"Oh, that's nonsense," Tibby said. "Complete rubbish. Really, it is. Honestly, I swear. I've never heard such nonsense. Have you, Andrew? I mean, really. The idea."

She chattered on and on, her voice giving way to nervous laughter from time to time, and Kizer understood that what he had said, that he would always be a reminder to her of her old, wretched life, was true.

Mr. Bell clapped his hands together. "I feel like celebrating," he said. "We should have a grand dinner this evening. We should have a feast. The prodigal son has returned. Isn't that worth a feast? Aren't you famished, Tibby?"

She took Kizer's hand. "It's time to forget old wounds, at least to forgive them." She folded his fingers into a fist and then closed her own hand around it. "We're family," she said.

They dined at the Arlington, and then later they walked up the street to the headquarters of Heavenly Springs, a three-story building with six Tuscan columns along its front. Inside, Kizer could hear dance music coming from somewhere above them.

"I added the top floor," Mr. Bell said. "Your mother rehearses her theatrical group there in the afternoons. Saturday nights, we use if for dancing." With a sweep of his hand, he indicated the marble stairway. "Shall we?"

Kizer hesitated. "Is there an elevator?"

"We'll take our time," Mr. Bell said. "No hurry. Here, I'll help you."

He tried to put his arm around Kizer's waist, but Kizer pushed him away. "I'll manage, Father. You don't have to do me any favors."

"Kizer," Tibby said with a nervous laugh. "Don't be rude. We're having such a grand time. Don't ruin it."

"Oh, he didn't mean anything," said Mr. Bell. "He's absolutely right. I should have put in an elevator. Don't you worry, Tibby. We're painting the town tonight."

"Well, if we're going to paint it," she said, "let's make sure we paint it red and not black. We're not in mourning, are we?"

"No, we're not in mourning," Mr. Bell said. "We're all in fine spirits. Aren't we, Kizer?"

Just then, a woman appeared on the second-story landing. She was wearing a sleeveless dress made of black velvet and a strand of white pearls around her neck. "Tibby," she said, "you've finally come. Thank God. Come, give us a song with the band."

Tibby waved at the woman. "I'll be along in two shakes, Mira."

The lights brought out the olive tones in Mira's skin, and, looking up the stairway at her, Kizer thought of Camellia.

Then he felt his mother's hand stroking his arm, and he couldn't recall ever feeling her touch him in such a tender way.

"I must be a reminder to you, too. A reminder of so much misery. I know you've always been ashamed of me." Her voice was gentle and kind. "But I'm different now. I have friends here. I've learned how to love people again. I've learned how to love my-self. Hot Spring teaches you that, how to love the flaws in peo-ple. The longer you're here, the more you'll know it's true."

Kizer felt, then, that he could tell his mother the truth about Camellia, that she still carried his child, but he didn't know how to find her. He could tell his mother that, and she would do what his father had been unwilling to do. She would find someone who would make Little Jones talk.

"Mother, I have to tell you why I can't be jolly tonight."

"Tell me," Tibby said. "You can tell me anything."

He meant to tell it all to her, but just then a Negro man wear-ing a white jacket bowed to them. "Miss Tibby," he said. "It's good to see you. Let me take your coat, ma'am."

"Goodness, yes," Tibby said. "I was starting to swelter. It's so good to have you people around."

Kizer turned to his father with an accusing stare. "You employ servants?"

"Attendants," his father said. "For people's comfort."

Kizer couldn't tell his mother his story then, now that he un-derstood that she would always think of Camellia as one of "those people." So he told the story of Jeanne and how he had failed to save her.

"That poor child," Tibby said in horror, and Kizer was satisfied with her response. "That poor, poor child. The world can be such an ugly place, but you, Kizer—you've always had a good heart."

Mira called down once more from the landing. "Hurry, Tibby. Everyone's been asking for you."

"Come on," Tibby said to Kizer. "I want you to dance with me."

Here was his chance to redeem himself for refusing such an offer on their first trip to Hot Springs.

"You're my son," Tibby said. "I want to show you off."

So he went upstairs to the ballroom, and he danced with his mother, leaning into her. His left foot came down clumsily on the white maple floor, but he didn't care. It was enough to be there with his mother, more wonderful than he could have ever imagined. They danced in the light of the pagoda lanterns, danced beneath the crystal chandelier and the hand-painted peacocks and cherry trees on the ceiling. As they danced waltzes and fox-trots, other couples worked their way close to them so they could chat with Tibby and ask her to introduce them to her escort. Her response was always the same: "This darling young man?" she said. "This is my son. Kizer. He's been abroad, but now he's come home."

Just after midnight, Mr. Bell drove Kizer to the train station so they could arrange for someone to haul his trunk to the Arlington, where they were staying while the builders were finishing their new home in the mountains. Tibby had gone to their room to retire for the evening.

Kizer was thinking, as his father drove down Central Avenue past the bathhouses, that she was indeed a different woman than the one he had left that summer. She was sweeter, more serene, yet with a vigor he found exhilarating. She had told him about the theatrical group she directed and the Christmas show they were putting together. She was up at six-thirty every morning for a brisk hike up one of the mountain fitness trails or a vigorous session in the Fordyce's mechanotherapy room, favoring the rowing machine, the electric horse, or the tissue oscillator. A twenty-minute soak in a tub followed her exercise. Then she took an application of hot packs in the Turkish Hot Room, a needle shower, a rest in the cooling room, and finally a massage. After breakfast at the Arlington, she went to the hospitals—the Army and Navy, the Woodman of the Union, the Leo N. Levi Memorial, or St. Joseph's—where she performed for the patients. After lunch, she rehearsed her actors, and in the evening, she and Mr. Bell went dancing at the Eastman, Club Dreamland, or Whittington Park when the weather was warm. "I keep myself busy," she had told Kizer. "There's always something to be done."

"So you see what I mean about your mother," Mr. Bell said to Kizer as he parked at the train station. "She has a wonderful life here, a full life. Everyone loves her. I wouldn't want to see anything ruin that."

"You're referring to Camellia and the baby," Kizer said.

Mr. Bell pressed down on the foot pedal to engage the parking brake. "You made a mistake. Lord knows I've made my own. But don't be a fool twice. If you try to find this girl, all of us might lose more than you can imagine."

"Would you call your child a mistake?" Kizer said. "Is that what you've always thought of me?"

For a good while, Mr. Bell didn't answer. Kizer stared straight ahead, through the windows of the train station. He could see a dim light burning, and a janitor, a Negro man wearing overalls, sweeping the floor.

"If I do what you ask," Mr. Bell finally said, "arrange for someone to get an answer out of Little Jones, I'll have to become the sort of man I thought I'd put behind me forever. And I have to think of your mother. If people find out about that girl and her baby, I'm afraid to think how they might shun us. If your mother were to lose the life she has here, I can't say what might happen to her. It's not that I hate Negroes, Kizer. Really, it isn't. But I'll do anything to protect your mother."

"This is my family we're talking about." Kizer turned to his father. "Camellia and the child."

"No, this is a girl you lay down with, and the child is the result of your fornication. This is another man's wife. If she wanted any part of you, she would have told you the truth about the baby. She's trying to get on with her life. I suggest we all try to do the same." Mr. Bell opened his door, and Kizer felt the cold air outside. "Still, if it's the only way for you to be happy, I'll help you. I'll help you because you're my son—not a mistake—but a son your mother and I brought into this world with love, and I don't want to see you suffer. I'd only ask that you consider your mother. However she may have hurt you in the past, for God's sake, forgive her."

"I don't want to hurt Mother," Kizer said, "but I have to know where Camellia is. Please, Father."

"All right. I'll see what I can do."

It took only a few days. Mr. Bell telephoned Bert Gleason, who was home now from Paris, and Bert Gleason went out to Rhodie Hill and started asking questions. Mr. Bell received his telegram on an afternoon when Kizer and Tibby were on their way out for a trip to the observation tower at the top of Hot Springs Mountain.

"Kizer, I must have a word with you." Mr. Bell took him by the arm and led him over to the railing around the Arlington's portico. "I've heard from Denton on the matter that we discussed."

"Camellia," Kizer said. "Where is she?"

"She's in Tennessee."

"Where in Tennessee? Quick, Father. For God's sake, tell me."

"There's something that you should know first," Mr. Bell said. Then, in a kind voice meant to disguise the fact that he himself was thankful for this news, he told Kizer that Bert Gleason had discovered that even though Camellia hadn't aborted the baby, there was a chance that it wasn't even Kizer's. The boardinghouse owner, Sibby Long, had reported that before they were married Ike and Camellia had carried on in his room. "This Sibby Long heard them," Mr. Bell told Kizer. "Son, there's no way to know for certain that the child is yours."

This was the news that Kizer carried with him as he and his mother rode the elevator one hundred and sixty-five feet to the top of Rix Tower. As the elevator stopped at the observation deck, Kizer said to Tibby, "Mother, I have something to tell you."

Then the elevator door opened, and the wind rushed into his face.

"Brace yourself," Tibby said. She secured her hat by tying a pink sash beneath her chin. When she stepped out onto the observation deck, the ends of the sash ruffled out into the wind.

Kizer swore he felt the tower move. "Good Lord," he said. "Is this safe?"

"Is anything?" she asked him. "Come on, Kizer. We both know how quickly everything can change. You start out thinking you'll know yourself forever; then one day you look in the mirror, and you don't recognize the person staring back at you. That's what the liquor did to me. Now look how far I've come." She moved to the waist-high rail that ran around the perimeter of the deck and swept her arm out into the air. "I like it up here because it reminds me of how careful I have to be. On top of the world one minute, but if I slip . . ." She bent at the waist and leaned out over the rail. "Oh, doctor. It's a long way down."

Kizer took her by the arms and pulled her back to him. "Mother, stop. You're scaring me."

He remembered once when he was a boy, a cousin had swung a baseball bat and accidentally hit him in the eye. That night, his mother had tried to put hot compresses on the swollen eye, but he whined and complained that the washcloths were first too hot, and then too cold. Finally, Tibby, her hands unsteady with drink, cried out, "I can't take care of you. I can't." She threw on a coat and started for the door, but Kizer ran to it and spread his arms across it, knowing this was the only mother he had, imperfect as she was, and if he lost her, then where would he be.

"When I feel the wind up here," Tibby said, "I know what your grandmother must have felt that night before she stepped off the sleeping porch. How easy it would be. Just one step, and she'd be falling. She must have thought what a relief that would be, just to give herself up to gravity. I used to walk through our house and think what a chore it was to put one foot in front of the other. Now I come up here to remind myself to keep walking, to keep feeling my body and the earth and the motion that keeps me anchored to it. Nothing's ever safe, is it, Kizer? Not completely. That's what drunks know."

"You're right," he said. "Let's not talk about those days. Thank God they're behind us."

"Thank God they didn't ruin us forever. Now what is it you want to tell me?"

Suddenly, on top of the tower, the wind raking across him, Kizer was afraid to tell his mother about Camellia and the baby. His father was right; she was another man's wife. She had been giving herself to Ike all the time Kizer had thought her his, and now she had chosen. Just as it had been when they were children, she was gone. The only consolation Kizer could take from giving up on finding her was the one her mother had offered that Sunday morning when she had come to ask for the fifty dollars; letting Camellia go proved that he loved her.

Now he looked out over the mountain peaks to the blue sky dissolving into a white haze at the horizon, and the size of the world overwhelmed him. It was too big, and even though there was a chance that the child she carried was his, the risk of finding Camellia was too great. What would he say to her, and what would it mean for his mother, who was there now before him, waiting with her radiant smile, the same smile as she ascended on angel's wings on the Heavenly Springs bottle label.

"I wanted to tell you," he said, "how proud I am of what you've managed here. How much I love you, Mother."

She took his hand and squeezed it. "And I you, Kizer." She pointed out to the west. "Do you see the point of that mountain? That's Mount Riante." He could see a sparkle of glass and red, glazed tile. "That's the house we're building, your father and I. That's where we're going to live. Will you stay with us, Kizer?"

He thought of the war orphans in France. Mme. Blanchet had told him how they cried in the night for home. He thought of his grandmother hurtling through the air, the ground rushing up to meet her. He prayed that Camellia's child would have a good life, would know love, the love he felt now for his mother.

"Yes," he told her. "I'll stay."

31

One day, Uncle Me came to Little with a silver locket he had found in the drawer of the chifforobe. He opened it and showed Little the pictures of Camellia and Kizer. Little took the locket and studied the pictures, feeling a burning in his stomach to think of all the sorrow they had caused with their carrying on. The locket, with its small photographs hidden away, as if there were any way in the world to be discreet about this, only reminded Little of how Camellia, and even Eugie, had kept so much from him, and the thought filled him with rage.

"What do you know about this?" Little said to Uncle Me.

"I seen them." Uncle Me giggled. "Seen them fuckin'."

Little swung the locket by its chain and slapped Uncle Me in the face. He swung it again and again. "That's my daughter you're talking about like she's a whore." Every bit of anger that had lain dormant inside him the past months was coming out now, as he whipped the locket through the air. "I won't have that talk, do you hear?"

Uncle Me crouched down, his arms crossed in front of his face. "I seen them," he said again.

Little beat him with his fists, his hands coming down on his head, his back, whatever he could reach, beat him until Uncle Me finally pushed him away, and ran from the house.

*   *   *

At first, Little's rage was so great he was glad Uncle Me was gone. Then night fell, and the only sound in Little's house was the slide of his own steps across the floorboards, such a sorrowful scraping like the noise rats made when they got down in the walls or a bird, its wing tips scrabbling frantically as it tried to lift itself from a stovepipe. Little imagined listening to the sound of his own footsteps for years and years to come, and as he sat in the dark house, he began to regret what he had done to Uncle Me, an idiot who had only told the truth. If anyone should be brought to judgment, Little knew, it was Camellia and Kizer Bell, Eugie and Little himself. They had all, to some degree, been unable to say everything they had known and felt. Uncle Me had stated the fact of what he had seen. He had told the truth in a way no one else had, and Little, because it had been too much for him to hear, had driven away the only friend he had left.

He went into the bedroom where Uncle Me had slept and opened the drawer of the chifforobe. The moon was up and its light flowing in through the window cast a glow on the red ribbon that had been Camellia's, and the bottle from Mr. Smoke's, and the seashells Uncle Me had taken such pride in showing Little. Every so often, he would haul them out and lay them in Little's palm. "This one," he would say, "and this one, and this one, and this one." And Little would tell him they were pretty, and Uncle Me would grin. Little knew, at those times, what Uncle Me was feeling because he, too, had once found something beautiful and delicate in the world—the white lilac—and had brought it back for people to admire. Some nights, he would find a shell laid carefully on his pillow, and he would go to sleep, worrying the whorls and grooves with his fingers.

He lit a lantern and hitched his mule to his wagon. Then he drove it across the leveled and graded plain of what had once been Quakertown. From time to time, he called out, "Me." If there had been anyone there to watch, they would have seen the light of the lantern bobbing through the dark, would have heard the groan of the traces and the cries of, "Me, Me, Uncle Me."

At the creek, he turned the mule around and made his way to Frame Street. RCO's Ice Cream Parlor was closed, as was Billy Moten's Apothecary. Little kept looking for Uncle Me but saw no one along the street or down the alleys.

There was a single light burning in Dr. L. C. Parrish's office above Nib's Grocery. Little pulled back on the reins and stopped the mule. He got down from the wagon and wrapped the reins around a streetlight pole. Then he climbed the stairs to Dr. Parrish's office, and he knocked on the door's frosted glass.

"Come in if you're sick," Dr. Parrish called out. "If you're not, go away."

Little opened the door and stepped into the office, blinded momentarily by the harsh light of the goosenecked lamp burning on the desk. For a moment, he couldn't locate Dr. Parrish; then he spotted him in the corner by the parrot's cage. He was holding out peanut kernels for the bird to take.

"Well, if it isn't the devil himself," Dr. Parrish said.

"It's me," said Little. "Little Washington Jones."

"The way your name's being said these days, it might as well be Lucifer."

"I came to ask you a question."

"Ask away. What I don't know, maybe Marcus Garvey here will."

"Last summer, my wife brought our daughter here."

"Could be," Dr. Parrish said. "That seems like a long time ago now. Lots of water under the bridge since then."

"I'd think you'd remember this."

"A D-and-C." Dr. Parrish leaned his face in close to the parrot's cage and clucked his tongue. "That's what you're referring to."

"I don't know the fancy name for it, the name you doctors use. To my way of thinking, no name could make it something easy to hear."

"Dilation and curettage." Dr. Parrish fed the last peanut kernel to Marcus Garvey and then clapped the dust from his hands. "Abortion."

"Is that what you did to my Camellia? I can't tell you how much it matters that I know. It could mean everything." Little walked over to Dr. Parrish and touched him on the arm. "Isn't it your job to keep folks from suffering?"

"I cure ailments of the body," Dr. Parrish told Little. "People's souls are their concerns."

"Did you take the baby from her?" Little's voice was so soft, so full of anguish and dread, it was impossible for Dr. Parrish to refuse it.

"No," he said. "I did not."

Little drove his wagon to the end of Frame Street and turned to the east toward home. It was then that he saw the flames and smelled the smoke and knew that his house was on fire.

By the time he got to the house, flames were spewing from the window frames, curling up to the roof. He ran into the yard, thinking he would save something of Eugie's—her sewing basket, a dress from her wardrobe, the portrait they had asked a photographer to make on the day of their wedding.

He had to cover his face with his arms, the heat was so intense. He made it as far as the front steps, but then the porch roof came crashing down, embers searing his hands and neck, burning holes in his corduroy coat, and he backed away, choking on the black smoke.

From the yard, he looked through the window, through the shimmering tongues of fire, and saw Uncle Me standing in the middle of the living room, surrounded by flames, his hands over his eyes.

"Run," Little shouted, "run."

But Uncle Me just stood there, and all Little could do was turn away, remembering his father's stories of the Civil War and how in dry weather artillery shells could spark grass fires, and soldiers could find themselves surrounded, no way out, no way for anyone to save them, no choice but to burn. Little knew this was how Camellia had felt all along. He braced himself by grabbing onto the trunk of the white lilac, imagining that soon he would hear Uncle Me cry out, but there was no human sound, only the crackle and roar of the fire.

Three

32

Pearl Mattoon could say two words plainly—*no* and *good*—but she often confused them, said one when she meant the other, and became frustrated when Camellia misunderstood what pleased her and what didn't. Each morning, Camellia cooked oatmeal or fried cornmeal mush while the Reverend Heddy Mattoon dressed Pearl and said his morning prayers in their bedroom. Camellia moved about the cold kitchen, one of Ike's sweaters buttoned over her swollen stomach, feeling the baby, so close to time, squirm and bump inside her. When she rubbed her hand over her abdomen, she could feel the outline of the baby, the head up high, as the granny woman had told her. A breech. "Child," the granny woman had said, "we got to get that baby turned."

They tried holding ice to Camellia's abdomen at the spot where the baby's head rested. "Baby turns away from the cold," the granny woman said once. She held a coal oil lamp between Camellia's legs. "Ain't no living thing can help but come to the light."

But nothing worked—not the cold or the light, not hot baths or drinking glass after glass of water, or Camellia standing on her head.

"You gots a stubborn baby," the granny woman told her. "That for sure. Maybe you afeared and keeping too tight down there. Maybe you don't want to let this baby out."

"No," Camellia said. "That's not true."

On occasion, in the afternoons when Pearl grew restless, and Camellia was frantic to soothe her, she laid Pearl's hand—her strong hand, the left one—on her stomach so she could massage the baby, and Pearl said, "No," with a purr and a smile, and Camellia knew she meant *good*.

"I do believe, Miss Camellia," Reverend Heddy told her once, "that child is what keeps Mother going. Otherwise, I fear she might give herself over to the Kingdom."

"If she could only get her words right and tell me what she wants," Camellia said. "Most of the time, I'm just guessing."

"She wants to see that baby, her only grandchild. Won't that be a glorious day? She never had a daughter herself, and now here you are."

Camellia loved the cold winter in Tennessee and the way the snow swept through the valley and left everything white. It hung in clumps from the trees, covered evergreen bushes, filled in her footprints where she walked. Reverend Heddy imagined Heaven as a city of gold and eternal sunshine, but Camellia preferred to think of it as a place of snow, a blanket of white covering over every wrong anyone had ever done. She would have her baby, she told herself, there in Tennessee where the mountain ridges rose up on either side of her, and she could hide herself away in the snowy valley, and somehow, everything would be all right.

"You go slow," Heddy told her one morning, when suddenly, bent over to stoke the fire in the cook stove, she felt dizzy and stumbled backward into his arms. "You got this baby to birth. You need to be strong."

"Ike works that awful job to buy us food," she said. "Least I can do is cook it."

Pearl's stroke had left them with doctor bills they couldn't pay, particularly after Heddy had lost his odd job sweeping up at Robinson's Drug Store and delivering medicines to customers in town. One day, he had confused two packages and delivered a

packet of arsenic to a woman who had ordered headache powders. Fortunately, the doctor had been able to administer an
emetic and save the poor woman. Still, Mr. Robinson dismissed
Heddy and hired someone younger. So without Heddy's money
from the drugstore and Pearl's teacher's pay, the family looked
to Ike for support though it shamed Heddy to have to call Ike
back from Texas, where he ran his own business, and put him to
work for someone else, particularly when that someone else
turned out to be the railroad station in Chattanooga, where Ike
worked all week as a restroom attendant. He handed towels to
white men, cleaned the toilets after they used them, and tolerated the way they called him "boy," and "nigra," and "Sambo."
And when he came home on Sundays, riding one of the excursion trains, he brought all the anger and gall he had stored up
during the week.

"You don't have to be cross with me," Camellia told him once
when he snapped at her for asking him to fetch water from the
well.

"I take orders all week," he said. "Sleep on a cot at the Railroad YMCA—not a room, mind you, just a cot in the basement.
I'm sure not going to get bossed around by you on Sundays."

Heddy tried to ignore Ike's poor humor. Pearl pressed her lips
tightly together as if she knew there were no words on her tongue
that could make Ike understand how he hurt her with his rancor.

Sundays, for Pearl and Heddy and Camellia, became days to
survive, never knowing when they might say something that
would send Ike into a fit. Camellia came to dread the heavy fall
of his boots on the porch when he arrived and the way he would
shake the floorboards inside the house and rattle the collection of
glass dogs Pearl kept on a shelf by her chair. Much better were
the days when he was back in Chattanooga, and the air in the
house was somehow lighter for his having gone. Heddy sat by the
fire, his Bible open on his lap, while he read the Psalms to Pearl,
who sat near him, dozing. Camellia listened to the music of

Heddy's deep, rich voice as it spoke of mercy and devotion, and she felt guilty because she was so happy that Ike was gone.

It was Pearl and Heddy that she truly loved. She knew that in her heart, and feared that Ike knew it, too. She loved to watch the way Heddy kneeled behind Pearl, as if he were praying, and braided her hair. He brushed it out and then patiently started working it into a knotted rope that hung down her back when he was finished. "She likes that," he told Camellia. "Her hair has always been her pride."

Camellia could tell Pearl had been a beautiful woman. Even now that age had crept up on her, she had lovely hands, the fingers so long and elegant, and smooth skin in the hollow of her collarbone that gleamed like a young girl's. Camellia loved the way Pearl's strong hand was always reaching out to touch something— the glass dogs, the polished arm of her rocking chair, Heddy's face, or sometimes Camellia's own hand. She thrilled to Pearl's touch, so full of love, and then there would come the regret that always shadowed the joy she felt, the guilt that she could feel this way with Ike in Chattanooga, suffering for all their sakes. She felt the loss of her own mother more sharply and wondered about her father and Quakertown, which now seemed so far away.

Sometimes, when she walked in the snow, her steps were awkward and she thought of Kizer and his hobbled gait. How she had wanted to heal him. Each time she pressed her naked body to his, she imagined—oh, she knew it was foolish—that health might pass from her to him and by some miracle correct his deformity.

On her walks, she went past the high school, often late in the afternoon when classes were letting out, and the boys and girls were coming out the front doors. Some of them called to one another—"Hey, George. George, hey. Wait for me." Others, the more timid ones, walked with their heads bowed and their books pressed to their chests like shields. Not so long ago, she thought, she had been one of those shy girls.

One day, as she stood across the street from the high school, squinting to see through a fine sleet that had started to fall, she saw a teacher, a young man, come out the school doors. He stood on the steps, his hands on his hips, and lifted his face to the sky. His shirtsleeves were rolled to his elbows, and his necktie was flapping in the wind. The sleet came down on the round lenses of his steel-rimmed spectacles, on his yellow-white hair, on the fair skin of his face. He looked so much like Kizer, for a moment she imagined he had found her.

She was so startled, she hurried on down Main Street, past J. R. Darwin's Everything-to-Wear Store, the Hotel Aqua, Robinson's Drug Store, and the courthouse, where she turned and walked a few blocks to the east so when she finally turned for home she wouldn't pass the high school again. As she walked, she kept imagining that it could happen; Kizer could track her down. Wherever he was in the world, he could find her, and, oh, what a mess there would be then, what with the baby so close and Ike in such a temper. Suddenly the mountain ridges seemed to close around her, the world so small she couldn't hide, and she realized, a chill passing through her, the only reason the teacher at the high school had started her thinking all this was because deep down she wished it could be true.

When she got close to home, she could see Heddy at the window. "Miss Camellia," he said when she came through the door, "I didn't know what to do. You've been gone so long. I wanted to go out and find you, but I was afraid to leave Mother alone. I didn't know what to do."

Camellia unwound her head scarf, crusty with sleet, and laid it on the hearth to dry. "I was just walking," she said. "You know how I walk. Granny woman told me to walk to help my baby turn."

"Not this long." Heddy helped her off with her coat. "Usually, you're back long before now."

"Just felt like walking more today," she said.

"You be careful with that walking. What would Ike think if he knew?"

"We don't have to tell Ike."

"That's his baby," Heddy said. "He'd never forgive me if I let something happen to it. And Mother? I'd hate to think what it'd do to her."

The next day, Camellia walked past the high school, hoping that she would again see the teacher with the fair hair and the spectacles, but she didn't. She came again the next day and the next, but all she saw were the boys and girls coming out the school doors. On Saturday she stayed home and dusted Pearl's glass dogs, letting her hold them in her hand one by one as she tried to name the students who had given them to her. Words were coming back to her now, but often the wrong words, recalled only because they sounded like the ones she wanted to say. The right corner of her mouth drooped as if she were frowning, and the lid of her eye fluttered and twitched. "Corn," she said, and Camellia could only guess she meant *Carl. Sweater* for *Sarah, ring* for *Irene.* "Yes, Mama Pearl," Camellia said. "I know they all loved you, dear."

Then it was Sunday, and Ike was home, and, praise Jesus, he was laughing and joking and calling Camellia and Pearl his two best girls. He got down on his knees and pressed his ear to Camellia's stomach. "What do you think it's going to be, Mama?" he said to Pearl. "Boy or girl or one of each?"

Pearl tried to wave her right hand at him, as if to say, "Oh, you. Go on." But her arm flopped like a fish out of water, and then lay still on the arm of her chair.

A boy or a girl, Camellia thought, and felt a shiver pass through her, half anticipation, half dread. What would her baby look like if it turned out to be Kizer's? Would its skin be Camellia's buttery cream, or would it be fair and white?

She watched Ike help his mother walk to the kitchen table. He eased her into a chair, tucked a napkin into the collar of her dress.

Then he filled her plate and held bites of food to her mouth, wiped her chin after she finished chewing. "That's it, Mama," he said. "That's my girl."

There was goodness in him. Camellia believed that. He didn't deserve the hurt that might soon be his.

After dinner, he hauled water in from the well and set it to heat on the stove so he and Camellia could wash the dishes. It was warm there by the stove, and he stood close to her and told her in a quiet voice that as soon as the baby was born he was going to get a job as a sleeping car porter. The pay would be better—nearly seventy dollars a month, not to mention tips—and after he paid Pearl's doctor bills, he would put enough money back so he could open a barbershop there in Dayton.

"Get us a house of our own someday," he said. "How about that?"

"Lands," she told him. "I've never thought that far ahead."

"Well, you better start thinking, Mrs. Mattoon. We got us a baby coming."

"Then you'll be gone even more than you are now."

"Oh, I'll see the country, all right. But don't worry. You're the one I'll always come home to."

That evening, Camellia walked with Ike to the depot, where they waited for the excursion train to take him back to Chattanooga. They sat inside and watched the snow blow up under the train as it arrived. Camellia could see the faces of the passengers through the glass of the observation car, white people taking glasses from trays offered by Negro porters. She knew that when Ike boarded the train, he would ride in the caboose.

"If you become a porter," she said, "you'll be serving people like them."

"Beats spending every minute in a toilet breathing their stink. I swear, Camellia, I got to get out of that job. It makes me mean." He took her hand and slipped it into his coat pocket. She felt the smooth handle of a razor, the ridge of its closed blade. "Something I kept from the barbershop. I figure it might come in handy."

She drew her hand away as if she had stuck it into fire. "Ike, no," she said. "That's asking for trouble."

He kissed her on the forehead. "Don't worry about me, Camellia. I'll be fine."

It was the next afternoon, when she was walking past the high school, that she slipped on a patch of ice and went down hard on her back. One second she was watching the fair-haired teacher coming down the school steps, a shiny leather briefcase swinging from his hand, and the next second the world tilted under her, and she was looking up at the slate-colored sky, a flock of starlings wheeling and chattering above her through a gauze of snowflakes as big as clumps of cotton. Her breath came in ragged gasps. She knew this was how her father had felt when he had found out about her and Kizer, as if the world he thought he knew had spun beneath his feet and sent him sprawling. "My baby," she tried to say. "My baby." But she couldn't find the air she needed to make the words.

Then the fair-haired teacher was kneeling beside her, and she felt so sorry that he was staining the flannel of his trousers in the ice and slush, all because she had been careless, unable to stay away from the school where she hoped she would see this man who reminded her of Kizer.

"Ma'am," the teacher said, and his voice was shy the way Kizer's had been that first night at the travelogue. "Ma'am, if I help you, can you stand up?"

How easy, she thought, it would be to lie there and let the snow cover her. Then she felt a sharp pain in the small of her back, felt it spread around to her abdomen, and she wondered whether, without knowing it, she had willed the fall, so this baby she carried, this secret, might never be known.

"I'd be obliged to you," she said, and then she felt the teacher's strong hands lifting her to her feet.

"I'm going to take you in here to the school nurse," he said. His spectacles had slipped down on his nose, and Camellia wanted to straighten them for him. "Make sure you're all right."

"Lands, no," Camellia said, unable to imagine turning herself over to the care of white people. "I don't have the money for that."

"Money?" The teacher was holding onto Camellia's arm. With his free hand, he pushed his spectacles back up his nose. "Why, it won't cost you anything. I just want to make sure you're not hurt."

"Oh, I'm fine," Camellia said. "I'm right as rain."

"At least let me get my Model T and take you home so you don't have to walk on this ice."

"Oh, it wouldn't do," she said, and she knew it was what she should have said to Kizer the night he had asked her to get into his motorcar and ride with him into the country.

She heard the doors to the school swing open, and when she turned, she saw a portly man with watch chains glittering on his vest. "John," she heard him call to the teacher. "What in the world are you doing out there holding onto that colored gal?"

"I'll be going now." She eased her arm away from his grip. "Got to get home before this snow gets any deeper. You've been fine to me. No need for you to get into any kind of trouble, not a nice man like you."

"I just wanted to help you," he said.

"You did fine," she told him. "Go on now. Tell that man I was some crazy girl who grabbed onto you. I won't mind."

"But that's not true," the teacher said.

"True enough," said Camellia, and then she turned and started her walk home.

By the time she reached the house, her back had stiffened, and she walked with a stoop. She came through the door, and Heddy said, "It's happened. I knew it would happen. I told you to be careful on that ice."

"Just a little sore back," she said. "Here, help me off with my things."

He slipped her arms from the sleeves of her coat, untied her head scarf, helped her sit in his own rocking chair.

"Is Mama Pearl sleeping?" she said.

Heddy nodded. "I got her off to bed just after you left. Now what can I do for you, Miss Camellia?"

Camellia was ashamed, not so much because she had fallen, but because she had been watching this schoolteacher at the time, had gone out on the ice because she had wanted to see him, this man who reminded her of Kizer.

"I'm afraid you've got two patients on your hands now," she told Heddy. "If you wouldn't mind supper being late, I'd like to lie down for a while."

Camellia slept, but then, toward dark, the pains started, and she knew she was in labor. She clenched her teeth against the pain and tried not to cry out, so peaceful it was in the quiet house what with Mama Pearl still asleep and Heddy in his rocking chair by the fire. Camellia could hear the steady creak of the chair, the crackle of the fire, Heddy's mumbled prayers, and it was all a comfort to her, every sound of the place she now called home.

She could see snow piling up on the ledge outside the window, curving up across the glass. The wind rattled the panes, howled in the chimney. She knew the snow was falling hard and had been ever since she had first fallen asleep.

The next pain was so sharp she couldn't help but cry out.

"Miss Camellia." Heddy was knocking on her door. "Miss Camellia, are you all right in there?"

Camellia lifted her knees to try to ease some of the pain. "Baby's coming," she said, when Heddy opened the door and saw her.

"But it's not time," he said. "Not for another month."

"Coming early, I guess," Camellia said. "I suppose it didn't take kindly to that fall on the ice."

Heddy came a bit closer to the bed. "Has it turned yet?"

"No, it hasn't turned. You better go for the granny woman."

"Lord, I wish I could," Heddy said. "But we're in the middle of a blizzard. Hear that wind? It's surely drifted shut the hollow where that granny woman lives. Maybe I could get downtown to the doctor's."

Camellia shook her head. "We owe him too much money now."

"But your baby."

"Looks like you'll have to help me along with it."

"Oh, dear Jesus, I never birthed a baby before. And a breech."

"That's all right," said Camellia. "I never had one before. I guess we'll have to learn together."

Heddy rubbed his hand over his face. "Maybe I should get Mother up," he said. "Bring her on in here."

"Reverend Heddy, she won't be much help."

"Maybe not. But it might do me a world of good to have her here. Something tells me this is going to be a long night."

Pearl sat by the bed and held Camellia's hand with her strong one. Heddy had brought in all the coal oil lamps for light, and when he moved about, their glow threw his shadow high up on the walls. "What is it I'm going to have to do?" he kept saying. "Tell me again."

Camellia, between the pains which were closer now and more intense, spreading over her entire abdomen, told him what the granny woman had told her. If the baby was breech, either the feet or the bottom would come first. If the bottom came first, the feet were probably tucked up under it. In that case, Heddy would have to get the feet and bring them down and then wait until he saw the shoulders. He'd have to turn those shoulders and let the baby slide on down. "The neck and the head," she told Heddy. "That's going to be the tricky part. That's when you're really going to have to help me. You'll have to whirl that baby. Granny woman says we got five minutes, then, to get it out."

"I don't think I can do it," Heddy said.

"Got to," said Camellia.

Pearl, for the first time since her stroke, found the exact words she intended. "God will help," she said.

Camellia felt the powerful squeeze of her hand. "Hear that, Reverend Heddy. Mama Pearl says God will help."

Shortly after midnight, Camellia felt the water running down her thighs, and she knew the sac around the baby had burst just as the granny woman had told her it would. The sight of it was too much for Heddy. His shoulders were trembling, and his voice was choked with his sobbing. "I near killed that woman," he said. "That poor woman who took the arsenic. All on account of me. And now you want me to birth this baby. My grandbaby? Lord, oh Lord. What if I do it all wrong?"

Camellia was bearing down, contracting her stomach muscles the way the granny woman had taught her. Between the pains, which were coming every couple of minutes now, she lay back on the pillows and rested. "No time to feel sorry about anything we regret," she told Heddy. "This baby's going to come no matter who we are or what we've done."

Just then, a form filled the doorway. Camellia felt the balance of light shift in the room. She raised up on her elbows and saw a man covered with shadow. She could smell the cold and the snow on him, felt a chill pass through her. "I tried to raise someone," he said. "But I reckon you didn't hear me at the door."

He took a step toward the bed, came into the light, and Camellia saw it was her father. "Papa?" she said.

The snow was melting from Little's coat and hat, running down his face. "Baby-Girl," he said. "I came in on the last train that's going to be able to run for a while. I didn't have anywhere else to turn. I would have told you I was coming, but I was afraid you'd tell me no."

There would be time later for him to tell the story of all that had happened since Camellia and Ike had left. He would tell about the problems at Rhodie Hill, and Uncle Me, and the fire that had killed him. But at the moment there was only time for the baby.

What were the odds, Camellia thought, that her father would come at just the moment when she had been recalling what he had told her before she left him, that she shouldn't get so far from home that the people who loved her would be unable to find her if she was in trouble—and now here he was.

She wasn't ashamed at all to have him there at the moment of her delivery, to have him say to Heddy, "If it's all the same to you, I'll see to my daughter now." How many times she had watched her father coax plants from the ground, careful not to injure the roots, and that was what he was thinking as he got up on the bed and kneeled before Camellia, how when he had found the white lilac along Pecan Creek, he had known to work his spade under the root ball but not to try to lift the tree right away. He could still feel in his arms and hands the gentle rocking motion as he kept prying the spade under the roots until finally they came free.

"We're going to do fine," he said to Camellia. "You and me."

She was thinking of her mother, Eugie, who had agreed all those months past to keep her secret, had died never having said a word to anyone. She had loved Camellia enough to do that, and Camellia had loved the baby enough to risk everything for the moment when she would finally hold it in her arms.

Little could see the baby's toes, and he felt his breath catch in his throat. "This here's a breech baby," he said.

Camellia let out a long scream.

"What you got to do is get the feet together." Heddy was pacing back and forth alongside the bed. "Let them both come down. Yes, sir. That's right. And then make sure the hands aren't over the head. Isn't that the way the granny woman said it?"

"The arms and hands are clear," said Little.

"Good," said Pearl, and, again, the word meant exactly what she had intended.

Little drew back and looked at Camellia who was panting now, her eyes shut tight, the cords in her neck standing out, her mouth twisted in agony.

Heddy couldn't bring himself to watch the delivery. "You see the shoulders yet?"

"Yes, sir," said Little. "I see them."

"You got to turn those shoulders." Heddy stopped his pacing and twisted his torso to the side. "You got to whirl them."

"Whirl them?" said Little.

"Turn them," Heddy said. "That baby's got to come out sideways."

The baby was wet and slick in Little's hands, and he imagined he was reaching down into the damp, clotted clay of Quakertown again, feeling for a plant's roots. He eased the baby's shoulders around until he had turned it on one side.

"Have you got it?" Heddy asked.

"I've turned it," Little said.

"Neck's coming next," Heddy told him. "Then the head. That's going to be the tricky part. Bear down, Miss Camellia."

Camellia was huffing and growling. She pushed and pushed, not thinking about all the months of lying, the secret held from her father, from Ike, from Reverend Heddy and Mama Pearl. She wanted the baby out of her, out into the world where whatever was going to happen could begin.

Little let the baby's shoulders slip out, and what he didn't tell anyone—brought it into himself and held it still—was that the cord was wrapped around the baby's neck.

He had been aware, since he first saw the baby's toes, that it was lighter-skinned than Eugie had been, lighter than Camellia, and he knew that Kizer Bell had told him the truth. Little knew he was holding Kizer's baby in his hands. Even though it was mottled with mucous and blood, Little could see that the baby was white.

How easy it would be, he thought, to do nothing about the

cord around the neck, to let the baby strangle, but this child was what Eugie and Camellia had promised each other to protect, and now it was up to him, in Eugie's stead, to see that promise through. He slipped his finger in under the cord and loosened it from the baby's neck.

"Have you got the head yet?" Heddy asked.

"Fetch me a pair of scissors," said Little. "I've got to cut the cord."

He could tell there was no push left in Camellia. He got his free hand under the baby's neck, and he rocked it until the baby slipped free.

"Miss Camellia," Heddy said in a hushed voice. "Your baby is here."

Little showed him the loop of cord where his finger held it. "Cut it here," he said, and with sure hands, Heddy did.

"Slap the butt," Heddy told him. "You've got to get this young'un's lungs working."

Little smacked the baby's bottom, but the baby didn't cry. He took the corner of the bed sheet and cleaned the blood and mucous from the baby's mouth and nose.

Pearl squeezed Camellia's hand. Heddy started saying the Lord's Prayer. Camellia waited to hear her baby cry. "Oh, Papa," she said. Had she suffered all this only to have God take her baby away? Would that be the way he finally punished her?

The baby was no more weight than a gunnysack full of dirt in Little's hands. He brought its face to his, covered its mouth and nose with his own mouth, and blew out a gentle puff of air. Then he smacked the baby on the bottom again, and the baby, as if it hadn't agreed to be rousted from a pleasant sleep, began to squall.

Camellia, hearing that cry, was as happy as she had ever been. She was happy, and she was scared. Little laid the baby on Camellia's stomach, and she felt it squirm against her.

"You've got a girl," he said.

"Look at it," said Reverend Heddy. "It's the whitest little baby I've ever seen."

Little was trembling, the taste of the baby still in his mouth. He had offered the only thing he could, and it had cost him so little, one breath out of all the millions he hoped he had left to draw, one breath passing from him to his grandchild.

"Eugenia," said Camellia, holding the baby to her, tracing each finger and toe. "Baby Eugenia. Welcome to the world."

33

By morning, the snow had stopped, but it was evening before the trains started running again, and Heddy could make the trip to Chattanooga to tell Ike the baby had come. By that time, Heddy and Pearl knew all there was to know about the child because Camellia, despite Little's advice to keep quiet for the time, had been unable to stop herself from telling them about Kizer Bell. She had told them because, now that Eugenia was born, she wanted her to be able to always walk a straight path through the world, proud of who she was, instead of having to duck her head and hide from the truth. It was what Camellia herself had learned. No more secrets. No more lies. She swore she would never surround her daughter with shame.

"I can't change any of it," she said to Heddy and Pearl. The sunlight was dazzling in her bedroom, warm on her face, as she sat up in bed. Eugenia slept beside her, so sweet in the shirt Camellia had made from a flour sack.

"Is it that you don't love Isaac?" Heddy said. He was standing at the window, his back turned to her.

"I love him in my way," she said. "I love him just like I do everything else in my life now—you and Mama Pearl, my father and Eugenia, the snow and the sun. Everything like the blocks in this quilt." Camellia rubbed her hand over the stitches that pieced the squares together. When she had slept after Eugenia had come, she had dreamed that a group of women were sitting around her bed, sewing the quilt, making it for her warmth. Eugie had been there, and Granny Lesta, and Granny Ruth, and Mama Pearl, and even Tibby Bell. "God made the world and everything in it, didn't he, Reverend Heddy? He made Kizer Bell, and he made me, and even if what we did was wrong, I can't hate it, can't hate myself, because here I am with this beautiful baby, and I can't do anything but love her and everything else in the world because it all comes from God."

Pearl was still sitting by the bed, her good hand stroking Eugenia's arm, thinking how many boys and girls she had loved in her classrooms.

Little had gone out in the snow to burn the afterbirth, remembering how he had done the same when Eugie had delivered Camellia, burned it because the signs said if you buried it a dog might get hold of it, and then the mother would never have another child. He had burned it under one of the catalpa trees, but still he and Eugie had never conceived another baby, only Camellia, who was now a mother herself, mother of Eugenia Mattoon, this girl, part black, part white, in whom Little and Camellia would see themselves and Eugie and, for better or worse, Mr. and Mrs. Andrew Bell and Kizer.

"Sin doesn't come from God." Heddy turned from the window and faced Camellia.

She placed her hand on Pearl's which was still on Eugenia's arm. "Would you call this baby a sin?"

Pearl lifted her head and looked up at Heddy. Her eyes were wet with tears.

Heddy took in a deep breath, his nostrils flaring. "Miss Camellia," he said in a quiet voice. "What am I to tell him?"

"Tell him the truth," Camellia said.

Ike saw him in the mirror above the rows of sinks, his father, wrapped up in his coat, the legs of his trousers stuffed into his rubber galoshes. He had taken off his hat and was twisting the brim up in his hands. Ike noticed the tight set to his jaw, the same stern look Ike had seen hundreds of times when the Reverend Heddy Mattoon had stepped into the pulpit. Ike watched now in disbelief as Heddy came to him across the tile floor, the buckles on his galoshes jangling. Ike turned to face him, the hand towel he had been folding limp now in his hands.

"Daddy," he said. "Have you lost your sense?"

It was late and the restroom was empty, but Ike knew that at any moment a white man might walk in and find his father there.

Heddy had lived in Tennessee all his life, and he knew not to walk into a "whites only" toilet, but he wasn't thinking just then about where he could go and where he couldn't. He was thinking about his son, and what he had to tell him, and how much he wished it could all be otherwise.

"It's Camellia," he said, and though he spoke softly—more softly than Ike had ever heard him speak, his voice echoed in the room with its vaulted ceiling. "Son, she's had the child."

In that moment, Ike forgot that he was standing in a place he had come to despise—every inch of it—the porcelain sinks with their brass faucets, the marble vanity tops, the long line of wooden stalls he polished, the row of urinals across from them. He thought only of Camellia and the baby, their baby, who had now come into the world.

"Why didn't someone come for me?"

"We couldn't," said Heddy. "On account of the snow."

"A boy?" said Ike. All along, he had secretly wished for a son.

"A girl. Camellia calls her Eugenia after her mama."

Ike felt the muscles bunch in his jaw, crinkling the skin that puckered along the ridge of his scar. *Eugenia.* There would always be that name to remind him of what had happened in Denton—it seemed so long ago now—or perhaps the girl, her name, would be a balm, replacing as much as was possible the soul that had passed out of their lives. Perhaps the fact that Camellia had named the child Eugenia meant Ike's forgiveness.

"A girl," he said. "I bet she's a looker. And early, too. Couldn't wait to get born."

Heddy drew his shoulders back, the way Ike had seen him do so many times at a crucial point in a sermon. "Son," he said. "You got to brace yourself."

"For what?" said Ike. "Is it Camellia? The baby? Has something gone wrong?"

"That child," Heddy said. "It's not yours."

"Not mine." The towel slipped from Ike's hand and fell to the floor. "How do you mean?"

"I mean you're not the father of that baby. That's the fact. Lord, I wish what I had to tell you wasn't so."

Water was dripping from a faucet. Ike turned to the sink and gave the knob an angry twist. He kept his head bowed a moment, then raised it to look once more at his father in the mirror. He couldn't help thinking, How stupid, to come in the night with such news. What good would it serve?

Then his father came closer to him, and he laid his hand on Ike's back. "Son, there's more," he said, and now his voice was barely a whisper, and Ike suddenly loved him as fiercely as he ever had, loved him for being the one who wanted to stand by him, love him, at the time of his hurting. "That baby belongs to a white man. A white man named Kizer Bell."

Kizer Bell. For a moment, Ike let the name hang in the air. Kizer Bell, the cripple. The one Ike had always liked to keep waiting in the alley when he came to buy liquor for his mama. Who was the fool now? "Kiss the bride for me," Kizer had told him the night before the wedding. "Tell her it's from Kizer Bell." Ike remembered how Uncle Me had bumped into Kizer Bell in the doorway and made that vulgar sign with his fingers. Even an idiot like him had known what was going on. Who else had known? Ike wondered. Had it been everyone but him?

"Camellia told you this?" he said to his father.

"From her own mouth," Heddy said. "That baby's as white as butter."

Ike closed his eyes for a moment, and when he opened them and looked into the mirror, he saw a man, a white man, standing across the room, a cigar burning in his mouth. The man was wearing a double-breasted suit and spats. The silver stickpin in his tie gleamed on his chest. He had a camel's-hair topcoat draped over his left arm. Ike imagined he was one of the gamblers who liked to find a card game on the train up from Atlanta.

"Uncle," the gambler said to Heddy. "Uncle, I believe you're lost."

Ike felt his father's hand ease away from his back, one last loving caress of his fingers. "Yes, sir," he said. "Yes, sir. That's right."

"Come over here, Uncle."

"Yes, sir."

"Hold out your hand. Hold it out here now." The gambler drew on his cigar, and the ember in its ash blazed. "I don't want to dirty up this boy's pretty white floor. Do you, Uncle?"

"No, sir."

"Then you won't mind if I tap my ash off in your palm?"

"I expect that'd be all right, sir."

Ike turned from the mirror. "Sir, there's an ash can right over here," he told the gambler.

"I'm not speaking to you, boy. I'm talking to this nigger here." The gambler took the cigar from his mouth with his right hand. Ike saw his left hand snake out from under his topcoat and grab Heddy by the wrist. "I want you to remember this night, Uncle. The night you got uppity and came into a toilet for white men. Every time you look at your hand, you're going to see a scar. Every time you use it to turn a doorknob, you're going to feel it. Maybe that'll help you remember where you belong and where you don't."

Ike was moving before he even knew he had decided to move.

The razor was out of his pocket and open. He made sure the gambler saw the blade, the way he had seen the one that had cut his cheek. He backed the gambler up to the wall. The cigar fell from his hand.

"Here now, boy. What do you think you're doing?"

"Isaac," said Heddy, his voice stern with warning.

But Ike could only think of the men who had cut him, and of Kizer Bell. He grabbed the gambler by his hair and bent back his head. Then he brought the razor to the man's face.

"This is for all of you," Ike said. "All your kind."

Then he drew the razor down the gambler's face, and the man cried out, "Oh, Jesus. Oh, Jesus. Oh, God."

At first, there was only the thin line of the cut where the razor had slit the skin. Then blood welled up, and the man reached into his coat pocket and brought out a snub-nosed revolver.

Heddy saw the glint of the nickel-plated grip, and he called out, "Oh, merciful God."

Ike saw the gun, too, and he did the only thing he could think to do; he slashed the razor across the man's throat, and the revolver fell to the floor.

The gambler slid down the wall until it looked as if he had decided to squat down and sit on his heels. Blood spilled out onto his white shirt, and the camel's-hair topcoat, spilled over his shirt collar and into the vee of his lapels, staining the silver stickpin in his tie. He sputtered and coughed, gasped for air, and his eyes rolled back in his head.

"Oh, Lord," said Heddy. "You've done killed that man. All because I came here. All because of me."

Ike was backing away from the gambler, whose right hand was twitching, the fingers spreading open and then closing.

"Daddy, he would've killed us both," Ike said.

"You should've let him burn me," said Heddy. "Now you've got murder on your soul."

Outside in the waiting room, Ike could hear the call for the train to Knoxville. "You got to get on that train," he said. "Go back to Mama."

"But what about you?"

"I got to light out of here. Hide out for a while."

"We can tell the police what he was going to do to me. They'll go easy on you."

"Ain't no easy now," said Ike. "Ain't never been no easy for a colored man. You go on out of here. Get on that train." He pointed down the long aisle to the rear of the room. "I'm heading out that window yonder to the alley."

"Oh, Lord," said Heddy. "I'd rather that man burned my eyes out than to let you go away from me."

Heddy felt like a criminal as he boarded the train and started back to Dayton. He imagined everyone was looking at him with suspicious eyes. At one point, he even inspected his hands, his shoes, his coat for blood, but found none. You bring your children into the world, he thought as the train swept along the tracks, snow banked high at its sides, and you teach them what's right; then the world gets all mixed up, and it's so hard to tell what's right and what's wrong. The only thing he knew for certain was that he wouldn't be able to carry the news of what had happened in Chattanooga home to Pearl. He wouldn't be able to tell her their son had killed a man.

As the train pulled into the Dayton station, the sky was lightening in the east, and steam was rising from the mountains. The snow squeaked beneath Heddy's feet. The cold air stung his nostrils and burned his throat, and by the time he got home tears had frozen on his cheeks.

"I know it must have been a hard thing," Little said to him as he helped Heddy out of his coat. "I'm sorry it was my daughter brought you such a hard thing to do."

"You try to teach them," Heddy said.

"Yes, sir. I know you do."

"And then one day it's like you don't even know them, like they aren't even yours anymore." Heddy sighed. "At least you've still got your girl, and now a grandbaby. I envy you that."

"Reverend?"

"I don't expect we'll see Isaac around here for some time."

"Took it hard, I suspect," said Little.

"Yes," said Heddy. "He took it hard."

Little bowed his head, ashamed now of the way he had despised Ike after Eugie's death. The boy had been so desperate for forgiveness, and Little himself had now come in the night, a beggar seeking refuge, hoping that Camellia and the Mattoons wouldn't turn him away. And the baby had come, that glorious child, Eugenia. Little had suffered too much to take any pleasure from Ike's pain or to pass judgment on Camellia or even Kizer Bell.

"Daughter's always a daughter," Little said to Heddy. "Son's always a son."

Heddy was trembling by the fire. "I didn't know how cold I was. I swear I'm about froze to death."

Later, when Pearl was awake, he told her that Isaac wouldn't be coming home for a while, and she nodded. She sat by the window and looked out on the street. If Isaac would only come to her, she thought, she would tell him to be patient, to be forgiving, to be kind. Even if the words came out all muzzy, she would somehow make him understand. She would hold him to her, squeeze him with her good arm, until he felt loved. She would make him understand that too much hate could turn a heart to stone.

But all she saw on the snowy street were the children walking past on their way to school, their scarves whipping out in the wind, and from time to time, a stray cat prancing through the snow, or a motorcar rumbling past.

*   *   *

That evening, Little tried to make himself useful by sweeping the kitchen. He heard a meek tapping at the back door. When he opened it, he saw Ike standing there on the stoop, his arms crossed over his chest, a cap pulled down close to his eyes.

"Little Jones," he said. "I never thought I'd see you again."

"It's a long life," said Little. "People come and go."

Heddy was sitting at the kitchen table, his Bible open.

"Have you told them?" Ike said to his father.

Little went on with his sweeping, as if he couldn't hear Ike and Heddy, the way he had always tried to grant his customers privacy when he had worked in their gardens and some sort of family business had come up in his presence.

"I can't bring myself to say the words," Heddy said.

Pearl was in the parlor, still sitting near the window, a quilt across her legs. When she saw Ike step into the light, she tried to push herself up from her chair. She half-rose, the quilt sliding to the floor; then she gave up, and sank back down.

Ike knelt by her chair and took her hand. "Mama," he said.

Pearl was thinking what a sweet child her Isaac had been, timid and loving. Then he had gone to the war and come home, and a white man had cut his face, and he had learned how to hate people. Sometimes, the truth be known, she hated them, too, hated whoever had burned Heddy's church, even Camellia and the baby, and this Kizer Bell, and Little Jones who was there now in their way at the time of their grief. But it was always only a flash of rage, doused quickly by the thought that all God's creatures, again and again, fell short of his glory. Even she, who had tried to live a righteous life, had on occasion used her hand to strike a child, and her force and anger had shamed her. And once—a secret she had never told Heddy—she had let another man kiss her, the principal, Mr. Elgin, a bachelor with blue eyes, the first blue-eyed black man she had ever seen. He had come into her room one afternoon when the students had gone, and there at her desk he had leaned over and kissed her. She had reacted with shock and outrage—"Mr. Elgin, the idea!"—but oh, he had been so grand, and what she knew was that she had kissed him, too. Just for a moment, she had given herself to him.

She recalled that afternoon now, whenever she heard of anyone who had stepped outside their regular lives. You swore you knew yourself, she thought, swore you knew how you had decided to live, and then suddenly there was an opportunity, and you realized you had been fooling yourself all along. She wrapped her good arm around Ike's shoulders and drew him to her.

"I had to come home," he said. "I hopped a freight out of Chattanooga. Daddy came and told me about the baby—Camellia's baby—and ever since, it's all seemed like a dream."

Heddy thought how different this Ike was—soft-spoken, in a daze—than the one who had used his razor on that white man the night before. "Do you think I'd tell you a story?" Heddy said.

Ike got to his feet. "Some things just so terrible, you got to see them with your own eyes to know they're true."

Heddy pointed to Camellia's bedroom. "She's in there," he said, "with the baby."

Ike opened the door and saw Camellia sitting up in bed, the baby at her breast. In the dim light from the oil lamp, it was difficult to see Eugenia. Ike closed the door and came closer to the bed.

"Reverend Heddy said you wouldn't come," said Camellia.

"Had to see this baby," Ike told her. "Had to make you look me in the eyes."

He could see now that what Heddy had told him was true. The baby, its dimpled hands pawing at Camellia's breast, was as white as butter.

"I never wished trouble for you," Camellia said.

"Why did you go on and marry me then?"

"You were the one who was there," she said. "The one I could count on. I didn't want to be alone. And I did love you. You have to know that's true. Still love you, in my way."

Ike took off his cap and slapped it against his leg. "I wish I could be so much better than what I am. Lord, Camellia, I wish it was so. Can you say you didn't love him? Kizer Bell? If you can say that, I might try to imagine a way for us."

Camellia knew she should say it, say she had never loved Kizer. But it wasn't true.

"I can't say it," she told Ike. "There would always be that lie between us."

"You're choosing, then?" he said.

"Yes," she said. "I suppose I am."

Ike put his cap back on his head. "I loved you, Camellia. Loved you with all my heart."

"I know you did," she said.

Little had stepped out onto the porch to watch the stars come out above the mountain ridge when he saw a police car stop across the street and sit there awhile, exhaust rolling out of its tailpipe in great white clouds. Then the door opened, and the policeman, his leather waistcoat creaking, got out of the car and made his way through the gate and up onto the porch.

"You know Ike Mattoon?" the policeman said.

"I know him," said Little.

"Where was he the last time you seen him?"

"Texas."

"Texas?" The policeman laughed. "I'll guarantee you one thing. Time's coming when he's going to wish he stayed there." He pointed to the door with his billy club. "Take me on in there now. I got to talk to Heddy Mattoon."

Little opened the door and let the policeman step inside. Pearl heard the glass dogs clink together on her shelf.

Heddy knew the policeman, a Mr. Piper, because he had asked Heddy a few questions after he had made the mistake of delivering arsenic to one of Mr. Robinson's customers. Mr. Piper was a squat man with a square jaw. He liked to clench his teeth and point that jaw at people. Now he used the end of his billy club to push up the visor of his cap. "I'm looking for your boy," he said to Heddy. "I'm looking for Ike."

Heddy kept his eyes focused on the snow across the toes of Mr. Piper's boots, melting now on the floor. "Haven't seen Isaac since Sunday last," he said.

"There's been some trouble at the Terminal Station down in Chattanooga." Mr. Piper slapped the billy club against his palm. "Ike works down there, don't he?"

"Yes, sir. Folks know that's where Ike earns his money."

"Found a man dead in the toilet there last night. Someone cut his throat and now Ike's nowhere to be seen. Looks funny, don't it?"

Heddy raised his head and looked Mr. Piper straight in the eyes. "I wouldn't know anything about it, sir."

Mr. Piper jutted his jaw out at Heddy. "I'm going to have to look around."

"My wife." Heddy nodded toward Pearl. "You know she's poorly."

"I won't be bothering your wife." Mr. Piper tipped his cap to Pearl. "Ma'am."

He poked around in the pantry, went into Heddy and Pearl's bedroom and looked in the wardrobe. He started to open the door to Camellia's bedroom, and Heddy said, "My daughter-in-law's in there. She's took to her bed."

"What's wrong with her? She sick?"

"That's right," said Heddy.

Just then, Eugenia started to cry.

Mr. Piper scratched his jaw. "I heard that Ike's wife was near to pop. She have her baby, did she?"

"That's right."

"When?"

"Night before last."

"And no one sent for Ike?"

"We been waiting for the snow to clear."

"Tracks been open since yesterday evening," said Mr. Piper.

"Is that right, sir?"

"You damned straight it's right." He tapped Heddy on the chest with his billy club. "How come you didn't say anything about that baby? How come you just said that girl was in there sick."

"Sick from the birthing," said Heddy. "We haven't been able to send for the granny woman."

"You know I'm going to have to have a look. For all I know you got Ike hid in there."

"Isaac got nothing to hide about," said Heddy, and he felt the pain of his lie, felt how far he would go to save his son.

"Someone cut up that man, a Mr. Yarbrough from Atlanta. Ike used to be a barber, didn't he?"

"Yes, sir."

"Step aside now, Heddy. I'm going in."

Mr. Piper opened the bedroom door and saw Camellia in bed. "Beg your pardon, ma'am," he said, "but I got to search this room. Police business. You understand."

"I'm trying to get my baby to sleep," Camellia said. She was sitting up in bed, her back against the headboard, a row of pillows piled up behind her. Her legs stretched out in front of her and sank down into the feather mattress. She had pulled the quilts up over her shoulders, and she had Eugenia there beneath the top one, her mouth working at her breast.

"I don't see no baby," Mr. Piper said.

"She's under here," said Camellia. "She's nursing, sir."

Mr. Piper opened the wardrobe and poked his billy club through the hanging dresses. He got down on his knees and looked under the bed. He went to the window and beat his club against the curtains.

"When's the last time you seen that husband of yours?" Mr. Piper came around to the side of the bed. "He come home for your laying in?"

"Ike comes home on Sundays," Camellia said.

Mr. Piper used the tip of his billy club to lift up the corner of the quilt, and it was then that Eugenia turned loose of Camellia's breast and let out a cry. Mr Piper stepped away, and the quilt fell back over Camellia's shoulder.

"Good Lord, girl. That baby's as white as me. What in the world you been up to? Ike know about this? Hell, no wonder he'd go and cut a white man's throat."

Camellia watched Mr. Piper walk toward the door. Then he stopped, turned back to her, and pointed his club. "I'll be watching you all," he said. "We'll get that man of yours. Hell, probably do you a favor. Ain't that right, girl?"

"I don't know what you mean, sir."

Mr. Piper laughed. "Looks like you been wanting Ike out of the picture for some time."

When Mr. Piper had finally gone, there was no sound in the house for some time except the crackle of the fire, as if no one had the courage to move or speak. Then Camellia heard Heddy say, "I'm sorry, Mother. It's true."

He came into Camellia's room, then, and stood at the side of her bed.

"Has that policeman gone?" she asked.

"He's gone," Little called out from the parlor, where he had been standing at the window watching.

Camellia handed Eugenia to Heddy and pushed back the quilts. She swung her legs over the side of the bed, and Heddy saw Ike's legs, half-hidden by the furrow they made in the feather mattress. She pulled the pillows off on the floor, and there was Ike, his arms tucked in on top of him, his hands folded on his stomach as if he were a corpse.

He rose up from the bed, and Heddy felt thanksgiving fill him, having Ike there, breathing before him. Heddy gave Eugenia back to Camellia; then he said to Ike, "I want you to get down on your knees with me. I want you to ask God to forgive you for killing that white man."

Ike put his cap back on his head and went out into the parlor. "White man's been killing us for years, Daddy. Who you think burned your church back in the fall?"

"No one can prove anything about that church," Heddy said, "but I know what I saw you do."

"Can't be undone," Little said. He was standing back in the shadows. "If you don't mind my two cents' worth."

"God can forgive us," said Heddy. "If we'll ask."

"Forgive Camellia, too?" Ike said. "And Kizer Bell?"

"Yes," said Heddy. "Forgive them, too."

Pearl was trying once more to push herself up from her chair. Ike took her arm and tried to help her stand, but once she was on her feet, she pulled with her good arm, and he followed her as she kneeled on the floor. He kneeled beside his mother, remembering how she had once put her hand over his and showed him the gentle rise and flow of letters. Now there were no words. Pearl closed her eyes, and somehow Ike understood he was to close his, too. And in the moments of silence that followed, whatever plea for grace he could manage went out to the Heavens.

Camellia, watching, could still feel the outline of Ike's body beneath hers, could hear the frantic beating of his heart. How warm it had been beneath the quilts, she and Ike and Eugenia pressed together. In a moment, he would rise and leave his mother and father's house, and for months no one would know where he was. Then a letter would come, all the way from the West Indies, the closest he had been able to get to Africa. Pearl would sit for hours, running her fingers over the elegant handwriting, the last sign she would have from her son. "God bless that child," is all the letter would say. "She isn't to blame for any of this."

In all the years to come, there would be no further word, no word ever again. Camellia, from time to time, would find herself suddenly remembering how she had covered him with her body—the last bit of love she had ever been able to offer—and she would think, at least she had done that—at least, for that one night, she had saved him.

Epilogue
1943

And then it's Sunday, and after breakfast, Mama says to me, "Eugenia, girl, shake a leg." I hurry into the bathroom where I brush my teeth and tie a ribbon into my hair. Daddy Little is waiting in Mama's car. I look out the window and see him in the front seat, staring straight ahead. Then he dips his head a moment, and I see his fingers pinch the crease in a trouser leg and run down its length. The brown suit is new, a double-breasted with snazzy lapels and fine white pinstripes running through the cloth. He turns the rearview mirror toward him and leans over to check the knot in his necktie, also new, and the crease in the crown of his fedora. He slides his hand along the brim until he has the shape that best pleases him. Then he turns the mirror back, nudging it a bit at a time until he feels confident Mama won't know he's moved it, won't know he's been primping. Then he leans over and gives the horn a toot, and Mama calls up the stairs, "Eugenia, Daddy Little's going to have a fit if we don't get out there."

We're on our way to Denton, Mama willing to drive the forty miles there and the forty back, even though it will cost us all our ration stamps for gas, and she'll end up having to walk to school the rest of the month. "Do me good," she said. "I'm getting lazy. I used to walk and walk when I was carrying you, trying to get you to turn over and come out the right way. Lands, you were a stubborn child."

I came into the world sideways, and I believe I've been moving through it the same way ever since. White girls call me "Oreo Cookie," "Half-breed," "High Yellow." Colored girls call me "Marshmallow," "Whitey," "Snow." But when they hear me sing, all of them shut their mouths. My voice is full of all the hurt they've caused, and when they listen to it, they know, with an ache that leaves them mute, how much power they've given me.

"Trickus," "Bilky," "Rixo," "Putt." These are the nicknames Mama Pearl gave me when I was a baby in Tennessee, taking in the light and air of a place I would never know, the place where Daddy Little brought me into the world and gave me his breath, and a man named Ike Mattoon cut another man's throat and ran away from the law.

Mama and Daddy Little have told it all to me, told me about Granny Eugie, whose name I carry, about my daddy, Kizer Bell, and the secret that ended up spinning us out into the world, away from a place called Quakertown, away from Denton, where Daddy Little has never set foot since his house burned and he had to escape to Tennessee. He's never been back even though we've lived here in Dallas nearly twenty-one years, come here to Mama's friend, Miss Portia Washington Pittman, who found Mama a job teaching school.

"Nothing to go back for," he always said whenever I tried to get him to take me there. "Just a ton of heartache."

"What about Granny Eugie's grave?" I asked him once. "Don't you want to see that?"

He put his hand on my cheek. "Granny Eugie's in my heart," he said. "And she's in you, a part of her anyway, in this beautiful face."

But now he's been unable to resist. A few weeks before, a Mr. Gleason came to our house, and I took him into the backyard where Daddy Little was sitting on a stone bench beneath the Japanese maple.

"How in the world?" he said when he saw Mr. Gleason.

"I saw your granddaughter sing at the Fair Grounds Auditorium," Mr. Gleason said. "Heard her sing 'Sometimes I Feel Like a Motherless Child,' and everything came back to me. You made me cry, Eugenia."

Daddy Little stood up and put his arm across my shoulders. "When you've got a talent," he said, "you can't hide."

"I never should have run off to Europe," Mr. Gleason told him. "Back then when we were building that park. I should have stayed. It all went wrong, Little. It went terribly wrong."

Mr. Gleason had arranged for the city of Denton to erect a plaque at the city park that would tell the story of Quakertown, and he wanted me to sing at the ceremony, and he wanted Daddy Little to be the one to unveil the marker.

"Will you do it, Little?"

Daddy Little rubbed his hand over his face. "Don't know those folks who used to live in Quakertown would want me to be the one."

"A lot of those folks are gone now," Mr. Gleason said. "The ones that gave you a hard time. Some of them have left for other parts of the country; some of them have passed on. Mr. Smoke died a few years back. I hear that he was the one who burned you out."

Daddy Little nodded. "I figured as much."

"So you'll come up for the ceremony? Say you will, Little. It's been over twenty years. Such a long time."

"Maybe for you white folks. You didn't lose your homes. I expect for those people from Quakertown it all seems pretty fresh."

"We all lost," Mr. Gleason said. "White and colored. You don't know the ugliness I hear brewing these days. That night that mob wanted to burn Andrew Bell's house. That was only the start. All I see in front of us is trouble. I thought this marker would be something—some small thing I could do to help—and I know you're the man I owe the most."

Daddy Little turned to me. "What do you say, Grandbaby-Girl? Do you want to sing up there at that ceremony?"

I thought of all the stories he and Mama had told me. I thought of Granny Eugie, shot on the courthouse lawn, thought of Daddy Little standing in the cold night and watching his house burn while Uncle Me stood in the flames, his hands over his eyes. I thought of how afraid Daddy Little must have been to take the train to Tennessee, afraid that Mama would turn away from him. I thought of Kizer Bell, my father, a man I know only from what Mama has told me. A man who walks with a limp and must know, the same as me, what it's like to have everyone's eyes on you, a man who loved my mama, but finally didn't have the courage he needed to make her his.

"Daddy Little, I want to sing," I said.

He nodded. "All right then." He turned his head so he could look at Mr. Gleason. His lips moved slowly, forming each word with deliberation. "Tell us when, Mr. Gleason, and we'll be there."

When we finally are, the first thing that catches my eye is the white lilac tree just inside the gates to the park, its blossoms full and glorious, and I know this is the tree that Daddy Little found along Pecan Creek and paraded down Oak Street past the fine houses to Quakertown. The tree that shed its blossoms and dropped its leaves after Granny Eugie died. The tree Daddy Little tended and then left, certain he had seen it for the last time.

"I swan," he says. He pushes his hat farther back on his head and shades his eyes with his hand. "It's as pretty as it ever was."

To the right of the white lilac, Bert Gleason is setting up wooden folding chairs on a temporary stage, a rig of cement blocks and platforms. Just in front of the lilac, a pole set in the ground holds Mr. Gleason's plaque, a black cloth draped over it. Daddy Little lifts the bottom of the cloth with his finger so we can read the plaque. Its raised bronze letters say that in the nineteen twenties a Negro community called Quakertown thrived on this site until the city moved it to make room for the park. There were fifty-nine homes, the plaque says, and a prosperous business district.

"It tells the facts," Daddy Little says. He lets the cloth drop back to cover the words. "But it don't tell the whole truth. You need people for that, and even then you can't trust they'll get it right."

"Too much to tell," says Mama, "to put on a plaque."

The breeze ruffles the half-veil of her hat, and I try to imagine her on her wedding day coming through Daddy Little's yard. If we were to walk that same path now, it would take us through the park gates, out into a grove of trees. There are families, white, eating picnic lunches beneath those trees, their blankets spread out on the grass. There are children, white, tossing baseballs back and forth, splashing in the swimming pool, sticking their hands into the spray of a fountain, dashing back and forth across the bandstand. "You're it," one of them shouts. "No," says another. "You're it."

I remember all the names, chant them in my head: Poot Mackey, Bat Suggs, Billy Moten, Griff Lane, Tilman Monk, Hocie Simms, Nib Colter, Celia Dorrough, Mr. and Mrs. Oat Sparks, Willie Mack, Grandma Sue Moore, W. L. Briggs, Dr. L. C. Parrish, Sibby Long, Mavis Brown, Miss Abigail Lou.

Then, as if my chant has conjured them, men and women and children start to appear. They come from the east, from Rhodie Hill, the men with neckties lifting up in the breeze, the women with pocketbooks hanging from their arms.

A young man in an army uniform steps up to Mama. He takes off his hat and bows. "Miss Camellia," he says, "I'm Alvin Brown."

"Lands," says Mama. She puts her hand to her mouth. "You're Mavis Brown's boy. How you've grown up."

"Yes, ma'am." He tucks his hat under his arm. "Ma'am, I'd like your permission to escort your daughter up onto the stage."

Mama hesitates, and I know that she's thinking about herself and Kizer Bell and wondering what this invitation from Alvin Brown may start. Or maybe she's remembering how he bumped into Mr. Andrew Bell and caused him to shoot Granny Eugie. Finally, Mama sighs. "Of course," she says. "Go on."

On the platform, I sit between Alvin Brown and Mr. Gleason. "That's a pretty hair ribbon," Alvin Brown says, and I feel the blush come into my cheeks.

Before us, Daddy Little and Mama are making their way to the front of the crowd. I see people part to let them through. A woman wearing a hat as wide as a trash can lid grabs my mama by the elbow. "Camellia," she says. "It's Mavis Brown. Do you remember me?"

"You're Alvin's mother," Mama says.

"That's right. I bet you never thought he'd amount to anything."

"Never know what's going to happen, do we, Mavis?"

Mavis Brown points to the stage. "And that's your girl up there? You had me fooled that day you come into Dr. Parrish's office."

"So you've heard all about me and Kizer Bell?"

"Oh, we've heard." Mavis Brown nods, and the wide brim of her hat shakes. "But just look up there at your sweet girl. Hasn't it been worth it? Everything you've been through?"

"It has." Mama gives me a little wave. "It surely has."

She moves away from Mavis Brown, and I hear a murmur rise up in the crowd. I see people pointing my way, hear someone say, "Up there. That's her."

I fold my hands in my lap, and lower my head. Then I feel a woman's hand on my arm, and I see the bright flowered print of her skirt. "I've heard you sing, Eugenia," the woman says. "I'm Minnie Lee Wright. I started teaching school here after your mama left. Did she ever tell you that?"

"Yes, ma'am," I say. "She told me."

"You sing out, child." Minnie Lee Wright pats my arm. "You don't worry about those busybodies out there."

I raise my face, then, and I see Daddy Little in the crowd, talking to a man with a bald head. "Little Jones," the man says in a deep voice, and I know it must be Tilman Monk, who sang bass in the AME Church choir. "Plenty of us were cussing your name after we moved out to Rhodie Hill, but none of us stood by what Mr. Smoke did to your house. I just wanted you to know that."

Daddy Little nods. "Seems like a long time ago, doesn't it?"

"It does," said Tilman Monk, "and then some days it doesn't. We had a good life in Quakertown."

"I know it," Daddy Little says.

Mr. Gleason goes down into the crowd then, and fetches Daddy Little up onto the stage. He takes off his fedora and rests it carefully on his knee.

Then Alvin Brown gets up and starts the ceremony by reciting the Pledge of Allegiance the way he must have done each morning in my mama's classroom.

Mr. Gleason gets up next and speaks to the crowd. "It is a fine day," he says, "when we can gather to recall Quakertown and the lives that went on here." He stops a moment and lets the people look out over the park. "Many of you remember Little Washington Jones," he says, and I see Daddy Little set his jaw. "He's come back today to unveil this historical marker. Won't you welcome him?"

Everyone on the stage claps their hands together, but no one in the crowd does, and the clapping, next to the sounds of water splashing and people shouting to one another in the park, seems puny.

Daddy Little stands, and everyone on the stage stops clapping. He shakes hands with Mr. Gleason.

"Shaking hands with the devil," someone in the crowd says. "That's how we lost Quakertown."

Daddy Little lets go of Mr. Gleason's hand. He bows his head and turns his hat around and around, his fingers moving over the brim. Finally, he looks out at the crowd. I notice the stoop in his back. I think of all the burden he's shouldered, carried from Texas to Tennessee and back. All he must want, I imagine, is for his misery to end.

Now Mama steps up to the lip of the stage. "Go on, Papa," she says in a whisper. "Say what's in your heart to say."

His voice, when he finally speaks, is as soft as I've ever heard it. "I lost my wife here," he says, "lost my friends, my home, nearly lost my child. Those are the facts. You all went out to Rhodie Hill."

"You told us it would be heaven," someone says, and this time the voice that calls out from the crowd isn't so much angry as it is wounded, the voice of someone who has believed and, deep down, wants to believe again.

"I lived here most of my life," Daddy Little says.

"We lived here, too," says Tilman Monk, and his voice is like a clap of thunder.

"Yes," says Daddy Little, "and there was a time you were my friends."

Tilman Monk has worked his way up to the front of the crowd. Sweat glistens on his bald head. "After Eugie died," he says, "we wanted to stick by you, but then you started getting cozy with the white folks."

"They played me for a fool," Daddy Little says.

"We couldn't see that then. All we could see was that you were the one who got to stay."

Daddy Little bows his head again, and I see his shoulder blades rise and fall with his breath. A gust of wind comes up and sends a shower of white lilac blossoms drifting to the ground. He straightens and takes a step closer to the edge of the stage, closer to the crowd. I fear he's about to say he's sorry, and I can't bear to hear it, can't bear his shame.

But what he says is this: "If there had been a chance that you could've saved your homes—the houses where you loved your wives and children—you would've taken it, too."

There is nothing truer he can say, and when I rise and start to sing—"Sometimes I Feel Like a Motherless Child"—the women and men in the crowd stare off beyond me to the park where once there was a place called Quakertown, and each summer Daddy Little's white lilac tree bloomed, and one night he and Granny Eugie strolled home from the ice cream parlor, and he bragged about his yard, and she called him a high-hat nigger. My mama, tatting lace for her wedding gown, listened to their voices as they rose and fell. They floated to her through the darkness, and though she couldn't see Daddy Little and Granny Eugie there at the gate, the sound of their voices must have seemed as familiar to her as the trees and the flowers. Everything tied together like the loops and knots of lace she wove from a single thread: Daddy Little and Granny Eugie; earth and air; Mama and the secret that was me—Eugenia. I fill this place now with my song.

Lee Martin is the award-winning author of the acclaimed memoir *From Our House,* and *The Least You Need to Know,* a short story collection. He is the recipient of an NEA fellowship, among other awards. He completed this novel while teaching at the University of North Texas and is now associate professor of English in the graduate creative writing program at The Ohio State University.